Thanks for coming!

Dead M

and Other Stories from Voices Past

Jamie Rhodes

Illustrated by
Christa Leask

A collection of short stories dating from 1750-1900 inspired by the British Library archive collections

This edition published 2014 by mardibooks
www.mardibooks.com

eBook ISBN 978-1-909227-70-5
Hard Copy ISBN 978-1-909227-71-2

Illustrations by Christa Leask

A CIP catalogue record for this book is available from the British Library.

mardibooks has a small but growing stable of writers from around the world.
We publish in eBook format on Amazon.

To find out more visit: **www.mardibooks.com**

Dedication

To my English teachers, Terry Binns, Joanna Cowie, and Ghislaine Anderton, for inspiring, nurturing, and encouraging my love of writing.

And to all hard working teachers who do the same for young people everywhere.

Acknowledgments

Many people and organisations helped me to get this book out of my head and into your hands. In the order that they came to the project:

Margaret Makepeace at British Library; Deborah Williams and Piers Beckley from the Writers' Guild of Great Britain; Caz Moran, my brilliant mentor; Belinda Hunt and Jemila Abulhawa of Mardibooks; Gemma Seltzer, relationship manager at the Arts Council; Laura Kenwright, Sue Lawther, Lucy Beale and Paul Sherrard from writer development agency Spread the Word; Shenagh Goven of The Script Readers at the Theatre Royal Stratford East; 'T H E U N S E E N'; IdeasTap; The Free Word Centre; and my talented illustrator, Christa Leask.

Thanks to you all for your hard work and support.

Contents

About the Author

After graduating from Manchester Metropolitan University with a degree in philosophy in 2008, Jamie trained as a script reader for the Northwest regional screen agency and co-founded a filmmaking collective called Donkey Stone Films.

He has written several short films under commission, and is a full member of the Writers' Guild of Great Britain. He teaches creative writing and screenwriting workshops in schools and community groups throughout the UK. In 2013 his TV Drama script Folic Acid reached the later stages of the BBC Writersroom submissions round, and to date he has had two of his radio play scripts and one feature film script selected for readings by The Script Readers at the Theatre Royal Stratford East.

In 2011 he founded a charity, The Homeless Film Festival, through which he works with homeless people to develop stories and write short films. These films are shot and screened in cinemas nationwide alongside major feature films. Jamie was chair of the charity for three years, stepping down when he moved to London in 2013. In London he worked with students at London College of Communication to launch a screenwriting and filmmaking course at St. Mungo's Recovery College.

He has been involved with regional committees of the Writers' Guild of Great Britain since 2010, and is currently active on the committee for the London & South-East branch, helping to organise and speak at literary events.

He is an avid folklore enthusiast and has been a member of the folklore group Northern Earth since 2006. In this time he has collected a large catalogue of intriguing folk tales from all over the world. His writing is often inspired by these rare and unusual stories.

In 2014, he received a grant from the Arts Council to write and publish this book.

@JamieERhodes

www.jamierhodesonline.com

About the Illustrator

Christa Leask studied Textiles & Fashion at Manchester School of Art, graduating with a collection of interactive sculptures. Her collection exhibited at 'Preserve Your Instinct' exhibition at London's Sloan Square Joseph Store.

She worked at iconic British Fashion Label Pretty Green Ltd for three years as a menswear designer for print and embroidery, accessories and footwear, outerwear and tailoring.

In 2013, she set up Pierrot Doll Design Studio, working as a freelance illustrator, sculptor, and materials designer. She also works at 'T H E U N S E E N' as The Anatomist, creating sculptures, and developing materials and concepts.

Preface

A Note from the Author

Human beings are fascinating creatures and I believe that to write good characters, you have to observe the small but beautiful details of real lives. I'm a bit of a history geek and love writing historical fiction but obviously it is impossible to observe people who have been dead for hundreds or thousands of years. Hence the importance of the British Library's archive collections. You can hold the original reports from a ship's surgeon from two hundred years ago and see how his pen wobbled as the ship swayed with the sea; smell the pages of long unopened journals and diaries; some might even have an accidental thumb mark; see personal letters between friends, and note the crossings out and rephrasing as newly literate ordinary men and women of the past tried to show off their language skills, often in a seemingly competitive way. Documents like these give a unique window for observing the people of the past, and as I wrote these stories I found great joy in getting to know the personalities behind the pens.

Funding the Project

The British Library's 'Untold Lives' blog is full of fascinating snippets of peoples' lives and events from all over the world and spanning history. Margaret Makepeace and Penny Brook run the blog, and when I first moved to London in June 2013 I contacted Margaret to enquire about writing a few contributory guest articles. She was happy for me to do so and after a meeting in which we shared our passion for the untold stories of history, I suggested using the blog posts as a starting point for creative writing. I wanted to write a series of historical fiction tales inspired by the blog.

I am a committee member of the Writers' Guild of Great Britain London & SE branch, and over a few drinks after our monthly meeting I was talking to our other members about my idea. One of our members, Deborah Williams, suggested I apply to the Arts Council for funding to write and publish the stories in a collection. I never knew the Arts Council offered grants to writers and so was eager to apply.

Letters of support for the project were vital in me securing the funding, and so I set about rounding up allies to help me deliver the project. Through an organisation for emerging creative talent, IdeasTap, I met my publisher Belinda Hunt of Mardibooks. I also found out about Spread the Word, a London-based writer development agency and went to one of their publishing events at the Free Word Centre where I met Laura Kenwright, Sue Lawther and Lucy Beale. Spread the Word gave me feedback on the first draft of my Arts Council application, and came on board to advise me in putting on the reading events and workshops. These are part of the wider project of getting this book, and the knowledge I have gained through creating it, to a large and diverse audience.

Through the Writers' Guild I met Caz Moran, who became my mentor for the project. She's been brilliant throughout and has really helped a lot with my professional development. Her feedback on my work and encouragement when I was flagging were vital in getting me to the end. Piers Beckley, the chair of the Guild's London & SE committee, gave me a letter of support and also arranged for me to talk about the project at one of our Guild events.

The final stage of the project is getting my work to an audience. To do this I wanted professional actors to perform dramatic readings of the stories and so approached Shenagh Goven of The Script Readers. The Script Readers have held readings of several of my TV, Film and Radio scripts at the Theatre Royal Stratford East, and were happy to become involved.

With letters of support from all of these people and organisations, I arranged a meeting with a relationship manager for literature at the Arts Council, Gemma Seltzer. Gemma went through my application and offered advice about how I could improve it.

I submitted the Arts Council application in mid February, and six weeks later I found out that it was successful. Getting the grant really changed the outlook of my year. I was able to spend the next six months developing my craft, dedicated to my biggest passion; writing stories.

Throughout the collection, I have used material from the British Library's archive as a starting point. Some stories led me to utilise details more exactly than others, where I took on a more creative and fanciful approach to explore ideas that the archive material raised for me as a twenty-first century reader.

My aim in this fiction is to entertain and to spread a little light on the wealth of material in the British Library archives and to explore how my craft as a writer can bring alive a not altogether impossible re-imagining of our past.

***

In the tradition of Dickens and other pamphleteers, I offer this book not just as a whole collection in eBook and hard copy but also each story individually in pamphlet form as eBooks. Inflation dictates that the penny pamphlet is now the pound pamphlet, but perhaps those of you dipping into these fictional memoirs might take your pick.

Dead Men's Teeth
18th June 1815

This story was inspired by a post about early dentistry. In the British Library collections there are original advertising posters from London's dentists in the early 19th century. For a long time human teeth were the best possible solution when making dentures, and after the battle of Waterloo so many young men with decent teeth were killed that the dentures market became flooded with new 'Waterloo Teeth'. Soon, any teeth harvested from battlefields became known as Waterloo Teeth.

It struck me as grim but poetic that the relatively good teeth of a healthy young plough boy, cut down in his prime, would be recycled to help some fat aristocrat chew sweets. But there was something missing in the chain… How do the teeth get from the battlefield to the dentist? London's dentists certainly weren't going around the world chasing wars and returning with freshly harvested teeth. So, I had to create something that would be at least slightly plausible and entertaining.

I thought it should be young women who did the harvesting because men combing the battlefield should really have been in the battle, or they might be seen as looters. Young women could be grieving widows or nurses tending the wounded. They had to be quite poor young women used to manual labour, because pulling hundreds of teeth would be hard graft. They also had to be coordinated by someone in London who was wealthy and well connected to sell their harvest and ship the girls around the world to the battles. A person in this position would probably be male, given the time period, and bit of a dodgy character because it wouldn't exactly be the most honourable trade. Maybe he has his fingers in a few other illicit enterprises too.

Thus the world of *Dead Men's Teeth* was born. We are taken on the macabre adventure of a young woman recruited by a dodgy but dashing surgeon to pull teeth after the battle of Waterloo. It was a lot of fun to write this short story; one day I'd like to explore this world a little more; perhaps in a novel or a feature film script.

Quarantine

October 1882

The 'Untold Lives' blog post that inspired this story is about a ship's surgeon's report that can be found in the British Library collections. There was an outbreak of Cholera on the indenture vessel sailing from Calcutta to Suriname, and the ship was held in quarantine outside of Suriname for three weeks whilst the disease ran its course. The original report details what was eaten when and how many people had died, and I used this as a starting point making it more extreme for dramatic effect, exaggerating and adding to the details.

I wanted to use the image of a quarantined ship to convey my feelings about where we are as a species. We have come so far in our evolution, all of this capacity for conscious thought, appreciation of art, self-reflection, etc. is all great and I for one am chuffed to have it, but we still don't have any proper answers. We can't get to that final understanding.

When I try to think about this sort of thing, I feel like it's the same nagging feeling in the brain that is blocked when I forget a word mid-sentence. It's on the tip of my tongue, I can feel it there but I can't quite access it. I click my fingers and close my eyes, perhaps say things like 'that, what is it, erm… thingy, that word… the thing, like that other thing but not…' but of course I have to give up and move on, slightly embarrassed.

Why all this stuff? What's it all about really? We can't quite access that answer. We try to pretend we know by inventing religion, but of course this doesn't bring us any closer to understanding anything; we make it all up anyway. It just gives us an excuse to stop asking questions and convince ourselves that we've solved it. It's like a cul-de-sac for the evolution of the mind.

We left Calcutta a long time ago, but we can't quite dock in Suriname. The harbour is just out of sight over the horizon, we can feel it there, we know there's something there, but we can't get to it whilst we still carry a disease. What is the disease that keeps us in quarantine? I don't know. Maybe it's all the negative aspects of humanity that we need to iron out before we can go any further. Things like pollution, war, or cutting down rainforests. Or maybe it's all the social problems like inequality and racism. Or maybe it's being stuck with our animal bodies and finding there is much more fun to be had with sensory gratification. Given the choice between a day of mating and eating and napping in the sun like a lion, or a day of trying to solve the meaning of life, I know what I would choose.

Hopefully it will all become clear when we die. Maybe then we can finally dock in Suriname. We'll laugh as we pull into harbour and think 'Of course! Duh, I knew it was something like that!' But then, annoyingly, it won't matter anymore. We'll be dead.

Arrowhead

Summer 1832

This is actually a story I have wanted to tell for a while, but was not sure how. In March 2014 the British Library joined the 'Transcribe Bentham Project' with UCL, transcribing, digitising and adding its own collection of Jeremy Bentham papers to the project. In one of these letters there is a mention of Bentham's school, and this laid the seed of the idea for telling the story from the perspective of an out of work schoolteacher struggling to deal with the guilt of personal tragedy.

The story evolved over several drafts, to reach its current form and the initial link to Bentham was removed. To paraphrase William Goldman, 'There will sometimes be an element that is your scaffold. You need it all the way through the writing but at the last moment you realise it can come out, and improve the work immeasurably.'

Anyone wishing to find their own inspiration from the Jeremy Bentham papers can do so from the comfort of their own home through the 'Transcribe Bentham Project' website: http://blogs.ucl.ac.uk/transcribe-bentham/

Mary March
1819

I wrote the 'Untold Lives' blog post for this story based on a language dictionary I found in the British Library archives. The document looks like a small journal or diary and is one of only three surviving records of the language of an extinct tribe from Newfoundland called the Beothuk people. It is hand written and dates from 1818. For a lover of words and stories, it is a very moving item to behold.

There is a short prelude to the dictionary that details the tragic but heart-warming tale of a young Beothuk woman who tried to teach the European settlers some of her language. Her name was Demasduit, though the settlers called her Mary March. I felt a real connection with Demasduit as I studied the first-hand account of her life and tried to imagine how she felt. There is very little known about any religion of the Beothuk people, and so I had to invent a loose spirituality for Demasduit. This is completely fictional, but I hope not too fanciful.

The original document is written in English and so there is an obvious bias towards the colonialist settlers. I tried to take this into account, but also recognise that some of the strange behaviours that we are told about Demasduit are so odd and specific that I feel there must be some truth in them. For example, she had an air of superiority over the settler men, and would have them tie her moccasins. She was also mischievous and playful, sneaking up on people to make them jump, or openly mocking men who couldn't find a wife. She even stole the village priest's nightcap and made two little pairs of baby trousers out of it, returning the pom-pom bobble from the cap when she could find no use for it!

There is a wholeness and unity about the endeavour of creating the Beothuk-English dictionary, and so I wanted to use these themes in the story. These themes crop up frequently in human relationships, particularly with our significant others. As individuals we feel an innate lack in our Being and spend much of our lives seeking out others that might fill it. This is apparent even in the language we use to talk about relations to others; phrases like "you complete me", or referring to a spouse affectionately as "my other half."

Another thought that I find interesting on this matter is that no Being can be complete and whole without death. Death closes the bracket just as birth opens it. Like a putting a cork in a clear glass bottle. Whilst the liquid is being poured in, the contents swirl around, an indecipherable mixture of experiences, relationships, emotions…every aspect of life. Only once we stop pouring and put the cork in can the contents settle. Then we can hold the bottle up to the light to gaze in at the beautiful and complex cocktail of a person's Being. I had this image in mind as I wrote about this fascinating young woman.

The fact that the writer of the dictionary felt the need to write a long introduction of what little was known about Demasduit's life is testament to the impact that she had on the settlers. It is a beautiful but ultimately tragic document.

How I Did Long fer a Tattie Pasty!

c. 1849

This story is a bit of comical one. The American gold rush has always fascinated me; such a lawless situation gives a really interesting insight into the natural morality of human beings when there is no one around to control them. When I found this blog post about an interview with a Cornish tin miner who went to California with his brother to make his fortune, I had to do a story about it!

The interview is written in Cornish dialect and to be honest, I used it as a structure for the story. I took a few quotes from it, and built the world of Cornishmen in the Sierra Nevada hills around those quotes.

It is set circa 1849, but the exact date isn't too important. It is a tale of brotherly love and the violent lives that the miners led during the gold rush. Being the oldest of three brothers, the interview really struck a nerve with me. I sometimes go many months, and will likely at some point in my life go years, without seeing my brothers. Yet, however far we drift and however long our absence, it is always the same when we get back together. We might bicker and squabble, but I will always gladly take a bullet for them.

Wes Anderson's *The Darjeeling Limited* achieves a brilliant depiction of this relationship, and I strived to achieve similar with this story, albeit with two brothers rather than three (it's a short story and I wanted to keep it simple).

Interestingly, I found that there was such a huge influx of Cornish people to California that many towns and villages still have pasty shops to this day! I find this quite funny amidst all the glamour, celebrity and technology giants. A small reminder of California's humble beginnings.

Death or Australia

19th January 1788

When it was first decided that Australia should be colonised, British criminals who were convicted of serious crimes – and many not so serious – could be offered a choice of the death penalty or transportation to Australia. Surprisingly, some chose death. Australia must have sounded like the actual biblical idea of hell to the British convicts, and so I wanted a hardened criminal willing to take it on.

Again I went for the sibling relationship, as it is one that I know well, and find fascinating. I was also inspired by a brilliant novel about grave robbers that I read a few years ago called *The Sad Tale of the Brothers Grossbart*, by Jesse Bullington. However despicable the crimes of the heroes, when you see the beautiful moments of sibling rivalry and love, you can't help but want them to win.

The First Fleet arrived in Botany Bay in 1788 at night, and was made up of eleven ships carrying roughly 750 convicts, and 300 soldiers and settlers. Our brothers start the journey aboard the first convict ship, waiting for their chance of liberty when the ship might drop anchor…

Printed on the Thames

Winter 1789

The Thames used to freeze over during particularly cold winters. In the years when it froze, huge Frost Fairs would pop up. These were carnivals on the ice, full of vibrancy and colour, with beer tents, rudimentary fairground rides, bonfires, football matches, plays, dances… all sorts of weird and wonderful sights. Local printers would carry their printing presses onto the ice, and charge people to have little keepsake tokens printed. These were like postcards, perhaps with a short poem or limerick on, the year of the fair and the name of the person who bought it. The British Library collections contain several of these tokens printed on the ice between 1683 and 1814.

The phenomena of the Frost Fair struck me as quite surreal, and so I wanted to explore it through the eyes of a person under some narcotic influence. At the time of the fairs, the aristocracy would be taking opiates like laudanum for curing all manner of pains, as well as snuff and very strong gin. Cocaine drops came a little later on than the period in which this story is set, but I decided to use a little dramatic license as I needed an 'upper' as well as a 'downer' in my dabbling with the nature of reality.

This is a buddy story of two young aristocrats coming of age in the late 1700's. What fun they must have had at the Frost Fair. The Thames doesn't freeze anymore because London Bridge was rebuilt with less arches and support piers, which means the water flows a lot faster than it did.

Ignatius Sancho's Shop

2nd June 1780

Ignatius Sancho was a fascinating man who led a very unusual life. He is said to have been born on an Atlantic slave ship around 1729, and brought to England from the Spanish West Indies. From the age of two he grew up as a household servant in Greenwich, though this was still with the status of a slave by English law.

The Duke of Montagu took an interest in Sancho and paid for his education, and after the Duke's death in 1749 his widow took him into her service as her butler, leaving him a small annuity which eventually enabled him to set up in business as a grocer in Mayfair, Westminster.

Sancho blazed a trail for black Africans in Britain. He was the first black man to vote in a British parliamentary election, the first to publish any critique of slavery and the slave trade and the first to be accepted into London literary society.

Around the time I was writing this collection of stories, the British Library had recently acquired the archive of Ignatius Sancho's letters, and so I was eager to read them.

In my research I found that Sancho's little shop in Mayfair attracted some of the top (often celebrity) artists, musicians, actors and politicians of the time, as well as the next generation of young people aspiring to be like their idols. They all came to buy their tobacco, sugar, rum, and tea; slave products. Sancho could have refused to sell these goods on moral grounds, but they were the most popular and expensive products of the time. He would not have been able to make the money to keep his shop without them. It was a shrewd move.

He would chat with powerful and wealthy men regularly, about all manner of intellectual topics, becoming very close friends with many of them. All the while, over every cup of tea, every charming and eloquent letter sent, every little transaction in the shop, Sancho was influencing them to challenge slavery. His influence pulled together, for the first time, a group of people who could really work to bring about the abolition of slavery. The fact that he was a former slave, selling slave goods also drew public interest and put a spotlight on the slave trade. I can imagine the hipsters of the time saying things like:

'Have you been to that grocery shop in Mayfair? Ignatius Sancho's? Yah, it's really cool, an ex-slave selling slave goods. It's like, controversial, but really ironic at the same time... Yah, Laurence Sterne goes there. Him and Ignatius are like, best friends...sometimes we chat when I'm buying my snuff... I'm thinking about showing him my manuscript.'

And then of course, these 18th century hipsters want to follow in the footsteps of their idols and become the next generation of abolitionists.

One of the letters in the archive is Sancho's eyewitness account of the Gordon riots happening right outside his shop. The riots are nothing to do with him but, being a quite wealthy, property-owning African man at time when many people were living in abject poverty, he must have been at least a little nervous.

I wanted to use this threat to explore Sancho's mind. His moral dilemma and guilt about selling slave goods, his worries that all of his hard work influencing the powerful would be to no avail, his love of his wife, his pride about his shop, his yearning to see Africa, a land that he has only seen in his imagination... but I wanted to do this in an original and unusual way, personifying his sense of guilt and creating a surreal parable. A fairy-tale journey through which to explore his preoccupations.

Vulture Temple

Early 1900

An image more than a historical document inspired this story. As with all of these stories, it features in one of the British Library's 'Untold Lives' blog posts. It is an image of a 'Tower of Silence'. The towers of silence (dakhmas) are enclosed towers in which Zoroastrians expose the dead to be eaten by vultures, thus avoiding pollution of the sacred elements fire, water or earth. Zoroastrianism is one of the oldest religions in the world, dating back to roughly 1400 BC and tracing its origins to Ancient Persia. While they are no longer in use today in Iran, the Towers of Silence are still used by Zoroastrians in India and Pakistan.

The image that struck me is one of the vultures gathered around the rim of the tower, hunched in almost reverential mourning, waiting for the next body to be laid for them. It seemed that the tower was as much a religious site for the vultures as it was for the Zoroastrians. Keen to explore this idea of the religion of the vultures, I went about researching different species of vultures in India and looking at their behaviour.

George Orwell's *Animal Farm* was a big inspiration for this story. I want to write a short novella that satirises religion in a similar way that Animal Farm does with revolutionary politics. Vulture species squabbling over a human carcass feels like a good image through which to explore this idea. This short story sets up the religion of vultures and presents an episode to play out within it.

Sadly, in researching this story I found out that since the 1990's, 97% of Asia's vultures have been wiped out as a result of diclofenac given to cattle. Diclofenac stays in the

meat and is deadly poisonous to vultures. Vultures fill a vital ecological role, and as a result of their disappearance many tons of rotting meat lays unconsumed, spreading disease and contaminating the environment. These fascinating birds are now critically threatened with extinction, and I would like to take this opportunity to point you in the direction of the RSPB's SAVE (Saving Asia's Vultures from Extinction) campaign:
http://www.rspb.org.uk/supporting/campaigns/vultures/

Stolen From India

c. 1750

This story is inspired by a merger of two of the 'Untold Lives' blog posts. Firstly, one about Victorian prosthetics. The weapons used in this era meant that limbs would often be shattered in such a way that amputation was the only answer. Amputees must have been quite a regular sight throughout the Georgian and Victorian eras, and the prosthetics in use were varied and experimental. The other blog post is about the ghastly kitchens of the aristocracy. It was a common hobby for aristocrats with large kitchens in their homes, to practice the study of anatomy. They would cut up animals and boil their parts to try to understand how the body works. There was a huge grey area between culinary and scientific use of animal parts, with some anatomical works including instructions for cooking certain animals, and cook books advising on how best to dissect animals.

I wanted to blend these two ideas and create a macabre short story in the vein of H.G. Wells' *Island of Dr. Moreau.* I needed a wealthy military amputee with a huge manor house, and where better to find one than in the Companies of the British Empire. The man who inspired the character of the Master was not an amputee but a Major-General of one such Company; a large man with a reputation for having a ferocious temper. My character is completely fictional, and there is no reference to anyone living or dead. I am also a big fan of folk tales, and so decided to include an element of Indian folklore in the story.

Once I had all of these extreme and varied ingredients, I needed a perspective that would tie them together. The young gardener's boy stepped forward.

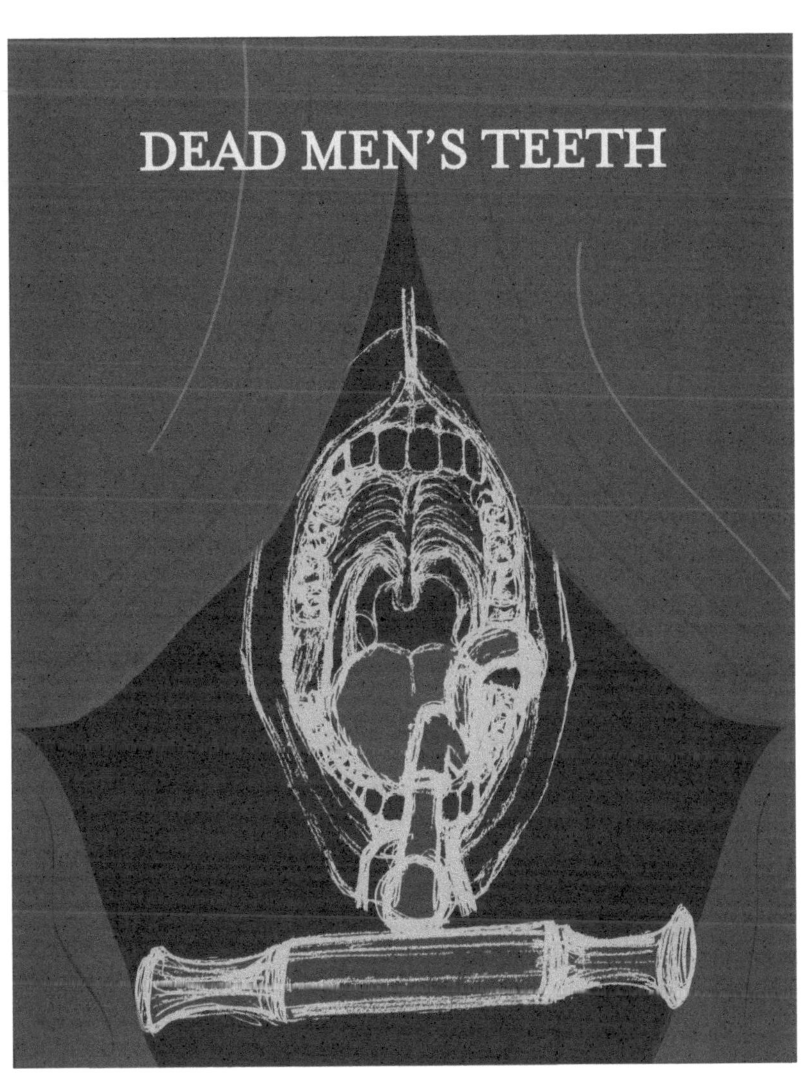

DEAD MEN'S TEETH

Dead Men's Teeth

18th June 1815

It was my mother's suggestion. She saw a notice when she was at the market. There was a surgeon in the city offering two guineas per incisor! Mother went along and swapped both of hers for four guineas. When she got home, she said I should go talk to the surgeon about assisting him with a job on the continent. Would you believe it? Assisting a surgeon! He was proper you know. A real surgeon at the Royal College. Not like the barber-surgeons. For his teeth work, he had set up a special practice in the cellar of a tavern by the docks. He told mother that some of the older surgeons at the College didn't like his modern methods, so he had to do his groundbreaking work somewhere they would never sabotage him.

He'd told my mother that on the continent Napoleon had escaped and a war was being fought again in France. Thousands of healthy young men were being cut down in their prime, their bodies left to rot in mass graves, or burned on funeral pyres. Their teeth were not needed anymore, but they would all be wasted in the cold earth. The Surgeon said he could make sure the soldiers' teeth lived on, fulfilling a purpose for someone in need. With his new methods, the peasant teeth of a lowly soldier could quickly be re-used. They'd be fitted into the mouth of some lord or duchess, and could be eating expensive meats and other delicacies in a few weeks or less.

The docks were safe enough during the day. Bustling with street vendors barking about their wares, workers trundling their carts. On such a hot day, the foul smells of the London summertime caught in the draped dirty bed sheets over the streets. The people of London seemed perfectly used to it, but by luck I'd been born on a small tenant farm outside the city. Life had been good and steady until my father had passed away four years ago. Since then we'd become desperately poor; we couldn't get the farm producing as well as it had done when he was alive, and the landowner would not reduce the rent. I was nineteen years old when he died, and still missed him. I had to take a job in the landowner's kitchens to bring some extra money in and support the failing farm. But, at least my mother and me had so far managed to stay in the countryside where the air was so much sweeter. I picked a sprig of lavender from the churchyard on my way into town, and held it under my nose to keep the miasmas at bay. It wasn't enough.

Next to the Kings Arms Tavern was a narrow doorway that led to an alley at the side of the building. I was sure it was the door that my mother had described, with the pattern of scratches and nicks on the front that could have been done on purpose. Carried along by the crowd, I saw the door too late and was washed beyond it. Gradually, I managed to pull myself to the side of the street and struggle back up stream to the door.

The door was a very thin piece of wood. It rattled unsteadily even under my delicate, trembling knock. I heard a heavy latch being lifted and the door was jolted open by a very small, wrinkled Chinese woman. Her face was drawn and her rheumy eyes sparkled deep within their sockets, as though she was about to commit some mischief.

'I'm looking for the Surgeon. I'm Mary's daughter,' I said, as slowly and clearly as I could. The little woman smiled a warm toothless grin and beckoned me through the door.

Beyond was a narrow, grimy alley. The floor was caked in hard-dried mud and the walls of the buildings on either side leaned over with age, their cold stone stilling the air. I had the impression of entering a cave. The little woman shut the door behind me, and then led the way down the alley to another small door built into the side of the tavern.

The little woman went through the door and, though I am not tall, even I had to duck down to follow her. The room beyond was a simple living quarters. There was a small low bed underneath the window in one corner of the room – though it did not look so slept-in as did the deep, moth-eaten armchair pointed at the fireplace. Just on the edge of hearing, the muffled sound of the busy tavern rumbled and clinked.

The little China woman opened a hatch in the floor that I would never have noticed. Below was a dark hole with a ladder, and a bright orange glow coming from the bottom. With quick feet that seemed strange for such an old woman, she stepped onto the ladder and began to descend, smiling her toothless grin at me as she went. I held my skirts closely around my legs, and followed her down into the orange glow.

The Surgeon's workshop was part of the tavern's vaulted barrel cellar. Flaming torches burned on the walls, causing shadows to dance between the barrels. At the far end of the cellar, in a large square lit by the most torches, was a workbench with various strangely shaped tools laid out upon it. Some glinted in the orange light, others were black iron. In the centre of that square was a sturdy chair, leaned back at a relaxed angle. The chair had levers for adjusting the different parts, and leather straps hanging limply from the arms and headrest for strapping patients down.

Still panting from her descent of the ladder, the little woman lifted an arm to gesture at the chair. She led me over shallow pools of liquid – perhaps ale leaked from the barrels. Together we made our way towards the chair, the puddles reflecting the torches like a patchwork of torn mirrors.

The little woman patted the seat of the chair, and pointed for me to sit in it. I refused, shaking my head at her. I would not be having any teeth removed and saw no reason why I should sit in such a terrible chair. The little China woman frowned her wrinkly face at me and we stood silently side-by-side awaiting the Surgeon. There was a ramp leading up from the cellar for rolling barrels up to the tavern. She kept squinting and frowning at the door at the top of the ramp. Light shone from a gap in the door-frame, eclipsed by shadow occasionally as people walked past. We listened intently to the muffled chaos of the busy tavern above our heads.

'What is your name?' I asked her, trying to speak very clearly. She looked up at me, her old rheumy eyes glistening in the torchlight.

'Zheng,' she barked, sharply. Her face creased into the gummy smile again. I smiled back.

'Em-ma,' I said slowly, pointing to myself.

'Yes. Your mother told me when she came here to sell her teeth.' I was shocked and surprised by the woman's grasp of English. Her accent was still heavily Chinese, but she clearly understood the words. Thinking about the way I had spoken to her before, as though she were a simpleton, made me feel a little guilty.

Suddenly the door at the top of the ramp was flung open. Blinding bright daylight surged down the ramp, carrying the noisy chaos of the tavern with it. I shaded my eyes, squinting. As my eyes adjusted to the light, I could see the silhouette of a man, framed in the open door holding a chalice. The cut of his clothes was that of a real gentleman, and the man held a powerful, almost royal, pose before turning and closing the door behind him. The tavern noise muffled once more, the man's well-heeled footsteps echoed around the vaulted cellar as he descended the ramp. Buckles on his shoes and belt shone gold in the torchlight, as did the glass chalice in his left hand.

At the foot of the ramp, he moved into the torchlight and I saw the man's face for the first time. The Surgeon. He was the most handsome man I had ever been so close to. My breath caught in my throat. He had a heavy brow, strong jaw and high cheekbones. I reckoned he would have been about thirty-six; there was a real old wisdom in his piercing deep brown eyes. He looked into my soul and smiled at me, showing the most perfect white teeth I had ever seen.

'Thank you for meeting me, Emma. My name is John William Anthony Laurence, and you are truly every bit as lovely as your mother told me.' His voice was deep and warm and very toffee-nosed. I could not help but blush and look away bashfully. 'For you, sweet lady,' he held out the glass chalice, 'only the finest French brandy.'

'Oh, no Mister Laurence,' I started to say, when he pressed the glass into my hand. I did not have the tongue for drinking fine alcohol, least of all in front of a proper gent!

'Please. Do call me John. I shall join you.' He went to the

workbench and from a chest underneath it, took another glass and a decanter of golden liquid. He poured himself a glass and held it up to mine. 'To our first meeting, fair lady.' With that, he drank down the brandy.

I tried to follow suit, but the brandy was so hot in my throat that I could only sip it a little at a time. After the first few sips, the burning sweetness became more palatable and I finished the glass.

Mister Laurence laughed heartily refilling our glasses, and then, slamming the decanter down on the workbench with a thud that rattled the metal tools, he took a coin from the purse at his belt and turned to Zheng.

'For you, Madame Zheng for looking after this young lady so well.' The little woman took the coin. She hurried back across the puddled cellar floor and climbed the ladder back to her room.

I was alone with Mister Laurence, The Surgeon. My heart was racing. I would have held my lavender to my nose, but I had tucked it up my sleeve to hide it. It seemed childish and silly to be holding lavender in front of so great a man. I sipped the brandy instead in an effort to calm my nerves. I suddenly felt very vulnerable. The feeling must have shown on my face for he was quick to reassure me.

'Do not worry my dear, I am a complete professional. My work is pushing the boundaries of science, and of the utmost secrecy. Hence you find me in these rather unsavoury surroundings, which I must confess I do find most unsettling.' His voice held such fire when he mentioned his work, but he appeared quite worried as he looked around the cellar.

I saw this handsome man in a different light. Brilliant though he was, he was also scared, not used to such lowly surroundings. It was good to find a man so passionate about his work that he would place himself at such risk, so far from the life he was accustomed.

'My mother said you needed an assistant for a job on the continent?' I asked. He flashed me his striking smile.

'My lady, it would be an honour to have you on my staff!' He took my hand in his and kissed it. For such a man to have such enthusiasm for me was most uplifting. My heart soared. His deep brown eyes lit up and I listened hard as he told me about his project on the continent. His powerful voice echoing through the cellar, he waved his arms around excitedly as he spoke.

Mister Laurence looked after the teeth of the top aristocrats in London. He said it was no secret that most of them needed false teeth and, grim as it was, best false teeth were ones made from real human teeth. His job was helping poor people with no money, to make money from the rich people with no teeth. This is why he paid my mother so much for her incisors.

My job would be to go to France with his other assistants and bring back the teeth of dead soldiers. Of course, my travel and food would be paid for, and I would be paid for every tooth I brought back. The value of each one would depend on its quality.

When he finished speaking he was quite out of breath. Smiling in the torchlight, he poured himself another brandy. The golden liquid glinted as it tumbled into the glass. I wasn't expecting to be doing the pulling of teeth myself, but didn't know how to tell him.

'I'm not sure I've a head for such work.' My voice trembled, I felt small and childish. Mister Laurence smiled warmly at me and took my glass.

'Nonsense,' he said, filling my glass with brandy, 'do you not work in a butcher's shop?' He handed the glass back to me.

'No, I work on a farm outside just town. And in the landowner's kitchen,' I replied.

'Oh, well, do you not to prepare poultry for cooking?' He held up his glass and smiled.

'Sometimes.'

'Well, it is no more difficult or bloody than preparing a goose or a pig for roasting.' He moved his glass towards me to clink it with mine. I copied him and the clink of our glasses chimed out through the vaulted cellar. We both drank. He drank deeper than me, though I was becoming slightly more used to the fiery sweetness.

'But a dead man is much different from a goose or a pig,' I said.

'When the soul has departed, we are all naught but flesh. Whether in the form of man or beast, without a soul, the flesh and blood is much the same.' His reasoning was cold, but he was a highly educated gentleman so perhaps he was right. I hoped so.

If he gave my mother four guineas for two of her teeth, I tried to imagine what I could make from a whole mouth of teeth. A thousand mouths full of teeth! I took another sip of my brandy.

'You gave my mother two guineas per tooth. How much are my teeth worth?'

'Oh my lady, your teeth are immaculate! A lady of your age, well, your teeth would be worth considerably more. Here, have a seat in the chair. Let me have a look.'

I paused for a moment. The chair, with all the leather straps, was quite frightening to look at.

'I won't be strapped in,' I told him.

'Of course, there is no need for that!' Placing my trust in the man, I sat in the chair and laid back. He leant over me. 'Open your mouth and relax.'

He put his rough hand on my cheek and leaned in close. The smell of his breath was sickly sweet from the brandy. Under that, his manly sweat mixed with a different unusual but pleasant scent. I remembered that this man was a real gentleman used to dealing with the aristocracy; he was likely wearing a perfume. I let my head go limp as he held it firmly in his strong hands, tilting it gently back and forth, left and right. He ran his thumb over my trembling lips, gently pushing each one back and peering closely at my teeth, so close to me now that I could feel his breath on my neck. For several moments he held me there. In the quietness of the cellar, I feared he would hear my heart beating wildly in my chest. I tried to keep my own breathing regular so as not to reveal to him the excitement I felt stirring inside me. Then, without moving away, he looked right into my eyes. Deep into my eyes. I stared back into his, helpless. In the flickering torchlight, they were flecked with gold. My breath caught in my throat again. He was about to kiss me.

Then he smiled. In an instant it was over. He drew back and stood up straight. I breathed again.

'Your teeth are priceless fair lady. Ten guineas per tooth would not be enough. Whatever you may say, I will not take a single one from you. It would be a crime against God to destroy so beautiful a smile as yours.' He stroked my cheek lovingly with his thumb. 'If you will go with my team to France, after the battles you can gather all the teeth you need to be comfortable for the rest of your life.'

'Will you not come with us?' I felt afraid.

'Sadly I cannot. An able-bodied gentleman such as I, walking the battlefields to save the teeth of the dead would cause outrage. I would never work in London again. I need to be here to meet with the toothless aristocrats and secure their business for when you return. I will be here waiting for you. What do you say? Do you want to work for me?' He looked at me intensely, pinned me to the chair with his gaze.

'I want to, truly I do, sir. But you know I do not know a single thing about pulling teeth.' For a moment I feared he would revoke his offer, until he smiled and his eyes danced excitedly again.

'This is the best news I have heard in weeks! Do not fret about the details of pulling teeth sweet girl. Come back here a week from today and I will be hosting a demonstration for all of my new assistants. You will learn how to pull teeth!' With that he filled our brandy glasses, and we drank together again.

Leaving the cellar, Mister Laurence gave me his arm and helped me pick my way back across the puddled floor. I had to climb back up the ladder and through Madame Zheng's little home so as not to provoke suspicion in the tavern. The brandy had made me a little giddy, and I stumbled on the uneven ground. As I put my arms out to steady myself, my lavender fell out of my sleeve and landed in one of the dark shimmering puddles of ale. I feared he would notice and think me a little girl, but thankfully it sank below the surface.

I bid Madame Zheng goodbye and hurried home. When I told my mother about the Surgeon's offer she was understandably a little worried for me. But, with the wealth at stake and the rarity of the chance for a girl of my standing to associate with so brilliant a man as Mister Laurence, she gave me her blessing.

The week would not go fast enough. The demonstration would be unpleasant, undoubtedly, but I was determined to learn well and do a good job for Mister Laurence. One of our pigs was due for slaughter in the landowner's kitchen and so I helped to gut it and prepare it. I made sure to get more intimate with the gore than I usually would; I would need to develop a stomach for such things. With Mother, I slit the pig's throat, caught the blood for black pudding, and carried the body to the kitchens very early in the morning before any other workers arrived. There I practised pulling out the pig's teeth with a pair of tongs, a jimmy bar, and my bare hands. It was not an easy or pleasant job. There was far more blood than I imagined possible, and I cracked several of the pig's teeth before I managed to wrench one out whole.

Eventually, the day arrived. I made my way excitedly back through the crowds along the docks to that little door next to the tavern. Madame Zheng led me straight through to the back room where the trapdoor was already open.

In the cellar there were four young girls stood with their backs to me in front of the Surgeon's workshop. Another, very finely dressed, older woman with a pipe in her mouth stood before them facing my direction. The Surgeon was nowhere to be seen but I could hear him working, pulling and tightening the leather straps on the chair. The older woman saw me.

'John, there's another little lamb here,' said the older woman, her voice gravelly with pipe smoke.

The other girls looked around at me and Mister Laurence popped his head up from his work.

'Emma!' He cried, 'So glad you decided to come. Come on girl, you'll miss the show!' He beckoned me to join the others quickly, so I hurried from the ladder to the workshop trying to dodge the puddles.

As I neared the others, they parted and I gasped out loud as I beheld the most shocking, nightmarish vision I had ever seen. There, strapped into the dental chair, which held such exciting memories for me from my last intimate encounter with Mister Laurence, was a human corpse. By the look of it, and the smell, it was not recently dead. The dark leather strap at the headrest was fastened tightly across the corpse's forehead. Grey mottled skin hung loosely around the head, bulging under the pressure of the tight strap. Mister Laurence laughed at my horror.

'Don't worry my girl, he can't hurt you! It's just flesh now remember.' He smiled his brilliant smile and patted the corpse playfully on the top of the head. 'Please, help yourself to a glass of brandy.' He gestured with a wave of his hand to glasses of the golden liquid lined up on his workbench.

I took one and stood next to the other girls who, to my relief, looked just as pale and ashen as I felt I must. We exchanged polite smiles and nods and sipped our brandies like proper ladies should.

'Shall I demonstrate?' asked the older woman, stood with her hands behind her back.

'Not quite, Nancy. Girls, this is Nancy. She got back from a fact-finding mission in France last week and the good news for us, ladies, is that Napoleon has most definitely returned!' He beamed at us all. 'Show them your teeth, Nancy.'

Nancy bared her brown-stained teeth at us like an animal. Her behaviour was completely at odds with her fine clothes. The Surgeon looked at her in confusion, and then coughed awkwardly, 'The ones you collected last time?'

'Oh,' she said, winking at us and feigning embarrassment. From behind her back she held up a small sack. It rattled as though full of dice, though we all knew what it really contained. Our suspicions were confirmed when Nancy tipped the bag upside down on the workbench and hundreds of teeth chattered as they tumbled out onto the wooden worktop.

'This is all that remains of ten such bags that Nancy collected during the battles last summer. Now the angry little man is back and will no doubt want another war. Nancy, please show them their tools.'

Nancy gave each of us a pair of simple forceps, a small sharp knife, and a strange key-like instrument with a small hook on the key end and a T-shaped wooden handle. The Surgeon held up his own set of forceps, far fancier than our simple ones.

'These are dental forceps. The front teeth can usually be removed quite easily using these.' He stood aside the corpse in the chair and took hold of one of the front teeth with the forceps. 'One sharp tug,' he grunted as he did so and the tooth came smoothly out of the skull.

Next he held up the T-shaped instrument.

'This is your best friend. It's called a turnkey. The back teeth are often much harder to remove.' He put the hook end into the corpse's mouth and turned the wooden handle. 'Get the hook clamped firmly around the tooth, then rotate the wooden handle, give it a wiggle, and voila!' The tooth came out of the skull on the end of the hook. 'Now, over to you, ladies. I have some business to attend to in the city. Nancy will supervise; I want to see every tooth out of that skull when I return this evening!'

'What about the knife?' I asked.

'Rest assured my inquisitive Emma, Nancy will show you how to use the knife when you get to France,' he said. 'I've booked you passage aboard a packet boat, leaving from Dover tomorrow afternoon. I've business to conduct in Dover, so I shall travel with you and be there to wave you off. Be back here by sunrise tomorrow morning; the coach to Dover won't wait!'

With that, he clapped his hands and left the cellar via the barrel ramp.

The cellar seemed so much bleaker without him. We each took turns at pulling teeth from the corpse. One girl was sick when old jellied blood shot out of the grey gum like a popped blister and landed on her dress. She left tearfully soon afterwards. I was glad that my work on the pig had hardened my stomach to such things.

The three remaining girls and I continued to practise on the corpse. Nobody asked about where it had come from; Mister Laurence was part of the Royal College and, as a medical man, must have been able to get access to such things with ease. Nancy gave us guidance and taught us the words for the different types of teeth. She praised our successes, and gently berated us when we tugged at the teeth too wildly causing them to crack. They were no use to anyone if they cracked.

After each successful removal, she poured us another brandy. We drank together and giggled like sisters, it was actually rather fun! The pleasant atmosphere returned quickly, despite the best efforts of the dead man lounging in the dental chair.

Later in the afternoon, a young tavern boy came down into the cellar to collect a barrel. Catching sight of us girls cackling merrily around the corpse, he wailed in terror and fled back up to the tavern without his barrel. We fell about laughing so heartily that tears streamed down our faces.

When all the teeth had been removed, Nancy showed us how to store our tools and knife safely in our skirts. Carrying them about openly in public would draw attention, and it wasn't always practical to carry a handbag. We promised to see each other in the morning, then climbed the ladder and left the cellar.

Madame Zheng smiled her old toothless grin at me and waved goodbye as she stirred a pot of stew hung over the fireplace. The stew smelled good and wholesome. It occurred to me that I hadn't eaten since breakfast.

My head spinning from the brandy and the laughter, I made my way merrily back home and straight to bed.

Wearing my best travelling dress – it was not fine and expensive like Nancy's, but it was well cut and made of a sturdy but light white cloth – I arrived back outside the tavern early the next morning just before the sun rose. The road was eerily still and silent. Ghostly wisps of fog hung just above the road; the pre-dawn haze, bathed in moonlight. Nancy was there already; she had taken a room at the tavern that night, and emerged from the darkness of the doorway carrying a large travel bag. Her sudden appearance startled me and I reached for the knife hidden up my sleeve.

'Good girl,' whispered Nancy. She gave a hushed cackle, 'You get the idea. Just don't pull it in haste.' She winked at me.

Two of the other girls arrived shortly after me. First came Rebecca, who was a little younger than me with pretty freckles around her nose and a savage scar along her right arm. She was a butcher's daughter and she said the scar was from an accident with one of her father's knives when she was young. Then came Anne; she was a quiet woman, older by several years than Rebecca and me, with vibrant golden ringlets and a strong hooked nose. I did not know her working background but she said she lived near the docks on a street further along the river. When we emerged from the doorway to greet her, she fully drew her knife with such swiftness and violence that I had to dodge out of the way or be gutted. The final girl from yesterday hadn't arrived in time, or hadn't arrived at all, we would never know. Our party was down to four including myself.

A large black carriage entered the far end of the street and rumbled towards us, the horses' hooves echoing through the stillness. As it drew nearer, the clouding of the horses' breath seemed to wrap around the whole carriage. The driver had his heavy coat pulled tightly around him, his collar up against the wind, and wide-brimmed top hat low over his eyes. He pulled gently on the leather reins, which creaked against the leather of his gloves. The carriage slowed to a halt next to us, wheels grinding on the dirt road, curtains drawn across the windows. For a moment there was silence. Then the door suddenly swung open and the stepladder folded out with a clatter. The Surgeon strode gallantly out, his broad masculine shoulders filling the narrow doorway. He held out a hand to Nancy first and helped her into the carriage. I moved behind the other girls; if I went last I could choose a seat whereby Mister Laurence could sit next to me. With the other girls in the carriage, only the Surgeon and I remained outside. He smiled at me and I held his gaze in mine for a heartbeat. As I placed my hand in his, for a moment I felt a lingering squeeze as he helped me into the carriage, and then it was gone.

Inside the carriage, to my disappointment, Nancy bade me sit on the side with the other two girls, facing backwards. She sat opposite Rebecca, furthest from the door and when the Surgeon climbed in, he was forced to sit next to Nancy, but opposite me. This turned out better than I had planned for it meant he must spend the long journey to Dover looking directly at me. I tried to smile sweetly at him as he climbed in. He leaned out to pull the door shut, then knocked on the roof with his large fist. The carriage jolted into motion.

The journey to Dover took many hours. We were forbidden from opening the heavy maroon curtains until we were far outside London, trundling through the Kent countryside at quite a speed. When Mister Laurence eventually drew them back, the beautiful sunrise flooded into the carriage, bathing us all in gold. The other girls stared at the rolling countryside outside of the window, but I had seen the countryside many times; it was the man opposite that so interested me. He caught my eye and smiled excitedly. I could only blush and look away out of the window. Our feet touched four times during the trip, when the carriage jolted sharply over rougher ground.

By early afternoon we had reached Dover harbour. The Surgeon shook me gently awake, and I blearily looked around the carriage, a little confused and embarrassed. Fortunately the other girls were also asleep. Nancy stirred them gently; she was like a mother during the trip.

The bright sunny afternoon was blinding and I was forced to shade my eyes as I stepped down from the carriage, helped by the gentlemanly hand of Mister Laurence. The sea stretched out to the horizon, glistening like a shimmering field grazed upon by fishing boats.

I had never been aboard a boat before, neither had the other girls. We were all very excited as we stood on the deck of the small postal boat they called a packet boat, with about thirty other passengers. From the back of the boat we stood waving to Mister Laurence as the boat pulled away into the ocean. He blew us kisses but I knew they were aimed at me. I returned them all and watched him until he was lost in the crowd on the harbour front.

Once into the open ocean, the little packet boat bulled through the waves without mercy, smashing each one into froth. Nancy reached into her travel bag and brought out some jellied eel pies for lunch. We ate them with relish, but the pitching and rolling of the boat made it difficult for food to settle in the stomach. Rebecca and I had to lean over the side and were very sick. Nancy and Anne kept theirs down. Their laughter rang in our ears as we watched our dignity spatter down the side of the ship and into the ocean to be pecked at by the waiting seagulls.

Even when we reached dry land, the rocking motion wouldn't leave me. Nancy had managed to learn a few words of French during her previous trips and at the port in Calais she arranged our lodging in a small back-street tavern for the night. I was to share a room with Rebecca and Anne, whilst Nancy took a separate room next door. She left us a few coins to get some supper from the tavern and assured us that they would speak English if we pointed and spoke loudly enough, then went out for the evening. Apparently Mister Laurence had asked her to meet one of his friends in the town about some other business, and she needed to find out where the battle fields were to be found.

As I lay in my bed that night, exhausted from the journey and full from supper, I swayed dreamily as though wrapped in a canvas hammock aboard a huge frigate ship. Deep muffled voices from Nancy's room next door clouded my head as I drifted off to a deep sleep.

The next morning, we were woken before dawn again. Nancy had hired us a coach pulled by two horses. She told the driver to take us to Brussels where the Duke of Wellington and his soldiers were based. The driver seemed to protest but I could not understand why. Nancy simply repeated her few words of French louder and more aggressively, and handed him a few extra coins. This seemed to pacify the driver's protests and we all climbed into the coach.

It was night-time when the carriage finally rolled to a halt. Even before Nancy opened the door, we could hear the raucous drunken noise of soldiers and taverns. It was quite intimidating. We stepped out from the carriage and stood in a public square. The air was warm and the buildings on all sides were tall and slim, squeezed together around the square like teeth in a giant mouth. Several of the buildings threw light from their windows into the square. Men came and went from these buildings in drunken packs. We were stood outside of one of these buildings and the merriment within was spilling out into the street. Our carriage pulled away and lined up near the other carriages on the opposite side of the square, no doubt hoping for some more business from the soldiers.

Nancy called over one of the other smaller carriages and in her loudest, and most aggressive, French voice persuaded the driver to take us to Waterloo.

Some two hours later, he refused to go any further. Try as we might, he could not be persuaded. He left us on a country track and sped back the way he came. We stood in the middle of the dark, moonlit dirt track, listening to the hoof-beats fade away into the night. Walking further down the track, my eyes became used to the darkness and I saw a line of orange lights in the distance. As we drew nearer it became clear that this was the camp of a huge army, the line of lights from the fires spanned the horizon for miles in each direction.

At Nancy's suggestion we didn't go right into the camp; if caught we would be accused of being prostitutes and perhaps simply ejected from the camp, or if we were extremely unlucky we could be asked questions. Either way, Nancy did not want us to attract attention. Instead we found a barn on the farmland nearby and slept in the hay.

There were other camp followers in the barn, likely soldiers' wives or thieves, or both. Some people were already sleeping, others simply watched us as we entered. Shiny eyes staring out from the darkness. Nobody asked questions. We found a clear spot, and after such an exhausting day were grateful to fall into the hay.

The deep bellow of canon-fire awoke us the next morning. The clashing steel, the peppering popping of musket fire, the defiant battle cries, the strangled whinnying of a horse falling under a pike, all rolled into one orchestra. It was a truly thunderous sound, the music of battle kept in time by the regular booming of the cannons. I stood up quickly and looked around, feeling desperately that I had missed something.

Nancy was awake already; she sat against a hay bale smoking her pipe, eyes distant and wrapped in thought. I looked around the barn to see whether the other residents were still there and found most asleep, others, like Nancy, simply stared vacantly and listened to the violence outside. Rebecca started to stir, awoken by my movement more than the raging battle in the distance. Anne was nowhere to be seen.

'Where's Anne?' I asked Nancy.

'Probably answering Nature's call,' she said, without breaking her blank stare.

'Is it safe to go out there?'

'Depends how far she went,' Nancy shrugged.

Rebecca sat up next to me.

'Should we go and look for her?' she asked. Nancy just shrugged again.

'Can't do anything until they finish killing. Got a couple of hours yet I reckon. Check your tools.'

We sat on the floor around Nancy. She took some cloth

drawstring coin purses out of her bag and gave us three each.

'If you fill them, come and find me, I've got plenty more.'

I took the purses and stuffed them into the pockets of my dress. I still had my forceps and turnkey hidden in the folds of my skirt, and the knife up my sleeve.

Anne came back into the barn and sat down with a smug look on her face. I noticed she had fresh blood patched all over the cuffs of her dress!

'Looks like I'm ahead already,' she announced breezily, and opened her hand to reveal seven whole teeth still wet and bloody.

'You stupid girl!' Nancy shouted, full of rage, 'Do you know how far and wild those muskets fire? You could've been killed!'

'S-sorry,' mumbled Anne, 'I thought you'd be impressed.'

'I don't want you risking your life,' said Nancy, as she took hold of Anne's right hand.

I watched in horror as Nancy she drew her knife and ran it smoothly over Anne's wrist. Anne shrieked. The blood-soaked cuff of her dress came loose, but the flesh beneath was unharmed. Nancy cut the cuff completely off and did the same with the other side, discarding them both in the hay.

'Next time, roll your sleeves up. Can't be going home with blood-stained sleeves. Folk'll ask questions.' She passed some of the coin purses to Anne, 'Keep your teeth in these.'

The battle raged outside. We sat in silence.

As the morning wore on, the rallying battle cries were drowned under the cries of pain. By the afternoon, the cannons and musket were silent. An eerie quiet fell over the barn. I could still hear the moans of the wounded, but no longer the strangled screams from the freshly skewered.

We looked at each other, then at Nancy. She nodded and led the way out of the barn.

A metallic taste tinged the air outside, a mixture of gunpowder and fresh blood carried on the wind. Rebecca said it smelt a little like her father's butcher shop. We walked up to the ridge on which the camp had been the night before and looked out over the plain below. The full scale of our task was horrifying. The mile-square carpet of dead bodies was alive with crows and flies, whilst those who were mortally wounded moaned and writhed in agony.

We had to get to work fast before the undertakers came with their carts to collect the dead. Nancy rolled her sleeves up high, almost to her shoulders, and bid us do the same. Then we began.

The teeth of fresh corpses proved much more difficult to pull than the old rotting corpse we had used back in the tavern cellar. That day felt like a lifetime ago as I stood straddling my first fresh corpse on the battlefield at Waterloo; a young Frenchman by the uniform. French or English, it didn't matter. The teeth could be sold to the lords and ladies of London as the teeth of fallen officers of the Royal Horse Guards. Nobody could prove otherwise, and everybody wanted teeth with a good story behind them

The young man's incisors were the easiest to get out, but that was to be expected really. The teeth were in fairly good condition. Five-guinea teeth for his best, a couple of molars at the back were fairly worn and probably only worth a guinea or two each. I guessed he had been grinding his teeth in his sleep for weeks, worrying about the battles. At least his worries were over now. He was gone and all that remained was simple flesh and bone.

The dark, staring eyes were nowhere near as beautiful as

the Surgeon's, but the young man had been handsome enough in his own way. I felt sadness for him, and disgust at the task before me. Yet, I had committed to the job, Mr. Laurence had given me training and equipment and paid for my passage; I had to complete the job for him. I shut my mind off from what the dead man used to be, and told myself once more that this was simply flesh that lay before me.

I put my foot on the man's face to get some leverage as I pulled the better of his molars with my turnkey. The horror of the job proved much easier to shut off from without the eyes staring up at you, so I quickly developed a technique. Once I had taken all of the best ones, I moved on to the next body and began again. After several bodies I found that the best, healthiest teeth did not suck wetly when pulled out. They took a lot more effort, strong and young enough to fight back, desperate to remain in the skull. When pulled properly they would thunk out of the rigid gum and keep their long root. I got some beautiful six and seven guinea teeth by targeting only the best. Some, I cracked, I was still learning after all, but there were plenty more.

'Don't twist the forceps!' I heard Nancy shout. That was the rule with the forceps; if you twisted, you'd crack the teeth. They were no good to anyone then.

When I learned to consider the meat before me as being the same as pig flesh, the more destroyed the visages and horrific the head wounds became a blessing. It was far easier to use a hand to simply pick out the best teeth from the bloody mess of a skull, than it was to grunt and groan trying to extract them by force. We had the cannon and musket balls to thank for that.

So absorbed was I in my task that I had filled my first

coin purse within an hour, and had started on my second one, when I inadvertently stumbled upon a wounded – but not quite dead – young man. I had just used my finger to part his lips and choose a tooth to begin with, when the body let out a moan.

'Help me,' it breathed.

I jumped back in fright and looked around the battlefield for the others. We had become quite spread out, and none of the others were in earshot. The man had the throbbing purple mass of half of his bowel hanging out of his gut, and his face was as pale as the corpses surrounding him.

'Help,' he breathed again, through quivering lips.

'Sir, I, I don't think I can,' I said, quite shaken.

'Please,' came the whispered response. I looked around again, but there was nobody nearby to help. I looked closer at the gash across the man's gut. His uniform had been sliced open, and the flesh beneath. The man's insides were clear to see. The throbbing purple intestine was not cut, but there was no way I could push it back inside and seal him up again.

'I'm so sorry, I don't know how to help,' I said. I felt useless, and tears welled up in my eyes. I wished the Surgeon was there, he would have known what to do.

'Mercy,' breathed the man. I knelt over his head and looked into his staring eyes. The life there was very faint. His dry, cracked lips parted again, 'Mercy,' he whispered. I wiped my eyes and knew what I had to do.

I drew my blade from my sleeve, and realised our good Surgeon's purpose in giving us a knife. Used in the right way, a sharp blade can bring as much relief as it can pain.

'Goodbye sir,' I said to the man, and kissed him gently on the forehead as I ragged the knife through his throat.

I left him with his teeth in tact; given our unexpected but

very intimate shared moment I felt uncomfortable with taking them. There were plenty more on the battlefield.

The little incident had thrown me from my rhythm and once I had taken the best teeth, I stood up straight to look around. There were others combing through the slaughter; thieves stealing rings and pistols, military men looking for the wounded, and the death wagons had started arriving. It was impossible for us to get all of the teeth; even if we had twenty girls working we would not manage half of it. The most upsetting sight was the weeping wives searching for their lovers amongst the slaughter. The corpses were still more than mere flesh to them and seeing their despair made the flesh seem human again. Keeping well clear of them – for it would be truly awful if one should catch me with my turnkey in the mouth of their loved one. I looked away and focused on the task in hand. This was just a job; a butcher doesn't feel sorry for the sow when he carves up a boar.

I had soon filled my coin purses and so picked my way across the battlefield to get more purses from Nancy. I considered her from a distance and noted that she had grown plump and quite wealthy working for the Surgeon. She had been to battlefields many times, and seen the horrors of war. Mister Laurence trusted her. I hoped that one day he would trust me too. She was bloody up to the elbows. I looked at myself and saw that I was the same. When I asked for more bags, she handed them to me with a proud smile.

The other girls came back to Nancy too, and we worked near to her for the next hour or so. I managed to fill three more bags before Nancy called a halt.

We returned to the barn and washed our bloody arms in the animals' drinking trough, as quick as we could. Our bags of teeth would need to be hidden in our skirts so as not to attract unwanted attention. To best do this, Nancy gave us all a needle and thread and we quickly stitched the tops of the bags closed against the inside lining fabric underneath our skirts. Nancy had filled the most bags by far with twelve, Anne had seven, I had six, and Rebecca five.

The mourning trail was to be our ticket home. Carriages were dropping a never-ending stream of mourning women and children on the track that led to the battlefield. We found an empty one, the horses grazing calmly nearby, and though the driver would not take us all the way back to Calais, we reached the central square in Brussels by sunset.

The square was bustling with celebrating soldiers. Wellington must have won. It didn't matter to us, Nancy said we had a boat to catch and hurried us to one of the larger carriages. She was in some hurry. Our skirts rattled with teeth as we scurried across the mouth of the square. Ignoring the catcalls from the soldiers, we climbed in to a carriage. We three girls sat panting inside whilst Nancy bartered with the driver. He did not sound keen to make an overnight run to Calais. After much arguing I heard a large number of coins being counted out, then Nancy threw her bag into the carriage and climbed in after it. The carriage jolted into motion and we soon left the chaos of the square behind.

In the peace of the carriage, Nancy took the brandy out of her bag and shared it around. We swapped stories from the battlefield and drank to our successes. I told the others about the poor fellow that I had helped with my knife and they all agreed I had done the right thing. They'd all had to do similar. Pulling teeth was hard labour, and we all complained that our arms ached. Nancy laughed and playfully mocked us. Going back to harvesting grain on the farm after the thrill of harvesting teeth on a battlefield would be very dull. If my harvest from Waterloo proved large enough, perhaps I wouldn't have to.

We finished the bottle of brandy and much to our dismay Nancy had no more left. She said we would be collecting more at Calais for Mister Laurence, but until then we would have to remain sober. She was on edge. The bumping and jolting of the carriage did not allow sleep to come easily, but after such a tiring day we all eventually drifted off, heads nodding.

The sun was just rising when we stopped in Calais, right by the waterfront. Nancy clipped us all around the head to wake us up and leapt out of the carriage.

'Hold onto your skirts and hurry! We have to be on that boat!' she shouted. Still dazed, not fully awake, we followed her orders and leapt out of the carriage after her.

The waterfront was just coming to life as we dodged and scurried past the fishermen and market traders. Nancy turned right onto a long wooden pier sticking out into the ocean. We hurried after her, our feet pounding on the wood and teeth rattling in our skirts. At the end of the pier was a small packet boat, bobbing gently on the waves, preparing to launch. The crew watched, smiling as we careered towards them. Nancy handed her bag to one of the men in the boat and leapt in after it. There were no other passengers on the boat, and once we were all aboard, the crew immediately untied the mooring and we launched out into the ocean.

'Didn't think you were going to make it, Nancy,' said one giant grizzled sailor.

To my surprise Nancy put a hand on his cheek and kissed him quite passionately! Rebecca and I giggled to each other. Anne frowned in disgust. Nancy eventually pulled away.

'Don't ever doubt me darling,' she said, patting his cheek lovingly.

When we were well out of sight of land, Nancy and her sailor went to the back of the boat and lifted a tarpaulin that lay over five large barrels. I saw her nod approvingly, and then she filled her brandy bottle from one of the barrels and returned to her seat next to us.

Nancy's sailor and his few crew members shared their food with us. Thankfully I managed to keep my stomach this time. The sea was much calmer than it had been on the way out.

Eventually Dover harbour appeared on the horizon. Nancy's giant grizzled sailor lifted a large brass telescope to his eye and stared for some time.

'Bastards,' he growled, 'They're checking the boats.'

'Police?' asked Nancy. The sailor nodded. 'Can they see us?'

'More than likely.' He tapped his telescope, 'I can see them. We'll have to come back for those five.'

He barked a series of commands at his crew, but I couldn't make out a word of it. The crew quickly started running about the ship with long lengths of rope. They tied the five large brandy barrels tightly together and pushed them over the side of the boat! All of that fine brandy! Each one splashed into the ocean with a deep gulp. The rope snaked off after them over the side. Before the end of the rope disappeared into the sea, one of the sailors tied a large wooden 'X' to it and threw it overboard. The wooden 'X' floated on top of the water, the rope disappearing deep into the murky depths below.

Nancy tugged underneath her skirt and pulled out her

bags of teeth. She handed four bags to each of us and bid us stitch them into our skirts.

'They'll want to question me, but I can get you three past. Cry. You're widows. Walk slowly so that you don't clink. Go straight to Madame Zheng.' She spoke intensely. 'Tell John he'll have to wait for his brandy.'

As we pulled into harbour, there were a dozen policemen stood on the pier. One officer smiled and strode forward, taking the mooring line from one of the sailors. Anne, Rebecca and I, sobbed like the best of the grieving widows I had seen on the battlefield.

Nancy and the sailors were taken into custody, but the police took pity on us grieving widows and even helped us to find a carriage back to London.

We were in shock as we rumbled and jolted along in the carriage. Everything suddenly felt very wrong after our brush with the police, and without Nancy we were motherless. Rebecca and I sat on one side of the carriage, our hands held, comforting each other. We did not feel like opening the curtains; the bright day outside was at odds with our mood. Anne sat opposite us, she did not seem at all sad. I had carried Nancy's bag and left it on the floor of the carriage, Anne reached into it and took out Nancy's bottle of brandy.

'Worth the risk if you ask me.' She held up the brandy and took a deep swig, 'Damn fine brandy.'

She offered it around to us, but it felt wrong to sup the golden liquid without Nancy. Anne went on drinking regardless. She kept on twitching the curtain back to check outside, as though waiting for something, and shuffling about uncomfortably on her seat.

The reason for her edginess became clear when we were deep in the Kent countryside.

She reached under her skirts and pulled out a flintlock pistol, aiming it shakily from me to Rebecca and back. I had seen similar weapons at the hips of some of the dead soldiers on the battlefield.

'Hand over your teeth ladies,' she smirked, cocking back the hammer, 'Or I'll take them, and the ones still in your pretty little mouths!' The carriage hit a hole in the road and jolted sharply. The sudden movement took Anne by surprise; the pistol exploded in her shaking hands. Rebecca screamed.

In a small space and at such close range the noise was deafening. Blue gunpowder smoke filled the little carriage. I wondered why the carriage didn't slow down.

As the smoke cleared I drew my knife and lunged at Anne. In one smooth movement she dodged and rose from her seat, drawing her own blade. With wide, unstable stances, we stood opposite each other in the pistol smoke. The knife felt awkward in my hand. It was one thing to slit the throats of dying soldiers to ease their pain, but quite another to fight an equally armed opponent. Anne did not look awkward; she held the knife with experienced hands.

Rebecca sat slouched in the corner, blood pouring from her right shoulder. She kicked the handle on the carriage door behind Anne, which swung open to reveal the fields racing by outside. Anne glanced around and I saw my chance. Before she could turn back, I threw my weight at her, shoulder first, and knocked her out of the open door. Her scream was cut short by a thud as she hit the floor outside.

The driver still did not slow the horses. I leaned out of the door to look back and saw Anne begin to move in the grass. Turning back, I noticed the driver up top looking around at me.

'You want that I should stop, miss?' he asked, shouting over the rumble of the carriage and the thundering of the horses' hooves.

'Drive on sir! Watch the road ahead!' I shouted back. The man was obviously used to making trips from Dover to London. He knew not to ask questions of travellers picked up from the docks, especially ones who arrived by a packet boat greeted by a dozen policemen.

Back inside the carriage, I tore a rag of cloth from the hem of my dress and did my best to stop the blood pumping from Rebecca's shoulder. She groaned anew with every jolt of the carriage. I put the brandy in her hand and bade her drink deeply.

By the time we stopped outside Madame Zheng's door, Rebecca was blind drunk. She did not seem to feel the pain in her shoulder, but was alarmingly grey and ashen about the lips and eyes. With money from Nancy's bag I paid the driver extra to clean his carriage and keep his silence, then took most of Rebecca's weight around my shoulder and hauled her out into the street. People nearby eyed us suspiciously as I brayed on Zheng's door so loudly and sharply that I feared it would break.

After a moment, Madame Zheng answered. She took one look at us and helped us inside. Locking the door behind us, she took some of Rebecca's weight from me and together we carried her down the alleyway. Inside Zheng's little home, we lay Rebecca on the bed by the open window.

'Get the Surgeon!' I said, desperate. Rebecca was looking paler as the dark red blood soaked her grubby white dress.

Madame Zheng was leaning over Rebecca. She had her sleeves rolled up and was using a cloth to wipe the blood from Rebecca's wounded shoulder.

She looked up from her work and screwed her little

wrinkled face up at me in a scowl. She pressed the cloth hard onto the wound in Rebecca's shoulder.

'Hold this here. Press hard,' she said, in her strange voice, pointing at the cloth. I took her place putting pressure on the wound, and she hurried up the few steps to the door that led into the tavern. The sound of the busy tavern filled the room for a second before she closed the door behind her.

For what felt like an hour I stood over Rebecca, pressing the cloth hard on her wound. I had tried to speak to her, to keep her awake, but Rebecca had lost consciousness. She was still breathing, but very shallowly. I feared that if Madame Zheng and Mr. Laurence did not come back soon, Rebecca would be dead.

Then the door to the tavern burst open. My heart leapt as Mr. Laurence strode manfully into the room. Madame Zheng followed close behind him, carrying a large metal cauldron full of water and more cloths over her shoulders. She put the cauldron of water over the fire. The Surgeon came and stood next to me at Rebecca's side. His breath smelled of the sweet brandy.

'My lady!' He bowed elaborately and then looked down at Rebecca, his mind racing. He held his fingers to her throat and seemed to be counting, and then leant over with his cheek next to her mouth to feel her breath. He pinched her under the arm, and she moaned a little.

'Anne shot her,' I said.

'Yes,' he replied, drawing a small rectangular box from the inside pocket of his jacket, 'Madame Zheng, boil me some water please.'

Madame Zheng pointed at the cauldron already on the fire and the Surgeon gave her a smile and a wink. He opened the small box and tipped several shiny metal objects into the water.

'Where is Nancy and why do you have her bag? Tell me what happened, don't spare any details!' He took over from me with putting pressure on the bullet hole, and I stood back.

As I recounted my tale, Zheng fished Mr. Laurence's shiny surgical tools from the boiling water with a pair of tongs. She laid them out on a tea tray and placed the tray on the table next to the bed. The Surgeon selected a scalpel blade and small pair of tweezers, then leant over Rebecca and began extracting the bullet from her shoulder. It was amazing to watch him work so skilfully, despite the brandy on his breath. Whilst he operated, he gasped and scoffed at various points in my story, sighing regretfully when I spoke of Nancy's arrest. Zheng boiled some clean bandages and towels, ready to dress Rebecca's wound.

'And what of the teeth?' asked the Surgeon, still not looking up from his work.

I rattled my skirt and then went outside to the alley to pull the purses from their hiding place, returning with them held proudly before me. Mr. Laurence glanced up from his work and whistled with delight.

'Aha!' he cried, and held up a small pistol shot in his tweezers. 'Got the beggar.'

Rebecca moaned in fresh pain as blood flooded once more from the wound. Like a cat, Madame Zheng leapt on the wound with a clean bandage putting pressure on the wound.

'Right, bind her up and get her some water. Chop, chop!' Said the Surgeon, sitting down in Madame Zheng's deep armchair. 'Rebecca will be fine, well, I expect she will always have a little stiffness in that shoulder, but she will live. Now, Emma, have you ever been to America?'

I told him I had not. I did not even know where it was.

'Given the facts of your little tale, and you tell it so well my dear, I think it might be best if we left the country for a while!' he beamed as he spoke. 'Wars have been going on in America for decades, their surgeons are terrible, and the rich have developed quite a taste for sugar!' he laughed.

'You mean for me to come with you, Mr. Laurence?' I could not believe what he was saying, my heart raced and I felt a little faint.

'Of course! I couldn't leave you here! You're clearly a most skilful worker my sweet. But you must please call me John.'

'What about the others?' I would feel terrible leaving everyone behind, and now in danger of arrest. The Surgeon craned casually around the armchair to look at Madame Zheng.

'How about it Zheng? America?' He bellowed. Zheng simply gave a curt nod. He turned back to me. 'Nancy will be fine, she's a wily one, and with the teeth you've got there, your mother will be set for life! I'll make sure Rebecca gets her fair pay. Come on, Emma. What do you say?'

John William Anthony Laurence held out a hand to me and looked into my soul. Reading me with his beautiful eyes and charming smile.

How could I refuse?

QUARANTINE

Quarantine

October 1882

She was to be held in quarantine until the sickness had run its course. Bloated and gangrenous, our frigate wallowed in the murky water like a corpse waiting for rot or redemption. Stranded in an empty void, the blurred line of somewhere and nowhere; we could neither dock nor return until the disease had cleansed us. After months at sea, striking an unerring path towards our goal, we could now only wait. Just beyond sight of the harbour. Languishing in the abyss.

I am convinced it was the cramped, dank conditions in the Coolie[1] 'tween deck that had caused the disease to spread like wildfire. As the ship's surgeon, I had done all I could for them, but most would not survive another month. The disease had grown in strength since we began our voyage, and there were quickly too many infected to contain it.

We hurriedly took on three hundred Hindoo labourers in Calcutta, destined for the plantations of Surinam. The Hindoos were cheaper to feed, being vegetarian, but many lacked the solid constitution for long voyages. I warned the Captain – God rest his soul – of the risks of rushing the

---

[1] See glossary.
Collective term referring to indigenous peoples to Asia. Accurate term in context of story history. Not used here in any way in a derogatory fashion.

recruitment process, but was assured all medical assessments had been properly conducted. I did not believe it at the time, but could not question the Captain's word. He may have left me behind and taken a different surgeon on the voyage; there were always others seeking work in the ports. So, I kept quiet and took the job. Lord how I wish that I hadn't.

Every worker was passed fit for the indenture vessel, but the disease had been with us since we embarked. On clothes, or in the water, maybe one of the Coolies was already infected before coming aboard. It didn't matter. It was simply a question of whether we would reach our destination or be wiped out entirely.

After the first few deaths, the Coolies wanted to build a funeral pyre on the deck to burn the corpses – the Hindoos cremate their dead to help the soul escape – but thankfully the Captain forbade it. He persuaded the Coolies of the folly of such action aboard a wooden ship. The Captain was amongst the earliest fatalities.

I was in my cabin writing my report when the weak, sharp-knuckled rap at the door finally snapped my frayed spirits. Every day those knuckles rapped on my door. That rattle-boned harbinger of another soul departed. If I declined to acknowledge the rapping it would only repeat, if not straight away then within the hour. Over and over, sharper and sharper. With more bones and rattle each time.

This time, the rapping caused me to jump and blot the ink across my report paper and on my hands. I looked at the black liquid forking through the wrinkles and cracks in my skin, and watched it seep like a black blush across the paper. This was how the disease started. From a blot in the Coolie 'tween deck, it bloomed through the corridors and veins of the ship, poisoning her and infecting us all.

When the spreading cloud of black ink reached a spilled drip of candle wax, it was forced around it. After a few seconds, the drip of wax was an island in the growing black sea. I realised the image was a message meant for me. A sign that I needed to put a barrier between the disease and myself. To isolate myself. To quarantine myself aboard the ship even as she lay quarantined from the world. This would be the last time that I answered the bony knocking at my door. I held my handkerchief over my nose and mouth, and rose from my desk.

With the help of the surviving Coolies, we wrapped yet another emaciated body in his soiled hammock. We dragged and hauled the corpse up from the 'tween deck through the levels of ship. Past the crew's quarters, now only sparsely populated. I did not know any of the crew members particularly well, but felt a helpless sympathy for them as they lay quivering in their hammocks, gripped by the disease. They would not see the end of the quarantine.

As we dragged the stinking corpse-filled hammock up through each level, the stench of disease thinned but never left my nostrils. Above deck, other Coolies gathered. Gaunt and skeletal, their loose robes of grubby white and ochre draped from their bony shoulders. Many wore their typical cloth wrappings around their heads and their thick beards quivered as they chanted in their strange rhythmic language. Each one prayed individually so that a hushed cacophony sloshed around us as we dragged their dead countryman through the crowd. At the gunwale we hoisted the body over the side, consigning it to the sea with the distinctive splash that forever haunts me. We long ago abandoned all ceremony. This was death seventy-four. The body lingered at the surface for a moment, covered in a frothy mesh of ocean spray, then the moment passed and it disappeared below the surface.

I hurried back through the crowd of chanting Coolies and down below deck. Quick and decisive. A surgeon of my experience could expect around three shillings per emigrant landed alive. If I reached my target quota, I stood to make a handsome amount and would seek immediate passage back to England. But now, all thoughts of profit were irrelevant. I would be lucky to leave this ship with my own life.

From the water store I found a large cask of fresh water and rolled it along the corridors into my cabin. My racing mind wracked with guilt, but fuelled by the innate animal urge for self-preservation, I grabbed my pistol from the desk and headed for the kitchens. With the Captain and crew either dead or dying, the Coolies had the run of the ship. Weak as they were, they were large in number and could easily overwhelm me should they question my purpose. A group of five of them sprawled in the corridor, from the feverish sheen on their faces and the reddening around their eye sockets I knew at least three of them to be infected. I covered my mouth with my handkerchief and hurried past.

The kitchens were not the worst I had encountered on the many ships that I had been posted to, though catering for the large labour force meant they were vast. I began rifling through cupboards searching for anything that might sustain me during my self-imposed isolation. The wooden doors of the cupboards were warped as though melting – an unsettling effect of repeated exposure to steam from the huge cauldrons of boiling lentils.

Like most areas of the ship now, the kitchen was strangely subdued. Only the cook remained. Janu, a large leathery man, we recruited in Calcutta. A veteran of several voyages, and an affable fellow I sincerely hoped would survive the quarantine. We had a shared interest in anatomy. With him having spent his life carving up animals for cooking, he paid close attention to the details of animal anatomy and made some very interesting points about the circulation of the blood. I saw him the previous day and so far as I could tell, he had managed to avoid infection. He was usually guarding the rations, but he was nowhere in sight.

There had been no salted meat or fish left on board for more than a month, but I managed to gather together a few other things. Sea biscuits and dried peas I could soak in water to eat. The biscuits were crawling with maggots and weevils, but having visited many exotic countries during my years aboard ships, I knew insects to be a vital food source in some cultures. They would help to sustain me. From a cramped storeroom I took a left-over hunk of extremely pungent hard cheese, and bowl that could serve as both a drinking vessel and a means of soaking my peas and biscuits. Thankfully, I also found a large quantity of limes. They had hardened during the voyage but would still contain some of their juice and would be vital in keeping my body free of scurvy.

I would have foraged further, but the delicate shuffling of bare feet froze me. I crouched in the storeroom; my pilfered supplies bundled unsteadily in my arms. I knew it to be one of the infected Coolies from the sickening drag of his unsteady bare feet across the wooden floorboards. If he found me he would surely shout to his fellows and they would soon know I planned to abandon them to their fate. Though I had proved many times that I was helpless to contain or cure this particularly vicious strain of the disease, the Coolies still pinned their hopes on my title. If I was discovered with armfuls of rations the Coolies might attack me. Though I had no doubt they had not the strength to do me grievous harm, being in a close scuffle could cause me to contract the disease. I had already run that risk too many times in my futile efforts to cure the doomed.

At the thought of the infection I instinctively reached for my handkerchief, and in doing so dropped a tin of biscuits, which fell to the floor with a loud clang!

The footsteps outside ceased their shuffling. I held my breath. They shuffled again. Drawing nearer. I cocked back the hammer of my pistol but if I discharged the weapon, the noise would draw others. Maybe I could flee before they arrived. I put the rest of my supplies down and stood up. The footsteps came to a halt. I could sense the man on the other side of the door and pointed my pistol chest height at the storeroom door. As I steadied my nerves, I heard other footsteps pounding along the corridor leading to the kitchen. Sturdy shoe-shod footsteps echoing through the wooden beams, drawing ever closer. The storeroom door began to inch open, pulled from the outside.

Suddenly, a deep voice called out in the Hindoo tongue, full of aggression and menace. It was Janu, the cook. The door closed again and the thin, reedy voice of the Coolie replied with submissive tones. I heard Janu march towards the Coolie, and reckoned from the grabbing and wincing sounds that he was forcibly dragging the poor fellow from the kitchen back to the 'tween deck. He would not escape infection for long by putting himself in such close proximity to the disease. Janu's selfless preservation of the food supplies added to the guilt I felt at taking them. If he caught me taking food he would not treat me roughly like he did with the Coolies – though not technically an officer, I was a much respected member of the crew – but he would be gravely disappointed with me. He would ask me to return the food and if I refused, with the ship's officers dead or dying, he might be forced to act out-of-turn towards me. I had to get out of the kitchen before he returned from the 'tween deck.

The kitchen outside now empty, I worked quickly. An empty hessian lentil sack in the corner of the storeroom was perfect for my purpose. I filled it with as many provisions as I could lift, and hurried back to my cabin.

Struggling back along the corridor with my sack, I was pleased to see the loitering infected Coolies were playing cards. Some of the crew had given them cards to prevent them from becoming too melancholic during the long voyage. It was good for their spirits, though I knew not what games they played. They whispered to one another weakly and hoarsely in their strange Hindoo tongue.

As I passed by them, one put down his cards and began to approach me with outstretched hands, pleading for the help and salvation I could never give. The man leered at me with his sickening stench, his rotten teeth, sunken wet eyes, and puckered, hanging skin. His spittle-riddled mouth shuffled closer, breathing a vapour of disease and infection into the air before me. With my free hand, I held my handkerchief over my mouth and nose and fled down the corridor.

In safety of my cabin, I dropped the sack onto the floor and slammed the door shut. The heavy iron bolt had rusted in the damp heat of the room. It groaned and protested as I levered it shut, eventually sealing me in with a sharp thud as the rust gave way. It would not be enough once the death toll increased and the Coolies started their sharp knuckled rapping, begging me to heal them. The full water cask was heavy enough to be an effective blockade, so I stood it upright and with great effort managed to walk it up to rest against the door.

It would be three months before the quarantine officers came to inspect the health of any survivors. Hopefully then the quarantine would be lifted. If I was sparing I should easily have sufficient water for that time, but my meagre food rations would be more difficult to stretch.

Sealed inside, I surveyed the wooden crypt that would be my world until the disease had run its course. I had done my best to make my modest cabin homely during our voyage. Somewhere to retire at night after the trials of a hard day at sea. One small porthole window provided light and an occasional breeze in the stifling heat. I had a small desk pushed against one wall; my report book lay open on it, with an inkwell and a well-worn quill. Next to that, against the same wall, sat a stout bookshelf in which I kept several heavy leather-bound medical journals. On top of the bookshelf sat a small keg of rum – my personal supply – and a rather fine tankard that I had picked up from Denmark on a previous, happier, voyage. My bed was a simple rectangular pallet with a straw-filled mattress and single sheet; there was no need for anything more in this part of the world. The cabin was pleasant, but even so, the thought of being confined here indefinitely filled me with a monotonous dread. If I was to survive the quarantine period, it was my only option. I settled down at my desk to work on my report. It would be simple. Disease. Infection. Death.

I didn't know if I would deliver the report with my own tongue, or if it would burn with my corpse when the quarantine officers found no souls left aboard. They would set the ship ablaze to prevent our disease from infecting the world beyond.

As I lay in my bunk on that first night of my solitary confinement, the nocturnal rhythms of the ship held a new menace. However still the water might be, the ship could never quite rest. Her gentle rocking that once gave my room a womb-like peace and security, now made my stomach feel unsettled and my head swim. The subtle swell carried an unrelenting lapping of the water against her hull. I dreamt that the she had sprouted the oars of an ancient trireme, each one a savage thirsty tongue lapping up the sea like a giant beast desperate to rehydrate itself as the disease drained its vitality.

I awoke damp with sweat and flung open my porthole window. The cool breeze washed over my damp skin. The obsidian sea stretched out forever in the moonlight, swelling and swirling gently with the wake from the great beasts swimming just below the surface. The sight pulled the weight of dread deeper into my gut and I averted my gaze, looking instead upwards at the night sky. In this part of the world, the moon seemed a thousand times bigger than it did back in London, and the stars stood out sharply like diamonds on a black velvet cushion.

I breathed in deeply, filling my lungs with the pure clean sea air, and held that blissful moment in my mind as long as I could. Soon my own urge for water tore me away, back into my dank, festering little wooden tomb.

After fumbling in my desk drawers for a box of matches, I managed to light the lantern on my desk. With the room lit, I took a jimmy bar from my surgical toolbox and pried open the cask of water. Inside, the liquid was as black as tar. For the briefest of moments I feared I had brought the wrong cask, but the viscosity of the contents assured me that their blackness was merely a reflection of the dimly lit room. Indeed, upon holding my lantern over the surface, I could see that it was water. This far into the voyage, it inevitably had a little algae and was far from the pure water we had embarked with. But, mixed with a little rum and lime-juice I'd have grog of which Admiral 'Old Grog' Vernon[2] would be proud of.

Hours later, sleep still would not come.

I sat up in my bunk, staring vacantly at the cask against the door. Listening to the silence of a sleeping ship. Though the men seemed quiet, the ship herself was not sleeping at all. She creaked and whined as though talking with the unknown abominations that dwelt in the depths, fathoms below us. Conspiring secretly in a language known only to the wind and the tides. Half dozing, lost in my macabre imaginings as to what our ship might be discussing with the whales and leviathans, I was sharply roused by that sickening shuffle of bare feet.

Distant at first, hesitant, faltering. The footsteps made their way along the corridor outside my cabin, drawing ever closer. I snuffed out my lantern lest the light leak from under my door and betray me. Ragged, rasping breathing carried down the corridor and I instinctively raised my handkerchief to cover my mouth and nose. As the creature outside approached my door, I realised that the breathing was not the ragged, rasping caused by illness. Rather it was the hushed incantation of a prayer being muttered by the Coolie in his rhythmic Hindoo language. With the shuffling prayer now right outside my door, I held my breath. Waiting

---

[2] The English Naval officer who, in 1740, suggested watering down sailors' rum and adding lime juice to mask the water's foulness. It was not known why Vernon's sailors were healthier than the rest of the navy until 1747 when James Lind formally proved that scurvy could be treated and prevented by supplementing the diet with citrus fruits. The rest of the Royal Navy quickly followed Vernon's lead, supposedly calling the new drink 'Grog' after Vernon's nickname 'Old Grog', attributed to his habitual wearing of a grogram coat.

for the unmistakable sharp-knuckled rapping that summoned me to another victim. It seemed minutes rolled by and still the knock didn't come. The hushed chanting continued at my door, and then the shuffling stopped, but still I remained un-summoned.

Instead, the sound of a soft, padded finger ran slowly over the outside of my coarse wooden door. It seemed to be tracing a pattern, though of quite what I could not tell. Once the pattern was complete, the Coolie carried on his shuffling walk along the corridor. I listened for what seemed an hour until he was out of earshot. The cool breeze coming in through the open porthole had chilled the room beyond comfort, so I shut it before settling down to try and find sleep.

The heat of the morning sun had caused the room to fester. I awoke once more parched and stifled. The pungent hunk of hard cheese reeked through the hessian sack, the rankness of the stagnant drinking water was much worse by the light of day, and that inescapable stench of death and disease from the 'tween deck seeped up through the floorboards. At least I could empty my chamber pot out of the porthole into the sea, this I did immediately.

Unpleasant as the room was, isolating myself from the infected Coolies would greatly improve my slim chances of survival. Providing, of course, that the disease had not entered the room with me and was already in my body.

After acclimatising to the stench, I drank deeply from a fresh tankard of grog, and then filled my washbasin from the cask. There was nothing to prepare for, but hygiene and routine were of paramount importance if I was going to survive the quarantine with my mind and body intact. Stagnant though it was, the cool liquid washed the nightmares from my mind. I held my breath and submersed my whole head in the water. The world became wonderfully distant. The horrific deaths I had dealt with aboard this ship, and others, just a memory from another time. Under the water, all was calm and tranquil. I hoped that this was what the dead felt when we threw them over the side.

Pleasant thoughts of childhood and youth came to mind; fond memories of helping my father in his meat shop, and long summers home from boarding school when we would go to visit my uncle in the countryside. I thought of my wife, Harriet, and son, George. He had been almost walking when I left for Calcutta, and would surely have taken his first steps by now. Submerged in tranquillity, I held them both in my mind. The long voyages were harder to take being a father, but I had a bigger family to support and needed the higher wages. If I ever got back I would use the money I had saved from my previous voyages to open a small surgery in a quiet little village where I could be at home every day. I relished the fantasy. If only I could've held my breath forever.

The sound did not terrify me at first. Heard from under the water, as I travelled through my memories and fantasies, it seemed so harmless. Nothing to concern me. Then it came again. Sharper. With more knuckles.

As I pulled my head up, gasping for breath, the horrors of my reality rushed back to consume me. I lay on the floor, my head and shoulders soaked, and sobbed. The knock came again.

'Sir? Sir, there's more this morning.' The thick Indian accent was not familiar. When I didn't answer immediately, the wretched knocking came again.

'Over the side with them and let me rest!' I wailed through the door.

'What about names?'

'It doesn't matter now. Our families will be told. I will see no more corpses.'

After a moment's hesitation, the footsteps padded down the corridor and out of earshot.

With no reason to get up, I remained in my position on the floor, the water pooling under my head from my wet hair. I had never considered my cabin from this vantage point before.

For hours I let my eye explore every wooden plank and beam. Tuned my attention intimately to each one. The complex way that the grain of each beam flowed and bent around the knots. Each one uniquely wrought in a time when they grew from the earth as trees. I imagined the journey the beams had taken to reach this point. They had my eternal gratitude; for I could also feel the weight of the vast world from which they kept me safe. Below, millions of tons of cold liquid rested on the earth's crust, waiting patiently to return me to its mass. From the direction we had sailed, thousands of leagues of open Ocean, eaten up irreversibly as we progressed towards our goal, unaware we carried a disease that would prevent us from ever docking. Ahead, the place we would never reach until we could free ourselves of the malady. From the crow's nest it had been possible to see hints of the world that lay just beyond our grasp, but I could not risk climbing the mast again to look.

Something caught my eye that returned me to my immediate surroundings. Underneath my desk, right where the front-left leg joined the work surface, there was a small, thin scratch. No more than a hair's breadth, it nevertheless marked permanently some incident in the desk's lifespan. I ran my index finger over it and wondered how it might have happened. The scratch was an imperfection. A weakening. A thousand such scratches and the desk would be destroyed. Yet, taken alone, this single scratch was important and beautiful. It gave the desk a certain character. A story that no other desk could tell in quite the same way.

I was roused from my musing by that infernal dragging and chanting. More infected would have died in the night and the mess that the corpses left behind would spread the disease further. At least they died quietly, dehydrated flesh-covered skeletons had not the strength to scream. The dragging chant began below me, in the Coolies' 'tween deck. Slowly and sadly, but with a dogged determination, the Coolies hauled the bodies of their countrymen up through the levels of the ship. I listened to their eerie rhythmic chanting, growing ever louder as they reached the open deck. The hundred weak, shuffling feet dragged the corpses over the deck above my head. With the porthole open, the mysterious Hindoo language floated into my room on the breeze. It became intolerable, but this at least forced me to rise from my still prone position on the floor. I stood to shut the porthole, just in time to reduce the full effect of the inevitable splash.

The splashes continued unrelentingly throughout the day. Each one wrapped in the unearthly chanting and wailing from the surviving Coolies as they conducted their death rites in their strange Hindoo tongue. With each splash, I was reminded of the peace and tranquillity I had felt that morning with my head submerged in my washbasin. Without the instinctive animal panic to fight for breath, the dead could enjoy their submersion without fear.

To break the monotony, I filled a bowl with dried peas, biscuits and hard cheese, and then soaked the mixture in water in preparation for my evening meal. Weevils and maggots crawled out from the biscuits, trying to remain above the water. I empathised with them. The futility of their struggling. I watched them for a while and then put my finger into the water, allowing one of the struggling weevils to climb onto it. Its tiny feet crawled along my hand, feeling my grubby flesh with its mandibles. The wet, shiny wing cases on its back were like polished black onyx. I released it onto my desk and watched it fervently exploring the surface for a while.

Ignoring the splashes and chanting proved impossible. In a vain attempt to block out the sound, I tore up bits of cloth from my clothes chest and plugged my ears. Although this did diminish the harshness of the noises, it also gave my world a distant ethereal quality, and not in the pleasant, cooling way that the washbowl full of water did. After several hours it became merely the constant background noise that underpinned my life in that room. Each corpse took around half an hour to be dragged from the bowels of the ship, up to the deck and overboard into the sea, and each corpse seemed to take longer than the last as the Coolies grew ever weaker.

In the fading light, I sat reading a medical textbook when the chanting suddenly stopped. There were no more of the awful splashes. Solid, shoe-shod footsteps strode purposefully down the corridor towards my door. My stomach in my mouth, I reached for my grog and gulped down a large mouthful.

When the knock came, it wasn't the weak sharp-knuckled rap of the Coolie. This knock was from a meaty fist, firm and full of threat. I sat very still, holding my breath. Within six heartbeats, the knocking came again. Louder this time.

'Doc! Open the door.' Janu's deep Indian voice was unmistakable. He spoke better English than the Coolies, being an experienced ship's cook English was a language he had picked up from previous voyages. We had struck up a kind of friendship; surely he would understand me.

The door shook and I heard him wince as he put his shoulder to it. I leapt from my bed.

'Janu, stop! I'm alive.'

'Then why did you not help today? Why did you send the Coolie man away this morning?' He sounded hurt and confused.

'It's useless.' It felt pathetic to say, but it was the truth.

'You can help. You're a doctor.'

'It is out of control. Your best chance is to lock yourself away from the infected until the quarantine is over.' I could hear his breathing slow as he considered my words. He needed some sort of reassurance. 'I'll meet you when we dock.'

'You're lying!' he yelled, bashing loudly into the door again, 'you can help! Help me to carry the dead!'

His anger surprised me. He had always been very respectful and courteous during the voyage when we had talked about anatomy like good friends. In a small way I was glad that he could speak to me with such anger, it meant our friendship had been true. He had not simply being tolerating my company because he felt my station dictated that he must.

'The risk is too great now. You must keep yourself away from the infected Coolies.' I warned. Again, he took a moment before replying.

'You are a coward,' he said with a voice full of pity and disappointment. It hurt me to hear the word. 'But I hope I can remind you of your cowardice when we get off this ship. See you in Surinam, Doc'. He gave my door a friendly pat, which shook the bolts, before walking away down the corridor.

In all sincerity I hoped to see the fellow in Surinam, but throughout our voyage he had taken no precautions whatsoever when interacting with the Coolies. Not even so much as a handkerchief across his mouth. I knew in my heart that his chances were very slim.

My evening meal had spent most of the day softening in the bowl of water. The biscuits and maggots were a soft mush, and the hard cheese had swelled and was soft enough to chew. The dried peas and weevils were still quite hard, so I chewed cautiously and rolled them very delicately along my back teeth, breaking them down a little at a time. The meal tasted of rotten earth and pond scum, so I washed each mouthful down with a glug of strong grog.

The nocturnal terrors persisted and prospered. The black weevil I released from the broth had grown fat and large as a man, feasting on the rot and decay that pervaded throughout the ship. It stalked the corridors at night, its shiffling mandibles whispering dark oaths in a strange language and tasting the air. Its hard legs tapping and scratching at my wooden door. Stealthily as I could, I took my pistol from the bedside cabinet and crept towards the door. Pressing my ear against the wood, I could hear the creature outside shuffle away down the corridor.

Returning to my bunk, I spent the rest of the night trying to ignore the lapping tongues outside my porthole window with little success. The dawn brought the fetid heat back into the room and so began again my morning routine. I soaked my evening meal and washed my face. No knocking disturbed the tranquillity of my washbasin now and I enjoyed the water until the Coolies began again. Their chorus of dragging and chanting kept in time by the metronomic splashes of corpses into the sea.

As the days trundled inexorably on, the splashes outside became less regular, and the shuffling feet that dragged the bodies were fewer and weaker. The weevil kept up the nightly rounds of the corridor, filling me with dread as it scratched its grotesque limbs across my door.

Gradually, my nightmares spilled over into my daydreams.

Even in the light of day, the grain patterns in the floorboards and walls became the gaunt warped outlines of the emaciated Coolies. Trapped in the wood, their haunted sunken eyes staring at me from the baleful knots in every wall and surface. Each night the weevil creature passed by my door, and each time I readied my pistol. I sat up in bed waiting for the hideous teeth to chew through my door and the shiffling searching mandibles to reach in to taste me.

On the seventeenth night of solitude, after the remaining Coolies had finished their chanting and dragging, and the bodies had finished their splashing. I ate my meagre ration and rather than lying on my bed, pulled my desk chair underneath the porthole window to sit directly opposite the bolted door. I watched the door and waited for the weevil creature.

When all the light had melted from the sky, revealing the stars sharp and solid, I set to cleaning and reloading my pistol. After several hours I had started to drift off to sleep, my head nodding heavily. I needed to stay alert to be ready for the creature, and so I stood up and splashed my face with water from my washbasin and looked out of the open porthole window. The moon had begun to creep into view, full now and perfectly round. I watched it, mesmerised, just as it watched me.

Another hour passed and the full moon had almost filled the porthole, casting a pale white circle on my door, about two feet above the water cask. Then they came. The shiffling and clacking at the end of the corridor signalled the weevil's long awaited arrival. It approached slower than it had done before. Its hushed mandibles still muttering and its hard legs clacking against the wood. I rose from my seat to stand close to the door and leaned over the water cask to place my ear against the wood. Listening so intently and at such close proximity to the creature, my own breath seemed rasping enough to alert the abomination to my presence. I stilled it.

Clack clack clack. Shiffle Shiffle Shiffle. It would be upon me in a few steps. I raised my pistol to the door. The smooth metal barrel, crisp and cool in the moonlight, pressed against the dull grain of the wooden panel. I clicked back the hammer and stood with a straight arm. Through the pistol end I felt the beast scratching at the surface on the other side of the door. Its spiny arm directly in front of my pistol barrel. I held my breath, and squeezed the trigger.

Thunder. The sudden explosion deafened my ears, blanketing my whole world in that blessed aquatic tranquillity. From the door seemed to erupt in a hail of splinters, flakes of wood dancing like sycamore seeds as they drifted through the blue-grey moonlit gunpowder smoke. When the smoke cleared it revealed a ragged circular hole about the size of a lime in the middle of the door. It was in perfect alignment with the porthole on the opposite wall, and the full moon beyond that.

The shiffling mandibles and clacking limbs had ceased. Tilting my head so as not to block the moonlight, I peered through the hole. What lay beyond drew a wail of horror from the pit of my stomach.

Pinpointed by the pale moonlight streaming through the porthole and the bullet hole, a wet, terrified, sunken eye stared back at me. The eye was still attached to the most ancient, gnarled and emaciated Coolie I had ever seen. He was clearly dead, slumped against the corridor wall opposite my door, a gaping hole in his chest cavity. I could not tear my eyes from what I had made. Though the moon's beam picked out only his sunken unblinking eye, I could just make out the white bone of his rib cage exposed amidst the mangle of his chest. I felt a surge of guilt but tried to quell it with the thought that the old man, like the rest of us, was on a gruelling and tortuous path towards death. I had simply eased his passage. Try as I might, this logic was no justification and the guilt would not leave me. In my madness I shot an old man. He still clutched his bamboo cane in his claw-like fingers.

I awoke the next morning to the usual stifling, putrid heat. My head was still hazy from the nightmares that had plagued my sleep. I bid good morning to the Coolies in the wood grain, and set to emptying my bedpan, soaking my evening meal, and preparing my washbasin. I resolved to treat myself to fresh water from the cask, and threw the old water out of the porthole. There were only two weeks left before the quarantine officers would arrive to check if we were free of our disease, and I still had plenty of water for drinking. It was green and scummy, but still fresher than that which I had been using for my morning washes. Upon approaching the water cask, I leapt back, crying out in terror. There above the cask, in the bullet hole in the door, that baleful, sunken eye that I had hoped never to see again. It stared at me, unblinking.

'Sir, what have you done?' came the strained Coolie voice of the eye. Dropping my washbasin, I scurried back away from the eye. Pressed back against the side of the ship. I would have climbed out of the porthole if I could fit. Anything to get away from that eye.

'Leave me alone!' I cried.

'Sir, the old Sadhu![3] Why did you do this to him? You've doomed us all!' Spoke the eye, in an Indian voice full of despair, as it writhed in the bullet hole.

'I did all I could! It is beyond my skill to contain the disease! Please! Leave me!' I sobbed openly, the tears stinging my cracked lips. I clawed at the faces in the wood grain, desperate to be away from the eye.

'The Sadhu's night Shlokas[4] thanked the Gods for each day and made them merciful. Now there is no hope.' With that, the eye disappeared. I stayed in my position, crouched against the back wall of my tomb, listening the dragging of another corpse. This one began right outside my door.

When I had the nerve to move, I stood up on shaking legs and tore a sheet of paper from my report book. I used some melted wax from a candle to stick the paper across the bullet hole in the door. If one of the infected Coolies were to cough into or near to the hole, then the disease would get into my room and straight into my cask of drinking water. I also wanted to stop any other Coolies from peering through at me with their haunting eyes.

I buried my guilt at shooting the old Sadhu under the thought that I had vanquished the weevil horror that stalked our good ship's corridors. However, I could do nothing about her unrelenting thirst that kept her lapping at the water. Nor would she cease her wailing creaks as she bargained with the leviathans of the deep. The distorted,

---

[3] A Sadhu is a Hindu holy man.

[4] Hindu prayer chants performed commonly to invoke various Gods and Goddesses.

skeletal Coolies in the wood grain seemed to have changed position each morning, but unlike the eye in the bullet hole, they were not intent on me. They were content and peaceable.

The daily dragging of corpses by feeble, shuffling feet, slowed from a torrent to a trickle. Each day the interval between splashes lengthened, the dragging slower and more laboured.

I was laid inert on my bunk when the splash that would be the last finally came. I had followed the dragging from its origin in the 'tween deck at the start of the day, right past my door, and by late afternoon it was up on the open deck above me. As it dragged over the planks above my head, I could count the weak shuffling footsteps of only one man. Praying alone, his chanting was almost inaudible as he panted and wheezed, dragging his load to the gunwale. When the splash eventually came, it was followed by a thud as the burden bearer dropped to the deck in exhaustion. Then all was silent. Even the ship seemed to hold her tongue for several moments. A strong breeze picked up and whistled through the porthole.

For four days I heard no human noise upon the ship, all was silent save for the ship herself. Her continuous creaking and lapping became a comfort, a reassurance that I was still alive. I understood her as though I had learned her language. The denizens of the deep respected her, were in awe of her, such that if she were silent for too long I would pray to hear her voice again to keep them at bay.

On the fifth evening it became overwhelmingly hot. Whilst trying to keep down an evening meal, and having heard not a soul for almost a week, I resolved to venture out of the room. The heat really was too stifling; I was being cooked alive. I longed to walk above deck in the cool sea breeze.

It being the first time I would have left the confines of those four walls for what felt like a lifetime, I wanted to be at my best to meet any survivors. So I washed myself thoroughly, took the cleanest of my shirts out of my clothes chest, gathered my personal effects, and prepared for the world beyond my door.

The cask in front of the door was almost empty and I was able to move it with relative ease. Before sliding open the bolts, I peered through the bullet hole for the first time since the eye had left me in peace. In the corridor outside the room was a vicious dried bloodstain where the old weevil Coolie had ceased his cursed nocturnal pacing. There was nothing else unusual outside. Slowly and with no small effort, I wriggled the metal bolts from their fastenings. They came apart with a clang, as dusty ochre rust broke apart. Screeching on its hinges, the door swung inwards.

The air was much different out in the corridor, dustier and harder. With no deck-hands or Coolies strong enough to clean, the blood outside my door had been left to become rancid. The guilt and disgust at my crime surged up again from my stomach and I fought to push it back down. The blood was like none I had seen before; it was coagulated and sticky with the heat. The heat. I strode over the mess, disturbing a huge mass of flies.

Once I had left the blood behind, excitement built in every step. I wanted to run and stretch my legs but had not the energy. Giddy with the freedom, I followed the corridor around the ship to the one on the opposite side that ran parallel to mine. I wanted to check if Janu had followed my advice. If he still lived, perhaps we would be rowed into Surinam together. I brayed on his cabin door with my bony fist. Poor diet and lack of exercise caused the weight to fall off of me. I noticed for the first time that my fists were as bony and sharp as the Coolies. My rapping on Janu's door hurt my knuckles and brought back the old sickening feeling of the Coolies knocking on my own door. Instead, I took out my pistol and used the butt to pound the door once more.

'Janu!' I yelled as loudly as my parched throat would allow, grinning and laughing I yelled again, 'Janu!'

No answer came. The door was firmly locked. I brayed on it several more times with the butt of my pistol. My joyous yells turned to cries of despair. I knew he could never hear me.

With a heavy heart I left Janu to rest in peace.

On top of the deck the heat did not abate, yet the sun had almost sunk into the sea on the horizon. It was as though the heat was coming from the ship herself. In the same way that a pile of compost gives off heat as it rots, so too our vessel was decomposing as she wallowed in quarantine. At the front of the ship were the remnants of the funeral pyre that the Coolies had been forbidden from lighting. Thankfully they had understood the folly of lighting the pyre aboard a wooden ship, for it did not appear to have been lit. There were drag marks across the deck, leading to the gunwale. This had been the corpse road.

A single corpse lay on the deck, at the end of the corpse road, right next to the gunwale where the bodies had been thrown overboard. It was the final Coolie who had used his last shred of energy to consign the diseased corpse of his countryman to the sea. He had dropped to the ground in exhaustion and lain there to expire in the sun. Now the pool of disease visibly permeated through wooden deck around him, like the blot of ink spreading across my report paper. I kept well clear.

Over the edge of the ship, in the sea below, I noticed a small rowing boat. My heart leapt! It seemed too good to be true. Perhaps it was looters, willing to risk the disease for a little plunder. Or perhaps it really was what I had prayed for; the medical officer in charge of the quarantine station had finally sent the boat out to collect the survivors! There was a man in the boat, his hooded cloak pulled right up despite the heat. The first person I had seen alive in three months!

'Hoah there!' I called down at him. He looked up and gestured for me to climb down.

'Is the quarantine lifted?' I shouted. The fellow didn't answer me, but merely gestured again that I should get into the boat. Being where we were it was likely that he didn't speak English. I noticed a ladder had been thrown over the forecastle, and began to descend it. Unsteadily at first – I had not been physically active for some time – but growing in confidence with every step. I laid my hand on the hull of the ship, sad to be leaving this beautiful creature who had kept me safe for so long. She was warm to the touch. Alive, almost. Looking up at her one last time, her brilliant white sails shone bright red in the last rays of sunlight. I bid her farewell and climbed into the rowing boat.

As the silent oarsman rowed us across the bay towards the harbour, I looked over the water to and noticed another small rowing vessel. It was on the same course as us but roughly a hundred metres ahead. The boat had one broad shouldered occupant, and was being rowed by another of the dockworkers. I was filled with joy when I realised who it was. There was only one man aboard our ship with such broad shoulders.

'Janu!' I shouted, waving my arms. The man in the boat looked around. It was him! Truly! He had survived the quarantine! We would drink together again, play cards, and swap stories.

'See you in Surinam brother!' He called back. Delighted I sat back in the boat, and looked over my shoulder for one more glimpse of our ship. To my surprise, it was ablaze with raging fire! Perhaps some of the Coolies had survived and finally had their funeral pyre. Or maybe the Quarantine Officer had deemed it too unsanitary to dock, with Janu and I being the only survivors. I felt sad that so fine a ship would flounder at the bottom of the ocean. Though perhaps there she would enjoy the aquatic tranquillity, without thirst and without fear. She disappeared out of sight over the horizon, just as the sun had not an hour before.

As we approached the harbour, I wondered what strange new wonders lay ahead in Surinam. Perhaps the oarsman could guide me? I took a couple of pennies out of my pocket to pay him.

ARROWHEAD

Arrowhead

Summer 1832

In the summer of 1832 I took a post assisting in the delivery of classes at a remote boarding school on the banks of an estuary in the Suffolk countryside. Wearing my best top hat and tailcoat, with my least-scuffed shoes and overnight bag, I took the train from London early on the Thursday morning. The previous assistant had taken ill the night before, and I was only to be boarding there for one night as the summer school finished on the Friday teatime. It may seem a long way for two day's work, but the money, and chance to occupy my mind, was too good to refuse. After the accident in the canal I gave up my teaching position in the city and had not worked since. My funds from the sale of our house had almost gone.

It really was the most beautiful location. The lush green trees, rolling farmland, birds tweeting joyously, the boats bobbing on the estuary, and beyond that the blue sea glistening in the bright sunshine. Having been holed up in London with my thoughts for the past year, I had forgotten the majesty of nature. I savoured the clear country air. I had needed it dearly for too long.

It was a particularly hot summer, and I arrived at the school in the height of it. Classes passed without incident and it was good to be working again; I felt positive about myself. The evening was warm and golden, and with the chances of me returning to this part of the world very slim, I resolved to take a walk down to the estuary.

At the edge of the school playing fields a footpath led down through a short stretch of woodland. Trees lined the path, their immense bows arched overhead like a natural tunnel, the evening sunshine penetrating the canopy.

Strolling through the inside of a pincushion; insects danced like dust particles in shafts of gold, their collective buzzing punctuated periodically by the melodic call of songbirds. The place hummed gently, in the meditative harmony of a forest at peace.

I emerged into farmland. Tough, dry grass patch-worked by stout wooden fences. In the estuary beyond, boats nodded ponderously to each other in the gentle swell, grazing on their slate-blue field. A mirror of the agriculture in my foreground. I wondered if the sheep could smell the sea, and if it smelled like home to them. These weren't the smells of my home. To me, the smell of the sea is one of a thousand adventures embarked upon. Of conquests and exploration. The smell of a more romantic time, but one that I had only ever read about in the works of Defoe. Oh, how I longed to lose myself in an adventure story once more. My mind would no longer permit such an escape.

Before reaching the estuary bank, I was first required to navigate a network of dank little streams. The capillaries of the world, carrying nutrient-rich water through the ancient landscape. Things followed me. Rustling and chattering in the undergrowth. I never saw them, but turned my thoughts to them in acknowledgement. The air felt moist and organic. It had an ancient, timeless weight and tasted like the treacherous heavy fog that settled around the canals of London. A taste I had become all too familiar with during the past year. With the threat of being pulled away from the beauty of nature, I physically blew the fog from my thoughts – an exercise my doctor recommended – and returned to the present.

I walked gaily along a raised flood bank, the salty marshland to either side teeming with insect life. Gulls and dippers broke from grooming the mud flats, shrieking their objections at my intrusion into their world. Time wearing on, I hurried to the end of the bank, and there before me stretched the estuary shore.

With the tide low at this time of evening, a good stretch of shore lay exposed. Cloggy silt dotted with pebbles and rubble prevented me from reaching the water's edge; having only brought the single pair of shoes, I was reluctant to dirty them. Until, that is, I noticed that the receding tide had unveiled the remnants of an ancient wooden walkway. I had a keen interest in history and could not resist; I may never be back to this place and felt the urge to investigate. Perhaps I would find a memento to take back to London.

The ancient walkway was made up of rotten stumps running in parallel lines across the dark brown silt, lashed together by mouldering green seaweed. Rotting flesh stretched over the vertebrae of a long dead leviathan. Desperate for a token, I scanned the mud quickly for anything of interest. An old coin, a fossil, a piece of pottery; anything with a story. I had to have something. To my amazement, I saw what I was certain was a perfect flint arrowhead. Then another, and another. All around the rotten walkway, they pointed sharply out of the silt. I grabbed one, not caring about the mud. In my eagerness I nicked my thumb on the sharp flint point, still so deadly after thousands of years.

Looking around, now with the arrowhead in my hand, what before had held such wonder now seemed a macabre place of the dead. I wondered how many souls had been lost to the arrowheads in this prehistoric battle. I noticed for the first time that the crisp sea breeze could not penetrate the close, muggy rot of the silt bank. In the distance from where I had come, I could see the boarding school. Its opulent bell tower looming over the estuary, watching me. Perturbed by the increasingly dark tone of my thoughts, I set off towards it, walking slowly and carefully across the slippery silt.

It took me many minutes to reach the firmer ground of the flood bank and night was falling fast. The innate human fear of dark wilderness nagged at my heels. An itch in the pit of my stomach. It reminded me of that awful evening at the canal when darkness had descended so quickly on our lovely summer evening. I reburied the memory.

I started to jog. The marsh birds screamed at me again. Hidden from view by my singular determination to make it back to my dorm, they seemed to swoop and wheel above my head, screeching their rage. I traversed the dank network of streams leading into the estuary. The capillaries of the world now varicose. The things that followed me in the undergrowth, once so curiously, now held a darker menace.

I ran. Past the field of sheep, whose horns had grown and curled like so many devils. Around the next bend in the footpath, the forest lay just ahead. I slowed as I approached the entrance. A gaping, savage mouth, black as pitch. The moonlight could not penetrate the canopy like the sun's rays had not two hours past. Yet there my path led. The only way back to my dorm. With my last ounce of stamina, I plunged into the forest's yawning maw.

My imagination wild with fear, shadowy faces seemed to rush at me from the edge of the path, their gnarled muscular spines raking at my clothes. Panic renewed my vigour and I clutched my arrowhead tighter in my hand, racing on, bellowing my defiance. Then suddenly, it was over. I burst out of the forest and onto the school playing fields.

The adrenaline leaving my body made me light-headed. Panting and wheezing, I staggered up to the top of the field next to the tutors' dormitory.

Outside the dorm building, the soft, well-kept grass invited me to lie for a moment. I gladly accepted. Splayed out under the stars, still clutching my token tightly, I repaid my oxygen debt. Under the silence of the first rays of moonlight, I could hear the earth breathing with me. The landscape catching its breath after a busy summer's day. Together we watched the swarms of midges buzzing softly around us. I felt disappointed that fear had overwhelmed me so easily after such a positive day. Reflecting on what had happened, I squeezed the arrowhead tighter in my hand.

Having given the midges a wholesome feast, I bid the landscape goodnight and went inside to my dorm.

The room was sweltering. It stank. Poor ventilation and the hot summer's night gave a foul taste to the air. I opened the window slightly and filled my basin with water to cool my face and clean my shoes. Upon opening my hand, I discovered that by clutching my arrowhead so tightly I had cut my palm.

That night, as I lay in my bunk, turning the arrowhead over in my hands, I contemplated the decaying walkway. It had enticed me. Lured me. Its deathly aura spoke to my historic curiosity. My ancient implement of death felt like the most prized artefact, perfectly hewn from solid rock with a kind of primitive artistry. Small as it was, its weight was considerable. My wrists soon ached from holding it in front of my eyes, so I put it safely under my pillow.

Sleep did not come easily. The humidity. The stench. The nightmares. I awoke in cold sweats several times to check that the arrowhead was still safely under my pillow.

Nightmarish visions, so vivid, leaned over my bed, hovering off the ground. My wife; my little girl. Pressing down on my chest with impossible strength, their hair floating, still submerged. Ragged grey skin, torn and nibbled by the mouths of a thousand eels, fish and all manner of vile creatures that dwell in the murk of London's canals. Their eyeless sockets watched my terror with bird-like curiosity.

My wife took my perfect arrowhead, and fed it to me. Her hand clasped tightly over my mouth, forcing me to chew the sharp, solid flint, whilst I lay pinned by those whom I held the dearest.

Dawn found me sweat-soaked and haggard. I took another walk down to the estuary; the crisp sea air would clear the nightmares from my head, ready for class.

By the light of day the landscape was beautiful again. In the estuary beyond the fields, boats bobbed ponderously in the gentle swell, grazing on their slate-blue field. The dreadful dead walkway would now be beneath the waterline.

My arrowhead felt heavy. Heavy with the weight of dead generations. Like a spoken word, an arrow, once fired, cannot not be recalled. The flint arrowheads that ended lives all those thousands of years ago had ensured that countless individuals would never exist. These cursed arrows travelled through time, whilst their initial victims were long forgotten. It was a powerful object to possess.

As much I wanted it, as perfect and beautiful as it was, I should not bring such an object back into the world. It should not be marvelled at and admired, whilst its victims lay forgotten. It should be consigned to the silt where it can do no more harm.

Walking briskly back to the estuary shore, I sensed that it knew my intention. The thrill as it cut me increased tenfold. Again and again, I nicked the ends of my fingers as I fondled it in my trouser pocket. It was ecstasy. I did not want to let it go, as much as it did not want to leave me. At the water's edge, I held it aloft, my bloodied fingers shaking. The smooth ridges of the dripping flint glistened in the sunlight, like wet marble. It seemed so appealing to put my tongue on it. Surely I could not drop such a beautiful object into the water.

It was madness. I had only possessed the thing for one night and I felt it pulling at my mind, urging me to keep hold of it. I thought about my wife and daughter, and my sickening nightmares. Slowly, I forced my fingers loose. I gasped and wept as the arrowhead tumbled into the water. It lay there, shimmering and golden on the riverbed, more beautiful than ever. My will gave way. I leapt into the icy water, flailing madly as for a drowning lover. The putrid silt under foot slipped away and the last I remember was tumbling headlong into the current.

I awoke in a bed in a small sparse room, my hands bandaged like mittens. An old woman was sat next to me, her haggard wrinkled face staring at me.

'Where am I?' I asked, sitting up with a start. The old woman's face creased into a caring smile. 'Where's my arrowhead?'

She was the school nurse and explained that a group of boys training with the school's country running team had seen me fall into the water. They had fished me out, forced the water from my lungs, and carried me up to the school.

She had dried me off and bandaged my shredded hands, then lay me to recover. My arrowhead was next to me on the bedside table.

After sufficiently regaining my senses I thanked the nurse for her kindness, and put on the dry clothes she had laid out for me. I was relieved and put the arrowhead back in my pocket.

The nurse tried to persuade me to stay and rest, but gravely embarrassed, I was eager to be gone from this accursed place. I would wash and collect my things from my dorm, give my apologies and my thanks to the tutor, and the boys who surely saved me from damnation, and then board the first train back to London.

It took me the best part of an hour to get myself washed and presentable. My hands were a crosshatch of scratches where I had fumbled with the arrowhead. I could easily tell people that I must have scraped them on the riverbed when I fell in. My gums were also bleeding. The metallic tang of blood would not leave me, but at least I had the arrowhead, safe and sound in my pocket.

With my meagre possessions gathered, and my wet clothes packed into my overnight bag, I returned to London, clutching my arrowhead tightly all the way. I was clearly not yet ready to face the world.

Back at my grubby single-room lodging by the canal, I stood at my mouldy window looking down at the water below. Something of them was down there still. The arrowhead in my pocket nicked my fingers.

Wobee
White
Yaseek
One
Adjieich
Two
Kuis
Moon
Demasduit
Demasduit
Water
Ebauthoo
Eat
Odoit
Mammateek
House
Adothe
Canoe
Shoe
Moosin
Head
Keathut
Memel
Hand
Black
Mandzey
See
Ejew
Hear
Eenodsha
Demasduit
Demasduit
Demasduit
MARY MARCH
Demasduit

MARY MARCH

Mary March

1819

The side of my husband's head shattered outwards as the metal ball left his skull. A shower of blood coated the nearby trees, and left the snowy forest floor speckled red. His hunting knife fell from his hand and he dropped to the ground, severed from me. In that instant I felt incomplete. That little metal ball from the settler's gun had reduced me.

No birds sang in the trees now. The dogs that pulled the settlers' sled ceased barking and laid flat. The wind held its breath. Even the snowflakes seemed to settle more silently. The forest had been hushed into silence by the gunshot.

I sought the earth spirit. She had led me far from the hunting grounds this year, following the path of the caribou migration much closer to the settler village than usual. She had guided me to these settlers and would guide me again.

My husband's killer was quite a young man with heavy shoulders, golden hair, red ears, and a bony-ridged nose. His dress was strange and cumbersome, the typical style of the settlers from the coastal village. They were feeble of mind and body, but well equipped. Five of them encircled me, all strange shapes and sizes. Some too round and fat, others too long and thin. They did not fit well into the landscape here. Their pink cheeks puffed cloudy breaths into the cold air as they stared. Waiting for my reaction. I could not react;

I did not know what I felt. Horrified, angry. Isolated, empty, numb. All of these feelings swirled from my gut to my throat and back.

Swallowing to keep my stomach down, I walked slowly towards the young man whose gun still smoked. Other settlers raised their weapons at me so I held out my arms to show I meant no harm. The man with the smoking gun looked past me without emotion, lips moving, muttering words as he stared at the bleeding corpse. The other settlers shuffled nervously.

I was angry. This settler had left me without the half that made me whole, and I wondered if he knew how that felt. His lips stopped muttering and I reached out and ran my hand down his pale cheek. His bright blue eyes suddenly darted up from the corpse to look piercingly into mine, but I could see nothing behind his icy stare.

Poised to spring past the man and disappear into the forest, I heard the clicking of four weapons being primed to fire. Turning, I found myself staring into the noses of the settlers' long guns. I took hold of the young man's arm and clung to him closely and tightly, hoping they would not shoot whilst I was so close to their own. The man trembled. One of the older settlers, with a ragged grey beard, spoke in that harsh jagged language, and pointed towards a sled that they had brought to carry equipment. I could not understand him, but the young man that I clung to led me to the sled. He pointed at it. He pointed at me, and then patted his hand on the caribou skins that covered the equipment. They meant to take me with them.

I could not abandon my people, but perhaps if I went with the settlers they would grow complacent and I could slip away into the forest. Willing though I may seem, I would not be an easy prisoner. I lived under a *fire spirit* and was borne aloft its power. My moccasins had come untied and so I sat down on the sled, stretched my feet out to the young man with the smoking gun, and gestured for him to tie them. The other settlers laughed.

A flash of confusion and uncertainty slipped across his mask. The young man slung his long gun over his shoulder, and knelt to obediently re-tie my moccasins. His hands fumbled with the cold but he struggled on. Perhaps he felt guilty about what he had done, or perhaps he was used to servitude in his culture. Whatever the reason, perhaps he could be useful. He finished his task and nodded his head at me. I swung my legs around onto the sled, and we began to pull away. I looked back one final time upon the body of my husband.

He had not been as wise as my first husband, or as gentle, but he had looked after me well in our five seasons together. The half that had made me whole. It was our way; a search for completeness. Laid on his front, the red blood blooming across the snow from his skull, his lifeless dark eyes stared back at me. He was not there. The sled moved through the snow-covered trees and I lost sight of him forever.

I passed by several sets of fresh caribou tracks as the sled move through the forest. With their guns, the settlers could have easily taken one, but they did not seem interested. They did not understand the land and insisted on struggling to catch fish even when the season was wrong. Caribou were much better to hunt in this season.

At a break in the trees, the dogs became excited and started to run. The sled picked up speed. Looking around, I could see that the men were distracted. All focused on either their own feet, or the surrounding landscape. They were perhaps fearful of bears, or maybe that my tribe were following. Nobody would follow. My people were not large enough in number to risk the settler guns. I threw myself sideways, off the sled.

Rolling through the snow, I caught a glimpse of the sled speeding away from me. I struggled to my feet, a little unsteadily, and ran towards the trees. Running in the snow was never easy, but in that moment I felt there was a current pushing back. Barking erupted behind me, from the dogs and the men. They bellowed and yelled. The trees would not come any closer. A gunshot cracked the cold air of the clearing, the metal ball whistled over my head and thudded into the snow-covered trees ahead of me. I threw myself forward into the snow, my escape attempt over.

Lying on my front, I listened to the snow. A few heartbeats of peace. I held on to each one and pressed my forehead into the cold ground. I cast my thoughts to the earth spirit, asking that my tribe find a safe future without me. Footsteps crunched over the snow. Before they were too close, I gathered a handful of snow.

They led me back at gunpoint. One behind me, one in front, the rest waiting by the sled. As I walked I pressed the snow in my hand into a ball. The older man with the ragged grey beard took a rope out from under the caribou skins and threw it to the young man with the smoking gun. He would not look at my eyes as he tied me onto the sled, so I smashed the ball of snow onto the back of his head as hard as I could.

The other settlers laughed, but the young man only paused for a moment, shook the snow out of his golden hair, and carried on with his task.

After several hours moving slowly through the forests and across open plains, the sun was beginning to set and the trees cast long shadows across the snow. The settlers stopped in a shallow bowl amongst the trees, and the old man with the ragged grey beard spoke to the others with hushed rasping tones in that strange sharp language. I could not understand him, but I could feel a nervousness in the air. The thick hair on his face was clumped together by jags of ice. As he snapped his stare from one man in the group to another, the jags were shaken free and sank into the snow at his feet. He threw one final menacing glance at me, and made a strange sign. With one finger held across the middle of his lips, he blew air against his teeth. I did not know what the sign meant. Perhaps the man was a shaman, and the sign was to ask something of the settler gods. It did not feel friendly. He climbed out of the shallow bowl and out of sight over the ridge.

***

Darkness had fallen by the time the old man returned. He led the group out over the lip of the bowl. At the other side, the land fell away steeply and far below, I could see the settler village nestled like a crab on the rocky coastline. By the moonlight the black sea frothed and glistened, stretching away to the end of the world. One of the settlers, though I could not turn to see the man, took control of the back of my sled and we moved slowly and quietly down the hillside towards the village.

At the edge of the village, we paused and three of the men crept silently into town. I had seen this settler village before, but never this close. They had cut down many of the ancient trees nearby, and sliced them apart in lengths to build shelters. Their shelters did not look warm. When the three men had disappeared, out of sight into the darkness, the man with the smoking gun and the old man remained. They spoke in hushed voices and aggressive tones. It seemed they were arguing. The man with the smoking gun handed over a small sack to the old man. It jingled heavily as he walked away into the dark village. We set off in the opposite direction, into the forest around the village edge.

A little way into the forest, away from the main village, we came to a large settler shelter. A faint orange light shone through a large square hole in the side of the wall. The light shimmered on the snow outside, falling into shadow at regular intervals. I could hear footsteps inside, pacing up and down.

The man with the smoking gun came around the front of the sled and untied my ropes. He gave two firm knocks upon the door of the shelter with his bony fist. The sound of his bones against the wood echoed loudly through the still night air.

Cough, cough, cough. An old, small, hairless, head looked at me from the door. The man's face had the same bony nose as Smoking Gun, and though their eyes and jaw were different, I thought that they must be related in some way. I stood in the dim light from the open door, being held tightly by Smoking Gun. The man with the small hairless head retreated into the gloom of his shelter, like a toad into a hole, and gestured for us to follow.

My angry spirit had tired and my actions became hollow. Inside, warmth melted my fears. The cold night had bitten hard at my cheeks and feet, but the shelter was warm and smelled of roasting meat.

I was led along a short passage and into a large but low, wooden room. There was a fire against one wall, with a black metal bowl hung over it on a spit. Smoke and flames licked upwards around the bowl and into a long shaft above. There was a large square hole in one of the walls, with two pieces of thick blue cloth hanging from a stick above the hole. Smoking Gun pulled the pieces of blue cloth across the hole and tied them together in the middle. He left the room, but I could still hear him walking in another part of the shelter. In front of the fire, facing the flames, were two wooden seats. Hairless Head smiled at me and gestured for me to sit in one as he bent to sit in the other.

Smoking Gun returned with three small bowls and filled them with rich meaty water from the large bowl over the fire. I was reluctant to accept food from these men who had captured me so violently, but the earth spirit had led me here and kept me alive for a purpose. The smell of the food made my stomach grumble and I relished each mouthful.

When we had finished eating, Hairless Head stared at me for a moment, and then patted himself on the chest. With a wide mouth spoke, he spoke words that I could not understand. His eyes widened and he pointed at me hopefully, nodding his head. I said nothing.

Hairless Head tried again with his words. He patted his own chest and said very slowly:

'Rev-rend Lee.' Then he patted Smoking Gun and said, 'John Pey-ton.' Finally, he pointed at me and nodded. I understood that he had spoken the names of the two men, and now hoped I would speak mine. Both their wide eyes focused on me, willing me to speak my own name.

'Demasduit,' I said. They looked confused. They looked at each other. They spoke quickly. I heard what I thought was them trying to say my name back to each other.

'Mary,' said Reverend Lee eventually, pointing at me. He repeated his pointing and naming of the three of us again. It appeared that my name in the language of the settlers was Mary.

'Mary,' I said. Reverend Lee became very excited at this. He stood up from his chair and laughed with such joy that he broke into a violent coughing fit. John Peyton handed a metal container of water to Reverend Lee, and after a few drinks the coughing fit passed.

After another hurried conversation, John Peyton brought Reverend Lee some thin, crisp cloth, a sharpened feather, and a small pot of black water. After dipping the point of the feather into the black water, Reverend Lee used it to mark the shape of a small canoe on the crisp cloth and pointed at it.

'Tapathook[5],' I said. He scratched some small markings underneath the canoe, and then pointed at it again. Very slowly, he tried to say the word I had said.

'Tap-at-hook.' He could not say the word as I did, so I repeated myself slowly and he scratched some more markings underneath the canoe.

My *fire spirit* took charge.

We repeated this with an image of a bird, though it was not clear from his markings what type of bird he was trying to show me. Then he grabbed different objects from around the room, many I had never seen before and so could not give a name to. After what felt like hours, I was struggling to stay awake. John Peyton sat by the door with his head on his chest, and his long gun across his legs. He snored occasionally. Reverend Lee's energy would not reduce, but he finally noticed my large yawn and heavy eyes, and awoke John Peyton.

---

[5] Canoe.

John Peyton led me outside to a small wooden box that smelled like an infected wound. He stood with his back to me and his long gun cradled in his elbow, watching through the woods in the direction of the village. I would not go into the box. I did not understand why the settlers would make such a box. It seemed such an unpleasant thing to create. Instead I crept around the box and went into the woods to busy myself where John Peyton would not see. I could easily have run away then, but if I fled back into the wild in this cold I would be dead by morning. Reverend Lee's shelter was warm and he did not seem intent on harming me. At least not tonight.

The crunching of feet running across the forest floor towards the village took us both by surprise.

We crouched down instinctively and watched in the direction that the feet had fled. There, in the gap between two of the black square shadows of the setter shelters, the figure of a man darted. John Peyton hurried me back inside.

The atmosphere inside the house changed. John Peyton talked quickly to Reverend Lee and they both seemed very distressed, though Reverend Lee tried very hard not show me.

He smiled and took my hand gently in his, then, holding out a flame on a candle, led me to a different part of the shelter and opened a door. By the light from his candle, I could see that inside this part of the shelter was a wide bed with a large wooden box at the bottom of it. There were other wooden boxes of different shapes and sizes, with handles on them. Reverend Lee opened the large wooden box at the end of the bed and took out some clothes. He put the clothes on the bed, and left the box open. Putting the candle on top of one of the smaller boxes next to the bed, he patted the bed, the clothes and the large box at the end of the bed. After each item he said 'Mary', and then left the room.

Alone in the room, I sat down on the bed. It was very comfortable. I did not know what use the small thin clothes that Reverend Lee had said were mine would be. They would certainly not keep me alive in the cold.

Closing my eyes and laying back on the bed, I fell quickly asleep. My last thoughts were of how I would escape in the morning. Perhaps I would take the useless clothes and a few other items with me to show my sisters and brothers. There were some very strange things about the settlers; my people might benefit from knowing more about them. The earth spirit guide was holding me there for some purpose.

***

I awoke confused and lost with my mind straddling reality – one foot in the dream world and one in the waking. I rolled over on the bed and everything flooded back to me. The gunshot. Red snow. Settlers. The sled. The village. The shadow man. John Peyton. Reverend Lee.

I groaned and coughed, something had caught in my throat during the night and I struggled to clear it for a few minutes.

I lay still again, breathing slowly. Daylight cut through the room from a gap between two small square doors about waist high on the wall. I could hear the voices of settler children outside, and further in the distance, the clang of metal and rumble of carts from the village. From behind the door to my room, Reverend Lee was humming happily in another part of the shelter. Everybody was already awake; I had slept too long and missed my chance to escape.

Looking around, I realised that everything in my room was made of dead trees, hacked and sliced into all shapes and sizes. I sat up in the bed and shuffled off to peer through the gap in the boards on the wall.

Outside there were children playing amongst the small stretch of trees between Reverend Lee's shelter and the main part of the village. They chased each other and laughed. It was a very happy sight. I felt sad to think that they might grow into hateful adults who would do harm to my children. Perhaps I could do something about that before I left the village.

A simple metal latch held the small square doors together, and so I unhooked it and pushed the doors open further so that the children could see me. I untied some of my leather bracelets, and held them out to the children. They were too involved in their chasing game and did not look around, so I whistled at them and smiled. Leaning through the square gap in the wall, I held out my bracelets to the children. They fell silent and stopped chasing, staring at me with open mouths. Offering my smiles and bracelets seemed to intrigue one of the children, a little girl. Slowly, she took a few steps towards me, looking more closely at the bracelets. Once one child had shown enough bravery, they all began to shuffle forward and I soon had an audience of six small faces looking up at me in the hole in the wall. They took the bracelets and looked at them, turning them in their little pale hands, and speaking words that I did not understand.

'Mary.' I said, patting my chest.

The children giggled and spoke very quickly to each other. One of the children had mucus trickling from his nose, he sniffed frequently but it made no difference. I tore a section of cloth from the thin clothes that Reverend Lee had left on my bed, and, leaning out of the gap in the wall, used it to wipe the child's nose.

The children were trying to say things to me that I could not understand, when I noticed John Peyton walking through the woods. He had his long gun slung across his back, and was carrying a string of dead wild birds over one shoulder.

'John Peyton.' I said to the children, pointing behind them. They all turned and ran over to him, hugging his legs and almost tripping him up. I could not help but laugh at his awkwardness.

He saw me looking at him from the gap in Reverend Lee's wall, and hurried over to me, his face serious and angry. He slammed the wooden boards shut in front of me, closing me in the dark wooden room again. Outside I could hear him talking to the children in a very serious but calm tone. They were quiet as they listened to his words, and then ran away, their footsteps disappearing in the direction of the village. John Peyton's heavy boots entered Reverend Lee's wooden shelter.

I could hear the two men arguing outside of my room. John Peyton angry, Reverend Lee apologetic.

When they had both run out of words, my door opened and Reverend Lee entered carrying a wooden board with some food on it and a hot drink. He was dressed even stranger than the typical settler style, wearing a long black dress, with a thin white collar tight around his neck. On top of his hairless head sat a black hat with a wide rim. He put the tray down on the bed spoke to me, but I could only understand 'Mary', and then pointed once at the food before leaving the room. He put something in front of my door as he left, holding it open so that I could see him across the passage in the other room, sat in his seat by the fire.

The food he had brought me was hot milky grains and a cup of warm water. I sneezed and spilled some onto the bed, but managed to wipe it off using another piece of cloth from the thin clothes.

John Peyton was sat on a short seat in the passage outside my door with his back against the wall. I could see his heavy boots, the long nose of his gun across his knee, and swirls of blue mist from his tobacco pipe. I caught him once, looking around the door at me, but he looked away quickly when our eyes met. After finishing the food I walked past John Peyton, stepping quietly around his gun nose, and went into the room where Reverend Lee was sat by the fire.

Between the two fireside seats, he had put a flat surface on legs. On top of the surface was a pile of sheets of the crisp cloth, his sharp feather, and pot of black water. I sat down on the spare seat in front of the fire.

For the rest of the morning, Reverend Lee used his sharp feather to mark out the shapes of different things, and I spoke the word of the things for him. He would try to copy me, but his tongue could not fit the words. Then he would say the word for the thing in the settler language, and make me say it back to him many times in his language. The crisp cloth that he marked things on was called 'Paper'. He scratched lots of symbols into the paper, and would sometimes make me say something several times and very slowly, before we moved on to the next one. One of Reverend Lee's markings showed a man dressed like a settler and a man dressed like one of my people. Through his game I learned that the settlers called my people Red Indians. The game was quite fun at first, and made me laugh to hear him try to say words in my language, but it quickly grew tiresome. My *fire spirit* waned.

All the time, John Peyton sat behind us by the door, smoking his pipe with his long gun across his knees. A threatening reminder of my captivity. Sometimes he would get up and prowl like a mountain cat towards the big square hole in the wall, opening the wooden panels slightly and peering out. I watched his movements, and the strength in his shoulders as he moved.

After several hours of swapping words, Reverend Lee had such a large pile of paper that it was spilling onto the floor.

***

We were eating more meat broth when I heard footsteps crunch on the forest floor outside of the door. Knock, knock, knock, knock. John Peyton froze. He dropped his spoon into his bowl and looked at Reverend Lee intensely. Reverend Lee spoke two words. I did not know the first, but the second was 'Mary'.

John Peyton pulled off his heavy boots and held them in one hand. He stood and grabbed me by the arm, jerking me up from the seat so quickly that I almost dropped my bowl of broth. Reverend Lee frantically gathered his paper, calling out something in a high-pitched voice. Stalking silently with his bare feet on the wooden floor, John Peyton pulled me out of the room.

We did not go into the room where I had slept. Instead we turned down a long, narrow passage and through a door at the end. In the next room was another wide bed with a large wooden box in front of it. John Peyton opened the box, and inside was a small door in the floor. Quietly, but swiftly, I dropped down through the box and into a dark passage, so low that I could not stand up straight. John Peyton dropped his heavy boots down and then appeared next to me.

In the earth underneath Reverend Lee's shelter, John Peyton brought his long gun around from his back and clicked it, ready to fire. He pushed me further down the passage. I could hear Reverend Lee above our heads open the door to his shelter and speak. The earthy passage led us underneath the main room with the fire and the chairs.

Through the gaps in the wooden floor above our heads, I could see Reverend Lee. He stood nervously in front of old Ragged Beard. Ragged Beard sat down in one of the seats by the fire. He pointed at the other chair and bade Reverend Lee be seated also. I could not understand what they spoke of, but John Peyton's face was set in concentration. His eyes were fixed on the earthy floor, and he was looking with sharp ears.

The old Ragged Beard used a word that I had learned earlier that day.

'Red Indian.' He said. There were other words around it, but my ears were blind to the language.

The old Ragged Beard spoke angrily, he reached inside his coat and pulled out one of my bracelets! John Peyton looked up too, and saw the bracelet. He looked directly at me with great anger. I swallowed hard and looked away, not able to hold his fierce gaze. Reverend Lee struggled to speak words, shrugging his shoulders and shaking his head even more. Old Ragged Beard stared with eyes full of hatred. He threw the bracelet at Reverend Lee's face! It bounced off and landed on the floor near to my head. John Peyton moved quietly and pressed the nose of his long gun against the wooden floor above our heads, pointed directly underneath Ragged Beard's seat. Reverend Lee had covered his head with his hands, and was stuttering words. His leg started to shake and he broke out into a violent coughing fit. Ragged Beard stood up and strolled calmly out of the room. Underneath the floor, John Peyton's gun followed Ragged Beard all the way to the door. With my hand resting on the earthen wall underneath the shelter, I cast my mind into the earth spirit and asked that I remain hidden. I did not know why John Peyton and Reverend Lee did not want me to be found, but I felt that the earth spirit had led me here for a purpose and Reverend Lee had been kind to me. Old Ragged Beard seemed dangerous. We stayed very still and listened with great sadness to Reverend Lee's uncontrollable coughs. He seemed to sob a little too.

John Peyton led me back up to the main room. Reverend Lee had managed to compose himself and the two men spoke frantically. As they talked, John Peyton picked up my bracelet from the floor and tied it back onto my wrist, tightly. Reverend Lee opened the doors on the front of one of the long wooden boxes that stood against the wall, and from inside took a large pile of papers bound together by a piece of hard leather. With the leather bound papers under his arm, he hurried out of the shelter and towards the village. John Peyton locked the door behind him and sat in front of it.

***

With Reverend Lee gone, and John Peyton guarding the front door, I was left alone in the main room. I searched for the papers that Reverend Lee had marked this morning, hoping to ask John Peyton to teach me more settler words, but I could not find them anywhere.

Instead, to keep me busy, I took down the thick blue cloth that hung on the wall. I searched the house and found a needle, thread and knife. Sat on the floor by the fire, I set about making some nice blue moccasins for my family. Reverend Lee and John Peyton did not seem to want to harm me, and so I believed that I might see my family again someday. It would be nice to have some gifts to give them from my time with the settlers. For the babies, I took a long triangular cone of cloth that was laid on the bed in the room I had not slept in, and made it into two little pairs of trousers. The cone could only have been a hat, or a perhaps a bag with no handles. There was a small ball of fur attached to the point of the cone, but I could not find a purpose for it.

***

Later in the afternoon, distant singing came from the direction of the village. It was a slow sound that trickled through the trees and leaked through the walls of Reverend Lee's shelter. The voices were rich and high, singing for several minutes before pausing and then beginning again with a slightly different tune. Perhaps they were communing with their own spirits. I so wanted to believe this. I finished stitching the second pair of baby trousers, and poked my head out into the passageway that led to the front door to see if John Peyton heard the singing too. He was asleep on his short seat with his back against the door. His head hung on his broad chest, and the long gun was limp in his hands. He had put his heavy boots back on, and they were planted firmly on the floor.

I could have escaped through one of the square holes in the walls. My tribe would be hunting the last of the caribou for this season further inland and I could easily track them. I hated the settlers for what they did to the Beothuk people. I hated John Peyton for shooting my husband and cutting me in half, yet he did not seem to care. I hated the old man with the ragged grey beard, and his men, who had taken me by force. Yet, despite all of this, Reverend Lee's passion for the Beothuk words felt important. The earth spirit guide kept me there and I understood that helping Reverend Lee could stop the little settler children from growing up with fear and hatred for my children. I hoped that I could one day take Reverend Lee back to my tribe, and he could share our knowledge. My people would not respect me for staying, but we could not fight against the settler guns. It was true that the settlers could not survive well away from the coast, they did not listen to the land, but with their equipment they would find ways. We would be the ones forced to leave and find new lands. Or be killed.

I left John Peyton sleeping for a while longer. Instead of running away I gathered up my blue moccasins and baby trousers, along with a few other interesting items from around the shelter, and put them into the box at the end of my bed.

Reverend Lee returned soon after the singing had stopped. I had opened the small square doors across the long square hole in the side of the wall where the blue cloth had hung, and watched Reverend Lee leading a small horse through the forest towards the shelter.

'John Peyton,' I shouted. He rushed into the room with his gun raised, but lowered it upon seeing me pointing out of the hole in the direction of the village.

'Reverend Lee,' I said, as Reverend Lee led the small horse down the side of the shelter. John Peyton ran over to me, and pulled the small wooden doors shut across the hole, hooking metal latch on to hold them shut.

In the shelter, Reverend Lee swapped his strange black gown and white collar for a more usual settler style. He and John Peyton spoke very quickly, packing clothes and food into bags as they did so.

As the sun began to set, John Peyton went to pull the thick blue cloth across the gap in the wall. Reverend Lee was busily arranging loose papers and scratching symbols into one of the leather-bound piles of paper, when John Peyton spoke to him. He pointed at the rail where the blue cloth had hung. Both men stood looking very confused. They spoke for a few heartbeats and I heard the word 'Mary', then they came over to where I was sitting by the fire and stood in front of me. I looked up at their confused faces, and had to bite my lip to keep from laughing. Reverend Lee spoke gently and pointed at the rail where the cloth had hung. I looked around innocently. Perhaps if I gave them a pair of moccasins each, they would learn to make better use of the cloth than to just leave it hanging there.

I gestured for them to follow me into my room. We stood at the end of my bed around the box that Reverend Lee had said was mine, and I opened the top. Inside were fourteen pairs of moccasins and two pairs of baby trousers. Reverend Lee and John Peyton looked into the box.

Suspense wrapped around my chest as I waited for their reaction. To my surprise, John Peyton made a short sharp breathing noise, which I thought was the beginning of the coughing that Reverend Lee and I had suffered. After looking closely at his face, I realised he was laughing! Reverend Lee followed John Peyton, and soon both were laughing. I feared that Reverend Lee's cough would start again, and although it did a little, he was not consumed by it like he had been.

I reached into the box and pulled out two larger pairs of the blue moccasins, handing the men a pair each. Hesitantly, Reverend Lee put his pair on. He spoke quickly to John Peyton, who then also put on his blue moccasins. Reverend Lee took my hand in his, and with a smile spoke some words I did not understand, followed by my settler name, 'Mary'. John Peyton copied him, repeating the same words. Having the words repeated like this, I understood them to mean a form of acceptance of my gift.

'Thank you, Reverend Lee,' I repeated their words back to them, 'Thank you, John Peyton.'

***

That night my coughing was very bad. I could not sleep, and must have kept the men awake too. Reverend Lee brought me a hot sweet drink, and John Peyton wiped my head with a wet cloth. They brought a candle into the room and left it next to my bed.

The coughing passed, and as John Peyton was wiping my brow, I looked closely at the ridge of his bony nose. It had clearly been broken many years ago and had re-set, hard but with a slight kink. I watched his blue eyes. There was care there. He was the man who had severed me from my other half, but he was not like the old man with the ragged grey beard, or the other three men who had taken me. From the way he and they acted during my capture, I did not think that he knew them at all. It was strange to see him in this way.

Reverend Lee sat in a seat next to the bed, his head on his chest, snoring deeply.

Footsteps crunched on the forest floor outside.

John Peyton dropped the wet cloth and darted from the bed. He moved silently in his soft moccasins, and pressed his eye against the gap in the small wooden doors on the wall. He watched for many heartbeats, and I watched with my ears, but there were no other noises. The footsteps could have been a deer, or other animal.

John Peyton woke Reverend Lee, speaking to him with a whispering voice, and they both left the room. John Peyton returned alone carrying his long gun in one hand, a short gun tied to his hip, and another long gun slung across his back. He leaned the long guns against the wall, and sat down on the seat next to my bed.

The candle had almost burnt out, and I drifted in and out of dreams. In the seat next to my bed, John Peyton was asleep. At least he seemed to be.

The soft clink of metal against metal stirred us both.

There, poking through the gap between the wooden doors on the wall, a sharp metal knife glinted in the dim candlelight. It had clinked against the metal latch that hooked the two doors together.

We watched it for three heartbeats. It did not move. Another five heartbeats. Still, it did not move. Then, slowly, it began to unhook the metal latch that held the wooden doors shut.

John Peyton stood up from the chair, and moved like a deadly mountain cat around the bed, towards the knife. The latch now lifted off, the knife withdrew back into the night, and the door on the wall moved open ever so slightly. I lay on the bed, and watched in horror as the black nose of a long gun pointed in, directly at me.

His short gun drawn from his waist, John Peyton was crouched underneath the doors in the wall. Seeing the nose of the long gun pointing in, he sprang up and a single gunshot cracked the air.

The long gun fell away and John Peyton ran out of the room. I shuffled off of the bed and ran after him, almost running straight into Reverend Lee in the passageway outside. Before I reached the front door it burst open inwards and John Peyton backed into the shelter, dragging a dead man by the arms. He shouted something to Reverend Lee, who quickly ran into the main room and lit some candles.

With the body laid out in the main room, I could see that it was old Ragged Beard. John Peyton searched through the dead man's clothes and found the jingling bag that he had given to the man the night before.

The two men ignored me, and the dead man. John Peyton went to gather his guns, and Reverend Lee gathered his papers, leather-bound papers, and the sharp feathers and black water that he used to mark the paper.

Blood from the dead man was spreading underneath him and seeping through the gaps in the wooden floor. I watched it dripping into the earth room underneath the shelter.

***

John Peyton led me around the back of the house to where the small horse was tied up. The moon had set outside and the sun would be rising soon. The small horse, loaded with lots of packs and bags, stood politely under a shelter in the grey morning haze. Reverend Lee was also there, dressed in lots of bulky clothes and furs, holding the reins of the horse. I looked again at John Peyton. He had swapped the soft moccasins for his heavy boots, and wore a thick coat with his long gun slung across his back. His other guns were tied on to the horse.

We were leaving. The earth spirit was sending me home. I ran back inside the house. John Peyton chased after me, but I was quick enough to keep just ahead of him. I ran past the dead man on the floor, and into the backroom. I flung open the box at the end of my bed, and gathered the blue moccasins in my arms. John Peyton saw me and after a quickly search of the room, found an empty cloth sack for me. He helped me to fill it with the moccasins and baby trousers I had made, as well as a few of the strange little items I had found around Reverend Lee's house. With my bag packed, we went back outside to Reverend Lee.

With the tip of the sun just rising from the sea beyond the village, the three of us and our small horse made our way up through the steep forest. John Peyton set a fast pace, and it was difficult for Reverend Lee to keep up; he was much older than me and John Peyton. At the top of the hill, I threw myself over the lip into the shallow bowl at the other side where we had waited on the night I was first brought to the village. My lungs felt torn and my breath was ragged. I coughed violently, and brought up lots of thick mucus. John Peyton gave me some water and we both crawled up to peer over the ridge. Reverend Lee stayed in the bowl. He too coughed up a lot of mucus, but he quickly got the coughing under control and sat in the snow catching his breath.

Lying on our fronts in the snow, John Peyton and I watched the village far below. The sun had almost fully risen now, and people could be seen walking around. A little way apart from the main village, Ragged Beard's men were searching for our tracks in the forest around Reverend Lee's shelter. They would easily track us by the prints we left in the snow.

I slid down from the ridge, and went a little way into the trees at the edge of the bowl.

'John Peyton.' I said. He turned from his anxious conversation with Reverend Lee, and looked in my direction. I pointed at my eyes, and waved him over.

Finding a suitably thick branch, with many smaller branches coming off of it, I leaned on it with all of my weight, tugging and twisting until it snapped off. John Peyton watched me drag the branch across the snow, back to the bowl where Reverend Lee was waiting with the small horse. Using some of the rope that held our packs in place, I tied the main branch stem behind the small horse, leaving the smaller branches and leaves to drag on the floor like a brush. This way, if we walked in a line with the animal at the back, the branch would sweep our tracks. It would not get rid of them completely, but it would help the wind and sun could disguise our footprints.

John Peyton nodded when he realised what I was trying to explain to him using the best hand gestures I could think of.

'Mary.' He said, and pointed to his eyes. From one of the packs, he pulled out a metal mouth with sharp teeth like a wolf's. He put it on the ground a little way away from us and spread the teeth apart. At their widest point they clicked and stayed open. John Peyton stood up and found a thick branch in the snow. He threw the branch into the open metal mouth. I jumped in fright at the speed with which the jaws snapped shut! They split the thick branch in half as easily as if it were kindling. John Peyton smiled at me and handed me the closed metal mouth. I had never seen one before, and was fascinated by it. I wanted to know how to make one. It would be very useful for hunting all kinds of animals. I tried to spread the jaws but did not have the strength to open them very far.

I gave the metal mouth back to John Peyton and he positioned it just at the point where our tracks led into the bowl. He covered it gently with some fresh powdery snow until it was completely hidden, and then turned back to me and nodded.

We both looked at Reverend Lee who was grinning with delight at us. He looked from me to John Peyton and back, then clapped his hands and spoke excitedly. I did not understand the words, but John Peyton looked at me with a strange smile. He set off to lead the way deeper into the forest, patting me on the shoulder as he walked past.

***

For many hours more we snaked through the forest, the small horse dragging the branch behind us to cover our footprints. I could tell by the sun that we were not heading back in the direction of my people, but I was not ready to return to them yet. The metal teeth had made me more certain than ever that there were many things I needed to learn from John Peyton and Reverend Lee. I wanted to have more of their words, and to give them more of mine.

We stopped for water and I cleared my lungs again. Each cough felt like knives tearing at my chest. John Peyton ran back along our tracks. I watched him cutting across the trail we had made, and weaving amongst the trees to confuse any who followed us. Reverend Lee sat next to me in the snow.

'Reverend Lee,' I said.

'Mary.' He replied. I held out the container of water and tipped some into my hand, then held my hand out to him.

'Ebautho[6],' I said, in the Beothuk language. He tried to copy me and so I spoke the word again. Eventually he managed to say the word and we both repeated it together.

'Reverend Lee.' I said, pointing and the water in my hand, and then trying to signal for him to speak his word. He understood.

'Water,' he spoke. I copied him and we said our words together. It felt good.

John Peyton returned to us, and flopped down in the snow panting.

'John Peyton,' said Reverend Lee, holding out the container to John, 'Ebautho.'

'Thanks,' he said, taking the container. He looked at me as he took it.

'Ebautho,' he pronounced, badly. Then smiled and drank deeply before laying back to catch his breath.

A sharp screaming began in the distance, carried on the cold wind.

---

[6] Water.

John Peyton sat up quickly and clacked his teeth together like a wolf biting. We set off again, at a faster pace this time.

After another hour we reached a shallow stream. It tumbled gently over rocks and fallen tree branches, carving a route to the sea. We took our shoes off and plunged into the freezing water. An instant sharp squeezing pain stung my skin. Instead of travelling straight across the water, we walked along in the current for as long as we could tolerate the cold. I hoped that this would help us to lose the men who followed. After climbing out of the water further downstream, we dried our wet feet on our coats, and put our shoes back on. With numb feet we struggled on. At least they were dry and would warm up as we moved.

***

Night had almost fallen when John Peyton finally stopped. One of the giant trees had fallen over, and its roots had lifted out of the earth. This made a small bowl, with the soil-clogged upright roots of the tree forming a wall against one side. It would protect us against the worst of the wind, and make it impossible to see our fire from far away.

John Peyton had brought some dry wood in one of the small horse's packs. He gave me the task of starting a fire, whilst he used a length of rope tied between two trees and old ship sail to make a simple shelter. Again, Reverend Lee watched us work, his eyes full of admiration. He took out several caribou skins from another of the packs and placed them around the fire in the middle of the shelter. I pinched Reverend Lee's hat from his head and used it to shovel snow into piles around the base of the sail shelter, and bigger mounds at the two ends the were open.

It was a very small space, but we would be warmer huddled together. We even brought the small horse into the shelter. The strong little beast was very obedient to Reverend Lee, and lay down by the fire with us. John Peyton had brought some of the birds that he had shot the previous morning, and we soon had one roasting on a spit over the fire in our cosy little shelter. I found six fist-sized stones on the floor, and put them in the fire. The two men did not understand, but they knew that I had things to teach them. After the stones had warmed enough, I took off my moccasins and used the sleeve of my caribou skin coat to drop a hot stone in each one. The men nodded their heads when they saw what I did, and took their own shoes off to have a hot stone put in them. It would dry the shoes out where the snow had dampened them, and warm shoes are a pleasure to put on cold feet.

Wrapped in my coat under the extra caribou skins, with my head resting on the warm flank of the strong little horse, and a belly full of meat, I felt at peace. I watched John Peyton cleaning and re-loading his guns and wondered how they worked. He wrapped the handles of the guns in strips of caribou skin. Reverend Lee took his papers and equipment out of one of the horse's packs, and we played the word game. I knew it was important, but the exhaustion of the day quickly caught up with me and I drifted soundly off to sleep after only a few words.

***

I awoke to the sound of distant gunfire. As soon as my mind felt a small wisp of the waking world, my lungs erupted in a fit of coughing. It was only just dawn.

My coughing woke the small horse, which stood up in a panic and tried to kick the shelter apart. Reverend Lee also woke and tried to calm the beast down, but it was impossible in such a small shelter; he could not stand to take the reins. We both covered our heads as the horse kicked out at the sides of the shelter and threw its head around. Despite the danger of the hooves, my coughing would not end. Eventually the small horse managed to find its way out of the end of the shelter and once in the open air, calmed itself. The gunfire continued to echo through the forest seemingly all around us.

I could not calm my coughing. Reverend Lee knelt over me and rubbed my back, but it did not help. I coughed so hard that blood filled my mouth. I spat it out into the snow. Reverend Lee brought a piece of cloth to wipe my mouth. He pressed his hands together, closed his eyes, turned his face to the sky, and began muttering very quick words.

Between the spasms in my lungs I could hear the gunfight raging on. I crawled out of the shelter into the crisp golden sunlight and lay on my back in the open air. I cast my mind into the spirit of the world and asked that the pain in my lungs be finished.

It took many more minutes before the coughing subsided. Even once it had eased, it would not pass entirely. There was still a knife in my lung that I could not shift.

The distant gunfire had become less frequent. As I listened it ceased entirely.

I sat up and looked around, but John Peyton was nowhere in sight. Reverend Lee looked around in desperation. The forest fell silent.

My heart leapt to my throat when I heard the crunch of hesitant footsteps on the snow behind me. I turned to see who it was, and to my horror saw one of the men who had taken part in my capture. He was a very long man with a thick fur coat and patches of wiry hair sprouting from his face. His mouth chewed constantly on a ball of something in his cheek and he held a long gun loosely in his hand. Reverend Lee shouted something at the long man and held up a block of leather-bound papers with a cross on the front. He unbuttoned his coat to show his thin white collar to the long man. The long man turned from Reverend Lee and, seeing me laid on the ground, grinned with brown stained teeth.

'Red Indians.' I heard him say, and then he spat a black lump into the snow and walked towards me.

I scrambled into the shelter and looked for a weapon, wishing I had taken the time to make a bow and arrows. I had taken a knife from Reverend Lee's house, but it was in my pack on the small horse. Instead I picked up two of the fist-sized stones that had warmed our shoes and ran out of the other side of the shelter. The long man laughed at me as I stood before him, a rock in each hand. His laughter fired me into a rage. The brown-stained mouth gaping open, I aimed a rock at it and threw it with all my strength. It thudded into his jaw with a squelching crack. He growled like an angry animal and spat bloody broken teeth into the snow. I threw my second rock as he raised his gun at me. It clanged against the metal nose, distracting him, but it was not enough. He was too close and the tree-cover too sparse for me to escape on foot. I cast my mind into the spirit of the world and gave thanks for the time I had enjoyed. The long man clicked back part of the gun, priming it to fire. He would not miss from so short a distance.

Behind the long man, the snow suddenly erupted. The air cracked and the long man's face exploded towards me in a shower of blood and bone. He fell forwards, hitting the ground a dead weight. When the powdery snow settled again, there stood John Peyton.

He had buried himself under the snow, and must have watched the long man for many heartbeats before firing. I ran over to him and punched him hard in the chest. Why had he waited for so long? I could have been killed! I shouted at him but he did not understand. Hand gestures could not express the reason for my rage. The fire left my blood and I collapsed in a heap on the snow, sobbing with rage and relief.

Reverend Lee spoke to John Peyton and afterwards John Peyton picked something up from the snow came over to sit next to me. I did not want to look at his eyes.

In his hand, he held one of the rocks I had thrown at the long man.

'Mary.' He said, and waved the rock under my face until I looked up at him. He pointed to his eyes, and then pointed to my heart. He took off his hat and bowed his head at me.

We both looked at the stone in his hand. What was fist-sized to me seemed small in his hand. He put the stone in his coat pocket and stood up. Offering me a warm smile, he helped me to my feet.

The fire in my blood had blunted the knives in my lungs, but now that it had left me they grew sharp once more. John Peyton searched the body of the long man and found some more shiny metal discs. We packed down the shelter and carried on walking.

Without the threat behind us, John Peyton set a slower pace. We untied the branch from behind the small horse; we no longer needed to cover our tracks and so there was no need for the small horse to bear extra weight.

***

For two more days we walked through the wild. Nature's territory. Home to neither settler nor Beothuk. Each night when we made our shelter, Reverend Lee took out his papers and we swapped our words. Each morning I would try to cough the knives out of my lungs, John Peyton and Reverend Lee tried to help me but there was nothing that they could do apart from wipe the blood from my mouth. After my coughing fits passed, they spoke in grave tones. Walking became very difficult for me, and I sometimes breathed as hard as Reverend Lee even though he was very old.

John Peyton and Reverend Lee offered me a place on the back of the small horse. At first I refused, proud and strong willed, but the pain in my lungs grew worse with every rasping breath of the cold frosty air. John Peyton carried some packs from the horse and I climbed onto its back. I was not used to it, but riding was far more comfortable for my lungs than walking. Reverend Lee's cough did not seem to trouble him now, and this gave me hope that mine would also pass.

The trees marched by in a blur and I could tell by the sun that we were heading in the direction that my people would be camped.

As the horse plodded on, Reverend Lee and I swapped more words. He could not mark the symbols on his papers whilst we moved, but each night when we made camp he marked everything down in one of the leather-bound blocks of papers. John Peyton had brought more food and dry wood from the large settler village, and so we were comfortable each night. I did not feel so incomplete now. Neither man could be the half that made me whole, but we had shared our lives very closely. We had worked together to survive and shared a desire for the knowledge that would tie us together more tightly.

I wanted to help build the camp but the knives in my lungs were cutting deeper. Every morning I had to clear out the blood they had made, and even through the day I was in great pain on the back of the horse. Reverend Lee and John Peyton looked more sad and anxious each day.

As the journey continued, I was forced to slump forward, resting my weight on the horse's neck. Each jarring step brought more pain and blood from my lungs. At night John Peyton lifted me into our shelter and laid me by the warm fire. I struggled to eat and so he cut meat into very small pieces for me, but even then I felt great pain as the food slid down my torn throat.

Speaking with Reverend Lee became almost impossible. He wanted to stop the word game when he first understood that I was in pain to speak, but I insisted we continue. I could manage no more than two words each day, and it was painful to get them out of my mouth, but Reverend Lee's papers could help make the future better for the Beothuk. We needed to get the Beothuk words and the settler words marked together on the same papers. It was the earth spirit's purpose in guiding me to Reverend Lee and John Peyton.

There were important words that I wanted him to keep, words for love, words for friendship, words for the spirits of the world; but I could not express these as easily as words for water or canoe.

I held on to the hope that my lungs would heal when we found my people, and I could continue to work with Revered Lee. Perhaps he could use the papers to teach the children in my tribe, and the children from the settler village, and they would play together, and learn more from each other.

At night, when I could speak no more, Reverend Lee sat up in our shelter, and scratched the symbols into the papers bound in leather. Then he marked all of the same symbols again in another leather-bound block of paper.

On the last morning, John Peyton was leaning over me to wipe the blood from my mouth. The knives in my lungs were especially sharp and hot, and I could not take much air in each breath.

I watched tears fill his blue eyes. Felt their warmth as they fell on my cheeks. I knew then that I was not able to heal.

In the clear blue sky behind John Peyton, the branches of different trees entwined around each other. I felt him lift me in his arms. Very gentle and full of care.

***

For six heartbeats I held the smell of the crisp forest air. The air of my childhood.

John Peyton placed me placed me in the centre of the Beothuk camp. My people would have hidden in the forest nearby when they saw John Peyton with his long guns.

Around me, Reverend Lee placed the pairs of blue moccasins and baby trousers I had made. He surrounded me with all of the unusual settler items that I had taken from his shelter. John Peyton left lots of the sharp metal mouths, closed for my people to use. He placed his two long guns either side of me. Finally, Reverend Lee placed one of the leather-bound blocks of papers on my chest. All of the words we had shared on our journey. I hoped they would stay and share the papers with my people. They took off their hats and stood around me with their heads bowed.

The knives melted in my lungs. The earth spirit wrapped around me and I became part of it. More whole and complete than I had ever been.

AW! HOW I DID LONG FER A TATTIE PASTY

How I Did Long fer a Tattie Pasty!

c. 1849

Aw my dear! How I did long fer a tattie pasty! The old tin mines were turning poor, so my brother, Tom, and I took a steamer from Liverpool bound fer America. Plenty of work fer a Cornishman out there since they'd no proper knowledge fer mining. It's true what they say, that a mine's nothin' more'n a hole in the ground if there's no Cornishman at the bottom of it! A Cornishman could get the top jobs with the American mining companies. Top pay too. And Tom and I were miners of some ten years experience each, I'd maybe a few years more on account of being a little older than he. We were both of us about right and ready to make ourselves a fortune and come back fer a life of proper comfort and ease!

Tom, he went straight West to Californy, far and away out through wild Indian territory. He heard about the gold in the hills far out there, and went over that way with a few others. Well, I were full of sorrow at his leavin' but he wrote me often as he could. I stayed in the East[7] fer four years working on their tin mines before I went West. 'Twasn't so organised as the tin mines back in Cornwall, at South

[7] At this time the U.S.A was made up of only twenty-six eastern states, and so there was a distinction between the eastern states, and 'America' the land mass.

Crofty, Gleever, Dolcoath or Chasewater. They were long established mines, some thousands of years old. Only recent had our Cornishmen shown the Americans how to fit a Cornish engine to pump water out. Many were now overmen, or shift managers. They'd always look out fer their fellow Cornishmen, so finding work was easy. The American tin mines weren't so deep as ours either, I suppose on account of how new they were. They'd get deeper quickly, I assure thee! Never had I hauled so much out with so little struggle to find a good lode! You'd to know how to spot 'em though, and them Americans were not so clever at that, but as a Cornishman I could speak the language of the rocks. They'd give me the signals to see the tin.

Well, I like to see chlorite, and I'm not averse to a little bit of white flourspar,[8] provided it's white, I like to see a little of that around, but if it's green or blue, as a rule I don't like that. Even tourmaline in some places, the blue or royal blue colour, not the dead black colour, don't like seeing that, but if you see the royal bluish colour coming then you'll usually get tin around there somewhere. There's certainly some lodes where as soon as you look at the lode in the light you'll see the tin absolutely staring at you, it's like a sort of brown sand in some places and other places it's black and the light reflects off of it, just like diamonds, and as soon as you see it it'll hit you straight away, you can't miss it. Knowin' all this I could haul twice as much in a day as I had done in Cornwall!

Tom kept on writing to me from Californy. Always saying in every letter that I should go West and join him, writing about all the luck he were havin' there. There

---

[8] Flourite

weren't a need fer proper mining to get the gold out of them hills, said he, a man could just pick gold straight out of the rivers! One payday the captain of the mine where I worked back East affronted me something rotten, and so I told him I'd not be back. I went to find our Tom out west.

Getting' to Californy, I found me a way to Independence Missouri to join one of the wagon trains set on taking the Oregon Trail. Independence was a bustlin' little town, grown-up fast with all the people heading West. I waited at Independence until such a time as there were enough families and skilled men to make fer safer travellin'. You see, getting' to Californy meant crossing over mountains, plains and deserts all along on the way!

When the day came, hundreds of people there were. All a following the River Platte that were an oasis runnin' through the dry wilds. Aw my dear! I looked back and seen the wagon train a snaking back fer miles along behind! All the Prairie Schooners, as they liked to call their wagons, winding through the sea of dry scrubby grass. Some evenings the wagon camps were a whole lot of happiness, if we'd reached a good place in good speed. Well, some of the people got out fiddles, and guitars and banjos and we'd have a real merry time on an evenin'. Two months it did take us to get to the other side of the plains, and then there were the Rocky Mountains where the people started separating off. Those headed fer Oregon headed through the North Pass, whilst them that were fer Californy steered off south.

For all the folk doin' that journey West, getting' through them Rockies were no easy task. Our wagon train hit on them at the right time of year though, before the snows, so were able to manage it right enough. If we'd have gotten there too late, there'd be no hope of crossing 'em. Many did die trying in years past.

Even after that, before myself and the other pioneers could reach them gold fields in what fellows were callin' the Sierra Nevada, we'd to cross the Great Basin. Aw! That were some mighty dry desert there were! Scorching hot when it were daytime, and frozen cold at night. We'd had to time our journey right on leaving Independence town. Had to be sure we'd cross the Rockies before the snows, and be crossing the Great Basin desert in monsoon season to be sure there'd be water enough to keep us alive. And we did, and there were patches of water dotted about from the rains. 'Twas still no certainty there'd be water each day, but fortune did smile upon us and we made it through the desert with only a few casualties. I myself were bitten' by some sort of damn little scorpion horror, right on my backside, such that I couldn't sit down proper fer three days and felt sorry and sick. The one that did bite me got away before I laid eyes on it, but I saw others, nasty little thornish crabbish beasts. We each shook our boots out on a mornin' and watched the things scuttle away into the dusty rocks.

After more days trundling along, we passed some of them Indians called Paiute, livin' in their dirt huts. Some fellows in our wagon train were 'fraid and readied their Sharp rifles, but these Indians weren't lookin' like them Apache fightin' types further south. The fellows in our wagon train warned me the Apache would gut us and slice our scalps clean off and leave us still to bleed out slow. Some other fellows said the Paiute warriors had done similar too in little battles past. Well, that put a fear right in me, but these partic'lar Paiute ones were some sort of family. Young and old, they just watched us roll on past, peepin' at us like we was wolves a circlin'. Strange old people they did seem to me.

Californy was no easy place to find, there not being state borders yet out there like the government had made in the East. The only town they had were a place called San Francisco, and that were on the coast so I'd no cause to go there. Tom were in the hills somewhere and the main miners' camp were a place called Sacramento, and that weren't a place fer livin' right and cosy. I walked in there through clogging churned up mud between rows of tents, all bustlin' with fellows buyin' their mining supplies. The air did carry a tang of uncleanliness and mistrust about it; mucky-faced fellas watched me all ways and angles with suspicious eyes. Sort of stands to reason mind, what with all that gold about. Ask about as I liked, it were still a great trouble findin' Tom, people said there were many Cornish fellas up in the gold fields and that I should find it easier to just go out an' look fer him.

Well! It were certainly a beautiful bit of wildness and nature out there, I assure thee! I walked all the mountains and camps in the gold fields asking after him. Men of all sizes and faces and tongues were lured from every little nook and cranny in the world by the gold in them Californy hills. Some of 'em were using trays of quicksilver[9] to get the gold separated off. Their fingers shone silver from all their pickin' through the liquid metal, and their teeth and lips were covered too where they'd bitten the lumps to check it were truly gold they'd picked. Tom had wrote about the quicksilver baths, said they sent men strange, made their eyes dull and dead. Quicksilver or not, there weren't a man amongst 'em diggers looked in their right health, and none were liking my askin' questions on their diggin' time. However, when I at long last did find Tom, 'twas in the

[9] Mercury

queerest place I ever did see. All along a river winding through the trees high in the hills, hundreds of men knelt by the riverbanks and in the shallows, a man on either side as far up the river as the eye could follow, an' likely far beyond. Each had a shallow pan and washed through the dirt, picking out any shiny bits as they might find.

Well, Tom, he was knelt similar, and looked up with much surprise when I arrived. Aw! My dear 'twas good to see him! Thinner than four years past, but well enough. We embraced and sized each other up there on the riverbank and he first asked me if I'd brought a 'tattie pasty! Aw my dear! How? Out there in nowhere? Tom said there were a Cornish digger's wife stayin' in Sacramento, and on some rare chances, she'd make a tray of pasties and sell them off to the highest bidders! Well! I did not see such a wife, but told Tom we would surely find her right enough. He told me all about the gold he'd been findin' and I agreed to pitch in and work with him. I reckoned I could pull myself my own fortune out of that there river.

'Isaac,' says he, 'I must tell you how we must do it out here.' He pulled me close by him, 'Keep both yer eyes open and treat every man you may meet with as you would thieves, rogues and vagabonds. Don't speak too pleasant to any one of 'em, fer they only want to rob you, and always carry a loaded pistol in your belt. I always carry two, so you can have one of them.'

He took a pistol from his belt and handed it to me. Other men who were knelt close by in the river peeped up at us, real squinty eyes in their mucky faces. I noted well that they all carried at least one pistol. Quick as a lightning clap, Tom drew his other pistol and pointed it at one of the peepers! Aw! My little brother! A gunman! Well, the starin' muck rake looked down fast, attendin' back to his swillin' pan proper, I assure thee! Tom were quick to tuck his pistol back away in his belt. I'd not shot a pistol before; there weren't so much call fer them over in the proper mines in the east. They'd a government that made proper laws over there. The only gun I'd ever shot was back in Penzance to hunt game birds in the summer. Tom's pistol was a heavy, solid-made sort of thing and he showed me how to load it and cock it to fire. I took a deal of care as I tucked it into my belt.

'If any of these diggers want a palaver with you,' continues Tom, 'get ready to shoot 'em, or maybe he'll shoot you, and then he'll swear 'twas done in self-defence, and then nothin' will be said. We used to have a lynch law here and hang 'em up to a tree ourselves, but that's done away with now.'

Tom showed me how to use the pans to wash the dirt and spot the gold. Aw! He was a fast one at findin' that gold, I assure thee! As we set to with washing, he told me how he had been robbed once.

He'd taken to burying his gold each day under the hearth right by his camp, and had got himself a right tidy sum, and set his mind to take it all down to the bank in San Francisco. Thousands of dollars worth he reckoned he'd got! He needed some bags to carry it in and so shot some sort of bear, and some sort of deer. He skinned 'em and with that, made some bags. One bag he made large enough to go around a horse's neck like a collar, and then he cut a belt to go around his own middle, and fashioned some small bags to hang onto it. When he'd filled 'em all with clean gold, thousands of pounds worth 'twas, remember, a Spaniard man sold him an old horse fer twenty dollars that weren't worth twenty shillin'. Then away Tom went fer San Francisco to put his gold into the bank what's down there.

He was in a wood when somebody shot near to him. He kicked the old Dobbin to run, but the old horse would hardly move out of place. Bang again went the gun, and missed again. Tom said that the harder he whipped the old Dobbin the less the beast would move. He thought he'd be dead and finished. Then three of the ugliest men he'd ever seen jumped out and knocked him off of his horse with a big stick. They beat him bloody and near to death, and took his gold, but stopped just short of killin' him.

Since he was robbed, Tom sent his gold down to San Francisco every fortnight to the Bank. There were men what take the diggers' gold down fer 'em, and they do give you a paper to show fer it too. Aw! I were real surprised at this trustin' the men, but Tom said the paper meant it were safe enough, though, I did never know the reckoning behind it.

***

Fer eighteen months we worked there in the same place on the river. Aw my dear! 'Twas coarse living there! We lived almost like pigs we did. Such sour maggoty bread, and such rotten stinking biscuits, and such sour belly-vengeance beer, when we could get any. The sort of house we lived in weren't better than a cow house, one what we pair fixed upright with trees and branches and such like. As fer our bed, 'twas nothin' but straw and leaves on the dirt. And the water we'd to drink was the same as we washed the gold in, and 'twas always puddle water. Why, fer the two of us, fer all meals, we'd only one large sort of a saucepan to boil our broth and that, and no spoons but what we could make out of sticks. 'Twas a dismal place with no comforts to speak of. The Cornishman with the pasty-making wife packed up and moved on from Sacramento, on account of all the harassment the poor bal maiden[10] were getting. Well, I assure thee, Tom and I both would've given our largest gold nugget fer a tattie pasty!

I got good and speedy at washin' that gold. Like a hawk, I watched the river silt swilling and swirling in the pan. I spotted them little flecks of gold, you see, sparkling up from the reddy-brown silt, and then I'd to sort of slosh the dirt out real careful, leaving the gold in the bottom. There were a real knack to it there.

After eighteen months we'd pulled a large amount of gold from that river. I said to Tom that I reckoned we'd got gold enough now, and I should like to go home to enjoy our earnings in comfort.

'Why Ikey,' said he, 'what dost tha' mean? Where's your pride? Or 'ave you gone lazy? What's come to you to talk like that?'

I told him what's the good of being proud and stuck out here? Fer there's nobody to see your grandeur if you ever should show any, nor no church or meeting to go to if you ever should buy any smart clothes. As fer laziness, well! I certainly weren't like that!

Tom said he wanted to stay out at the diggings until he had enough gold to strut out down Penzance Promenade with the Mayor and bankers, arm in arm. Said he'd have shining coaches and servants, and a tall woman fer a wife who he'd dress out smart and fine.

---

[10] A bal maiden was a female manual labourer working in the mining industries of Cornwall. From Cornish language bal meaning a mine, and English maiden.

Well, I was shocked at my dear brother. The man who left Cornwall with me all those years ago weren't one to be thinking like that! The gold fields had done some changing to Tom's sort of approach to life. He were the same man alright, but a man with a change of values and importances. I did always blame the gold fer that. He didn't take it kindly when I told him as much.

'You do what you've mind to,' said I, 'I'll be going home to live a decent life whilst I've still got my limbs and health.'

He was sulky with me after that, and didn't hardly speak two words to me fer the rest of the day. We pair washed our gold in quiet, the little birds tweetin' and chirrupin' in the trees like they was wonderin' what we lot were at, wallowin' like pigs in the muddy stream. The slosh-slush-slosh of the diggers with their pans kept up all day, not stoppin' even fer lunch.

By the evening Tom had gained a better temper and admitted he supposed every man ought to have his own fancy. He said if I really must go, he would go down to San Francisco with me and see me off by the steamer, but that once I'd gone my old diggings was his. Thought he could get thousands more and come back to Penzance some sort of a squire or lord. I'd be full of sorrow to leave him, be he were set in his mind on diggin' a bigger fortune.

A few days later we left the diggings sites in the hills, and walked down to San Francisco. We arrived on a Tuesday afternoon 'bout twelve o'clock and it were a real bustlin' busy time. Put me in mind of Independence back in Missouri in a good many ways. Same excitement flappin' about the air, but with more rich fellas and more guns. Tom and I, we went straight to the bank. We put our fortnights gold in the bank, and took back enough money for some eatin' and drinkin'. When I showed 'em my all my papers they gave me another paper to take to the Liverpool bank when I got back there.

After the bank we asked about a steamer to Liverpool and were told that one called the Clara would be sailing fer Liverpool the next evening, so to pass the time we went to a sort of coffee-room Hotel fer something to eat and drink. Aw! We ate good and dearly loved it! The first proper food we'd had fer near a year. Tom ate so much roasted veal that he was poorly with it.

In the evening we went to some sort of bar in a place like a horses' stables with seats around and a table in the middle. They called it the 'Box'. There we were talking about home and that, and having some toddy and a pipe, when came towards us the ugliest man I ever did see. He was more than six feet long and thin as a weasel, with skin as yellow as a kite's leg.

'Will you like to play cards, gentlemen?' said he.

We neither of us had a mind to play cards and told the man so. Tom accused the man of being a card sharp, but he did deny it and made out like we were 'fraid of him. Well, sharp or no, the grimy kite leg were stinkin' drunk! I knew Tom was a real beauty fer cards and most likely could beat the man, but we'd rather sit and talk about home together a bit more. So we said no to the man again.

Well, the old whiskey weasel kept on keeping on at us! At last Tom got vexed and agreed to play one game fer 20 dollars apiece. Old yellow chops agreed and at the cards they went, glaring and eyeing each other over the decks. I held my watch in my hand to see how long they'd be about it, and in less than eleven minutes Tom had him beaten clean off and took the money.

Then the ugly old rake pestered Tom to play again! Tom wanted no more, we just wanted to drink our toddy and talk about home. When he refused, the long man called him a coward, and both of us shabby Englishers. Aw! I thought, like that there's enough! The tall man was standing up so I begins to measure him up, eyeing fer a place to strike him and knock him down.

'Don't touch 'im Ikey,' said Tom, 'I've guns enough fer he any day.'

With that, Tom stood up and made a sort of speech to about twenty people who were sat in the room. He told 'em about the man's impudence and goading of us to play one game, and that even beaten the ugly weasel would not leave us to our peace and talking. Tom asked the people in the room to see that if he played one more game with the yellow weasel face, they see to it that he got fair play. Well, this game would be forty dollars apiece!

'He's a bad behaved man,' said 'em all, 'we'll see that you shall have your fair play.'

Tom and the old fellow went to it again, and them that were watchin' were tense as a knot. In ten minutes Tom had beaten him. He was going to brush the dollars into his bag, when what did old yellow face do but pull a loaded pistol out of his belt and shoot Tom! Bang!

Tom had seen that the old fella meant to shoot him through the head, and exactly as he ducked down his head upon his chest, off went the pistol. In went the bullet into the nape of Tom's neck, and that did keep Tom's head lopped down one side like, as long as he'd live, and after too I suppose.

Well, Tom had seen what the old weasel was about and took out his own loaded pistol. In a moment he shot the fella right through the heart of him, dead. Aw my dear! If you'd seen old yellow chops! How he grizzled and squinted, and then down he fell upon the floor like a piece of wood, dead as you like.

With that done, all the other gentlemen came forward to shake hands with Tom and thanked him fer what he'd done. They gave him three roaring cheers and asked what he'd have to drink.

''Tis a sorrowful job,' said I, but the other gentlemen said nay, 'twas a good job. They were glad he'd gone. He'd been around fer weeks, sort of havin' a palaver with real peaceable fellas. Pesterin' and naggin' fer drink and cards, then drawin' on 'em when he didn't win.

'Hold up thy head, Tom,' said I.

'I can't, Ikey,' said he, 'I still got the ball stuck in my neck nape.' He turned around and showed me, 'I can feel it too,' said he, 'real sore.'

One of the other gentlemen in the room said he was a doctor, and took the ball out of Tom's neck, and cleaned him up right and proper.

The Clara didn't sail until the day after, so Tom and I and the rest of 'em had a pleasant evening of it! And there lied the old grizzler, dead and stiff on the floor. However, we threw a tablecloth over him, and left him to lie there with us all the night through.

In the morning we had a sort of inquest, and then they buried him out back in a back-yard area. Then Tom and I said our goodbyes and I left fer Liverpool. When I got there, I took my bank paper to the Liverpool bank and they gave me my money, all real and proper! I stayed one night in Liverpool and then headed home.

Back in Penzance, I got myself my very own freehold of about six or seven green acres, and a cow, a horse and pigs. Made me a happy home, with a sturdy little darling fer a wife and quickly got me a healthy baby. Tom wrote me letters regular, but his pride did suffer badly from the fact of having a lopsided head. He stayed on at the diggings for a good many months more, pulling more gold he said. I wrote that he should come visit, but his head would always be lopsided and so I suppose he were too 'shamed by it to come home.

In his recent letter, he wrote that he'd used his earnings to open a little pasty shop out there in Californy in a little town called Grass Valley! Aw my dear! Wrote that he were taking a tidy little profit on account of all the Cornish miners out in the gold fields. All of 'em a pining after their tattie pasties!

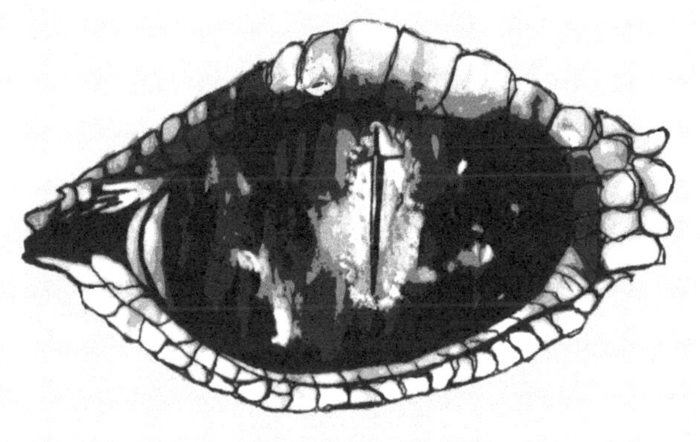

DEATH OR AUSTRALIA?

DEATH OR AUSTRALIA

Death or Australia

19th January 1788

Death or Australia? I was starting to wish I had chosen death. Some of the other convicts did. Mind you, trapped like sardines in the stinking belly of the *Alexander*, transportation had meant death for several of my companions. My twin brother John and I survived though.

Nine months it took from London, or something there about. Rats, bedbugs, lice, cockroaches and fleas tormented us day and night. The smell of the bilges was so foul that it stung my nose worse than anything I'd ever known before – and I grew up a sewer rat, foraging in sludge for anything of value dropped or discarded.

The thought of Australia filled me with dread. Backbreaking hard labour in the searing heat for the rest of my natural life. All for stealing a few crates of ivory. It wasn't even good ivory. I'd stolen better, and committed far more terrible and violent crimes. It weren't that we were bad men; we were just the best at leading the life that we'd been born to. The other criminals in London knew the work of the Sheppard brothers. With such a reputation, it was quite embarrassing to be caught for something so amateur. I'd been greedy and a little too confident.

Though they could never prove it, the police rightly suspected John and me of many other crimes. Sentencing us to death or transportation for life got us out of their hair for good.

One hot stinking summer night I sat hunched in the ship's hold in our metal gaol, my back resting against the knees of the convict behind me, when I heard much shouting and cheering above deck. The anchor was dropped and we stopped moving.

I looked up at John, sat opposite me with his back against the metal bars and his head resting on his chest. His clothes were no more than flea-bitten rags, his hair and beard shaggy and wild, and his gaunt face grubby with dirt and sweat. We were twins but far from identical. He was still large and powerful, but a shadow of the muscular man who broke into the warehouse with me for the ivory all those months ago. I was probably in a similar condition, though I had not seen my reflection in a long time.

'Reckon we're there, brother,' I said, and kicked him in the shin. He woke up with a start and looked around fearfully. Other men in the gaol looked around too. We listened as the crew overhead cheered and shouted, already quite drunk and celebrating the end of the voyage. They would not drop the rowboats and touch land until daylight as there was nothing could be achieved in darkness. It would be madness to go ashore in a strange land at night. I saw an opportunity.

'The promised land.' He said, with a gap-toothed grin.

The two red-coated marines standing guard outside our door had been drinking steadily since they came on duty. That was several hours ago, and they were swaying gently with the ship, their heads nodding with fatigue. One of them would fall over any minute.

'John,' I whispered. I nodded at the keys bulging in the guard's pocket. 'If he falls your way.' John turned around and saw the keys. He winked at me.

We had managed to escape early on in the voyage when the guards were drunk, quite a number of us too, but when we reached the deck we found ourselves in the middle of the open ocean. We were quickly rounded up by the armed red-coat soldiers and given thirty lashes each. That was many months ago, my scars had healed and the soldiers had become careless once more. They would be especially so tonight given that we had finally arrived. It could definitely be done.

I prayed that one of the drunken guards would fall our way. They were both young men, but older of the two was looking most likely to fall. Pink with sunburn, drunk and exhausted, the lad was not in his best health. I kicked John again to make sure he was ready and not dozing. He frowned at me angrily; of course he was ready.

If we escaped this time, we would surely be in sight of the coast and all of the crew and soldiers would be distracted and drunk. We could easily lower the rowing boats and disappear into the night. With a bit of luck we'd be free to make a new life in this unknown land. There would be women convicts on some of the other transport ships, and John and I had fantasised all voyage about running away and starting families with a couple of wide-hipped, street-hard women.

Then our moment came. The young guard stumbled as he swayed and fell against our cage. As easy and natural as breathing, John reached through the bars and picked the lad's pocket. The lad did not even notice as he stood up straight again, mumbling embarrassed apologies to the other guard.

Down the inside of my trouser leg I kept a sharp wooden splinter, like a stiletto, that I had pulled from one of the floorboards inside of our cage. Not being a large man like John, my splinter kept me safe and ready for violence.

John and I stood up. I didn't have to tell him my plan; having shared a gaol, a home, a childhood, a crib, and a womb, we were almost of one mind. With a look to the other convicts in our cage, they knew what was afoot and began to uncurl from their sitting positions. The guards didn't notice until it was too late.

In a flash John unlocked the cage and flung the door open. Before the guards could shout out or draw their weapons I had my stiletto through the throat for one, and John cracked the other's skull against the metal bars of our cage. The two lads crumpled to the floor in a heap.

John and I took the single-shot muskets from the dead guards before anyone else could get hold of them and then used the keys to unlock the rest of the cages. Soon there were well over a hundred convicts roaming freely and excitedly around the hold. True to typical criminal nature, they opened the hatches and went on the attack, shouting and swearing in one disorganised rabble. We did not. We remained behind.

With the hold empty and chaos raging above our heads, we calmly stripped the dead guards and put on their uniforms. We put our ragged convict clothes on the corpses, and dragged them into one of the gaols. Anyone who found them would simply assume they were two convicts killed in a gaol fight.

Looking like any other red-coats, we peeped through the open hatch at the chaos above.

Convicts and red-coats fought in lumps all around the deck. It seemed that the convicts had the upper hand, but the red-coats were armed and they would quickly regain control. We had to act fast, and so leapt clumsily onto the deck with our muskets primed.

The air above was cool and fresh with a hint of sweet gunpowder smoke, but we did not have time to enjoy it. Behaving as our new uniforms required, we discharged our rifles at two ragged convicts and then hurried to the rowing boats.

I kept a lookout whilst John lowered the smallest boat into the water. Nobody watched us; they were all too busy fighting and dying. The boat landed in the black water with a splash. We lowered ourselves over the side of the ship and dropped down after her. Once sat securely we took an oar each and rowed for our lives, away from the huge transportation barque and into the darkness.

It was a calm night and the sea had only a gentle swell. By the light of the moon I could see the coastline and so we followed it out of the bay, being sure to keep a safe distance from the jagged rocks. It was not until we were around a rocky peninsular and out of sight of the *Alexander* that we finally slowed down.

'Think you can row until morning?' I asked John, panting for breath. He shrugged.

'Probably.' By the moonlight I could see his gap-toothed grin. 'Bet you can't though.'

'Yes I can.'

'Pssht,' he scoffed like an ass.

I stopped rowing and took off my ridiculous red jacket, laying it in the bottom of the boat. John did the same. I rolled up the long white sleeves of my stolen uniform. John did likewise.

Our little forays into the smuggling trade had taught us much about navigating by the stars, so we headed north in order to avoid meeting the rest of the ships. The guards had mentioned ten other ships in our fleet, all coming up from the south. We rowed until the sky turned pink and the sun peeped at us, fat and orange on the horizon. Our rowing became much slower but we continued to follow the coastline, keeping the land in sight and getting as far away from the *Alexander* as possible.

Despite occasional draughts from open hatches during the voyage we had not had open air and the freedom was giddying. As the sea rose we saw with amazement this new world. Never in our lives had we seen such a horizon - thousands of miles in every direction - nothing. Landside or Oceanside the same. A mirage haze of shimmering heat rising before us. And the colours! After the cramped greys and browns of London, this open land was vibrant and vast. Deep reds, blues, purples, greens and dusty golden yellows. Like the stained-glass window of a church.

'God's country,' said John, smiling as he rowed. Despite the beauty of the place, the emptiness nagged at me. I shook my head.

'God forsaken country, more like,' I panted.

The sun got higher and hotter. We quickly became exhausted and weak. Dry mouth and hunger pains in my stomach, I was desperate to stop rowing. I looked at John. His brow streamed with sweat and his eyes were worryingly glazed over, but he rowed on. He would row himself to death if it meant beating me. Heat would kill us both if we did not find water and shade before midday.

I let my oar rest in the rowlock.

John made one more stroke and then let his oar go too. We sat in silence panting for breath. My lungs burned and I fought not to be sick. I knew John was doing the same, however calm he tried to look.

'Weakling,' he said, between breaths. I did not have the energy to rise to his goading.

'We'll wait a few weeks whilst we find our own little patch of land,' I said, then paused to take a few more breaths, 'Then when they've forgot about us, and are busy settlin' their colony, we'll walk back in like normal red-coats and free our wide-hipped women.' John couldn't even speak, he simply nodded.

'Water,' he whispered.

The shoreline was dotted with dotted with little rivers, so we chose one that looked deep enough for our boat and followed it. After rowing until we could no longer taste salt in the muddy water, we found ourselves surrounded by hot green swamp. The air was strange and sticky, and the flies mobbed us. We rowed carefully through, trying to remain in the deeper central channel of the river and prodding our oars into the gloopy brown mud every so often, testing for firmer land.

We found a sloped clay bank and hauled the boat up onto it. With the boat secure, we fell to our knees at the river edge and scooped the brown liquid gratefully into our mouths. Parched as we were, and after months of drinking green water from the stagnant kegs on the *Alexander*, it was the best water we had ever drunk.

So greedily did we sup, that we did not notice the huge monster, like some sort of dragon or demon, skulking towards us until it was too late. As I reached forward to scoop another handful of water, two golden cat-like eyes embedded in a thick scaly head looked up at me.

I yelled and leapt back, but the beast lunged. For a second, huge rows of razor sharp teeth gaped before me. The enormous creature could have swallowed me whole. It clamped its jaws around my left hand and I felt my little finger snap. My wooden stiletto was already in my hand. I jabbed at the beast's eyes but missed and the stiletto snapped against its thick scales. Unable to free myself from its grasp I was dragged into the water, screaming for my brother. Underwater I carried on jabbing at the beast, but it was useless. My lungs were empty and I was ready to pass out when it relaxed its grip to get a bigger bite of me. In that moment I pulled my hand free and managed to reach the surface for a breath. I scrambled for the bank, and was almost out of the water when I felt the jaws clamp around my lower leg and drag me back.

I caught a glimpse of John's boots and then, bang! I was free. I crawled up the bank away from the water. Another bang! John had discharged both of the single-shot muskets into the beast's head from point-blank range.

The giant water dragon laid still. Half in, half out of the water. My little finger hanging out of the side of its mouth.

Panting and shaking on the bank, I looked down at my bloody hand. The little finger had been torn off completely, and my ring finger was bent at an impossible angle.

John was still stood over the giant scaly monster, one musket still smoked in his hand, the other lay discarded in the mud. He stared in confused wonder and shook his head.

'You ever think we were made like we are by God with somethin' in mind?' he said, without taking his eyes from the monster. He sometimes got like this when we'd done some serious crime, but I did wonder if he was becoming more religious in the heat and the colour of this strange new world.

'What?'

'He made sure we got 'ere to send the demons and devils in this land back to hell,' he said, looking up at me with a thoughtful smile. 'We's good at sendin' stuff to hell.'

'Suppose that would explain why we got caught with the ivory,' I said.

'Exactly!'

My hand throbbed and swelled with pain, blood pulsing from the open wound where my little finger used to be. I held it up to show John.

'He's got a funny way of thankin' us.'

'It's only the little one,' John laughed at me. 'We know hundreds of men missin' worse than that. You should be grateful!'

I stood up and limped down to the demon. My leg was bitten and scratched, but it weren't bad enough to cripple me. Between John and me we hauled the giant beast fully out of the water. Tail and all it was longer than three of John. We cut the massive head off for a trophy to put in our new homes, so we could show our wives and children and grandchildren how we killed a dragon.

The tail was one thick muscle, so we sliced it into rough steaks to eat. We dragged the boat to the shade of some smooth, oddly scented trees where it could not be seen from the sea. There was plenty of dry scrubby grass and wood all around, so we built a fire and used the musket flint to light it. When the fire was blazing and crackling, we each speared a steak with the bayonet of our muskets and roasted the meat.

Our stomachs gurgled loudly as the meat dripped and sizzled, and we could barely wait for it to cook before biting into it. The meat was white and the texture of chicken, though it had an earthy fishy flavour. Not at all unpleasant.

Fuller-bellied than we'd been for months and more content, I set about fixing my hand. There was nothing to be done for my missing finger, but I lay a small stick next to my broken ring finger and John cracked it back straight.

The pain was so intense that I thought I would be sick, but I held my stomach down or else John would never let me hear the end of it. He tore a sleeve from the white undershirt of his red-coat uniform, and bound my hand tightly with it.

We reloaded our muskets, and laid in the bottom to doze in the shade. Sometime in late afternoon when the sun had passed its peak, we awoke. I hated waking up. Sleep was blissful and carefree, but being awake always meant pain and misery. We left our red jackets and the dragon head in the boat, covered it with bits of undergrowth, and walked further inland along the small winding river so as not to get lost.

It led us to some red craggy mountains that rose sharply out of the baked ground. I could see the dark mouth of a cave a little way up the mountainside and thought it might make a good home – temporary, of course, until we had the tools to build a proper house.

Inside, it was perfect. Deep enough that we could see the end and so not worry about any demons sneaking up behind us. High enough to stand upright in most parts, and wide enough for John and me to have some space to live and sleep. There were strange paintings of animals on the walls, and human hands. Whoever made them was nowhere to be seen now and so we reckoned the cave was ours. Until we could rescue some nice wives from the colony and venture further into this strange land. Once we found somewhere better, we'd take the time to build proper houses.

For two weeks we made our cave fit to live in. We counted time, making our own marks on the cave wall. We made a fire pit in the middle, with a spit and big wooden logs around it to sit on. The back wall had a short rocky ledge running along it, and we placed the dragon's head on that where it looked down over the cave. On my side of the cave, up against the wall I made a rough bed out of tree branches, dried grass and soft moss. John copied me. We ran into more strange and evil creatures as we foraged for things to make our home perfect and sent them all down to hell. Sometimes just with our bayonets to save on powder and shot.

I was coming round to John's idea of God. It was a strange but pleasant feeling to think that for all of our lives we had been doing exactly what God wanted us to do, but we had just been doing it in the wrong land. Even the two young guards that we murdered to make our escape were on the path of evil really; keeping hard-working people locked up in cages for months at a time. In the evenings as we lay in our bunks. John talked about our past crimes and explained how many of them could actually have been us doing God's work naturally, right and proper, without even knowing it. The more I listened, the more he seemed to make sense. It truly was an upside down land where John was right about things.

I was not sure how much some of the creatures needed sending back to hell. When on a scouting mission, we found a scrubby grass plain full of giant rabbit-like demons that stood on their back legs and carried baby rabbits in pockets on their bellies; they seemed harmless really. Their meat did taste truly wonderful though and so if God needed us to use our skills of a lifetime to carry out His bidding, we were happy to serve Him. We definitely had some making up to do. Or if John was right, He owed us, and this land of plenty was our reward for our decades of hard work.

***

One afternoon, when we were enjoying a lie down, sleeping off our lunch of giant-upright-rabbit leg, four naked black men with long sharp spears awakened us. They looked like the black slaves that I had known in London, but these had white markings painted all over their body. They pointed their sharp spears at us from the mouth of the cave, and shouted in a strange demonic language. It must have been the language of hell. I looked across the cave at John, laid in his bed against the other wall. He shrugged and picked up the loaded musket from next to his bed. I did the same and we shot two of the demons right through their black hearts. The other two ran away as their fallen friends bled out in the mouth of the cave. Considering how much like humans the painted demon men were, we reasoned that this was some sign from the devil himself. He'd had enough of our slaying his dragons and upright-rabbits, and wanted us gone from his land. The painted demon men were his messengers, come to stop our good work in our new lives. We reloaded our muskets before drifting back off to sleep.

We removed the dead bodies later in the evening, they looked too human to carve up and eat so we threw them in the river for the water dragons. My hand was still wrapped in the shirt-sleeve bandage, but it was healing very well. We were never ones to be ill for very long, John and me. It was one of the blessings we were born with.

***

'Think I'm ready to bring a wife home,' I said to John as we walked back up to our cave from the river. He smiled at me with the broadest grin that his big ugly face could muster, and clapped his great arm around my back.

The next morning, using the sharp bayonets of our muskets, we shaved our ragged beards and cut each other's hair. We washed in the river, taking turns to look out for the water dragons, and put on our full red-coat uniforms. Jackets, belts, hats, and sashes; it was far too warm but we needed to pass unnoticed into the colony. In the pockets of the jackets we found the identification papers from the two young guards. We would be caught if anyone checked the age, but at a quick glance they might be useful.

If we arrived in the boat that had been missing for two weeks they might get suspicious, so instead we walked back along the river and followed the coastline that we had seen from the rowing boat as we escaped. The day was roasting hot and the red-coat uniforms were quickly drenched in sweat.

The colony itself was beginning to resemble a small village. Some buildings were still being built, but I could tell from the guards on the doors that two prisons were already in use. John and I walked confidently along a dirt track that had been pounded into a rough street by hundreds of boot-shod feet. The sound of hundreds of axes clearing trees at the edges of the village hammered through the air. Land that had already been cleared was fenced off and some bony cattle, malnourished from their voyage, grazed on dry scrubby grass. Many red-coats rode on horseback, keeping a close watch over the convicts who laboured to clear the land and build the colony. We were grateful for our stolen uniforms. Of the two guarded prison buildings, one was significantly smaller than the other. The smaller must be the women's prison as there were far fewer women convicts than men. We approached the smaller building and I nodded at the two guards. They were much younger than John and me.

'Change of guard lads,' I said, with my best voice of authority.

'Why? Duty watch are on heat break. We're only here for an hour,' said one of the guards, looking in confusion at his mate. I shrugged at him.

'Take it up with the Captain.' I said, then narrowed my eyes at them 'maybe he knows you were doing something you shouldn't last night.'

'But, no, I-' started the young man. I held up my hands.

'Don't want to know lad. You'd best go see him.'

The lad passed me a large iron key and the two of them hurried sheepishly away. John and I took their places. We waited for a moment, standing in that pole-arsed way that guards do, and then ducked inside the door.

Inside there was one large metal cage holding around fifty sorry-looking women, all sat on the floor and wearing different clothes according to the jobs they had been assigned. I looked over them all. It was a long time since I had seen women and my fervour was making me rash.

'I am Jack Sheppard and this, my brother, John.' I tried to make eye contact with every one of them. 'Those of you from London will know our work. We are starting our own settlement in this new land, and have come to invite you to join us!' The women just stared at me blankly.

'Arsehole red-coat,' I heard someone mutter at the back.

'I'll prove it!' I said, and handed the key to John. Two women stood up quickly and approached the door. They were very similar in the face, though one was much larger.

John turned the key in the door.

We had become too confident again after our successful escape, and the fact of our being armed. Our belief in the rightness of our mission in this new world had dulled our wits. Bravado has no place in criminal activity. Planning was all. It was bravado that had got us transported and now bravado again would be our undoing.

I saw the sharp wooden splint too late. The smaller of the two women buried it deep into John's throat. I gasped as he sank to his knees, blood pouring from his neck. The larger woman was on me in a second, she cracked my skull against the metal cage several times with her huge hands and I fell to the ground blood pouring from my head.

As we lay on the floor bleeding out, women ran shouting out of the gaol all around us, some trampling our bodies. When it was quiet once more I felt the hands of the small woman unbuttoning my red jacket. Laid on my side, I saw the large woman removing my brother's clothes. I looked into his eyes and saw the life fade out of them. The bastard had finished before me. I let go and, into hell or heaven, I went with him.

PRINTED ON THE THAMES

Printed on the Thames

Winter 1789

'Edward! Why have you let me awaken with a headache!' I sat up in bed. 'Edward!'

A lump in the bed moved next to me. I froze. God I hoped she didn't wake. Quite a large lump this weekend. Red hair spread over the white pillow. That must have been the clincher; I went mad for redheads. Especially on the laudanum. Anything colourful… Wow!

The room was not familiar. The smell was; I called it the Sunday morning smell. Haha. Another victorious weekend. I couldn't wait to tell Wally.

The ornately carved ceiling to the large chamber was high and although the tall casements were slightly ajar, the heavy green silken drapes drawn across them prevented the chill winter air from freshening the room. My new tall beaver hat hung on the back of the door, crushed at an awkward angle. My father's rosewood cane broken on the bedside table. He would not be happy. I caught sight of my haggard morning-after features in the elaborate French mirror over the fireplace.

If only I had taken her back to my home, rather than the other way around, Edward would have poured a few glasses of water down my neck and made me a hearty supper. It was his job to prevent my hangovers. Where was he when I needed him?

I could be anywhere in London. Further even. Wally and I had been known to venture far and wide in search of a good game.

With a groan, I lay back down and held my head.

***

We started off wrapped in thick winter frock coats, trudging up the narrow slippery steps to the street above the opium den. Once again, we had inadvertently spent the night there.

Breath clouding in the freezing air, heads hung, throbbing. Wally and I were a sorry pair indeed. I felt that the universe was being rather unkind to us. She usually was on a Saturday morning.

We'd spent a raucous Friday night on the wine and finished up, as ever, at our favourite opium den on the south bank of the Thames.

My father was a rather dull financier, whereas Walter's father was a doctor. This meant Wally always had access to the best modern medicines on the market. By means of curing the horrid throbbing and groggy unease we both felt after our previous night's wine and debauchery, we shared a few more wonderful new cocaine drops, washed down with another glug of the laudanum wine. The wine was extremely bitter, but was a fast acting cure for all ailments. Too much laudanum brought on waves of hallucinations, but it was all in good fun.

At the top of the stairs I stopped dead in my tracks and Wally bumped into the back of me. We would not be taking a boat over the river; it had set solid like thick glass and was refusing to move. Even at this early hour, with only the first lazy rays of daylight slumped on the horizon, a carnival had sprung up on its surface.

With my world impinged upon by the beautiful vignette of laudanum, and the vibrant enthusiasm of cocaine drops – not to mention the opium still lagging behind my eyes, I could not help but laugh with joy at the rich colours and unusual sights before me.

A high street of stalls stretched out across the river, selling all manner of wares imaginable. Horses unsteadily pulled sleighs full of excited children. There were triangular frames with small ships, painted bright blue or green or red, suspended from a pivot. People sat in the ships, one at either end, laughing hysterically as they swung back and forth, getting higher and higher. They looked rather unstable, I felt.

Thespians had commandeered one of the boats that had frozen into the ice. They wore elaborate, colourful costumes and were performing a musical play. One man was trapped inside a barrel, his arms sticking out of the sides; and his legs out of the bottom. Crowds had gathered around the boat and laughed loudly as the actors pranced about the deck.

Well-dressed men were playing a game of football on the ice. They charged about wildly, legs and arms flailing as they chased a blown bladder. One man slipped on the ice and landed forcefully on the ground, causing an eruption of delirious laughter as he was dragged out of the way across the ice by the ankle.

Several printing presses had been brought onto the ice, and people queued in front of them waiting to get a token printed.

***

That was something. The token. It was probably her that made me waste the money on it. Husband hunters. The lot of them.

How did I get this one?

. . . A tavern?

She rolled over and dropped her heavy arm across me. I held my breath.

***

Looking at the carnival on top of the river, the world was certainly making more of an effort to be interesting than it normally did.

I turned to my good companion, Walter 'Wally' Robertson, to verify my reality, but found his rosy cherubic face slack-jawed and baffled. Despite the man's aptitude for the sciences (and he was top of all our University classes) a casual observer would think him a buffoon. He blinked stupidly as his tricorn hat blew away down the snowy street.

Wally caught his hat and tugged at my sleeve.

'What's going on, Henry?' He whispered.

'That depends,' I said. 'Does the river seem its usual self to you?' I pointed with my father's rosewood evening cane and noted that it did not bend like a liquorice stick as it did when the hazel laudanum was waxing.

'Not in the slightest,' replied Wally, 'it seems somewhat more vibrant and less brown than usual.'

'Do you see it flow?'

'No.'

'Do you see a carnival of sorts? People? Tents? Horses? Football? General revelry?'

'Yes.'

'Well, Wally, I suspect that our dreams are overlapping. We have made a rather profound breakthrough in discovering new capabilities of the human mind, and have in fact left our bodies lounging, pipes in our mouths, in the warmth and comfort of the den.' He did not look convinced.

'But my head is throbbing,' he said. Mine also hurt. I sighed with disappointment; Wally had no imagination, 'Sorry to disappoint you, Henry, but I believe we may be in the reality we regularly share, and what you see before you is the beginnings of one of the famed Frost Fairs.'

Wally explained that he had heard about the Frost Fairs from his grandmother. She and his grandfather met at the Frost Fair in 1740, and the two of them had a little printed keepsake made that sat in a frame in their drawing room. A simple little piece of paper with a poem and both of their names on it. At the bottom were the words 'Printed on the Thames'. It was a most appealing and romantic idea.

Almost fifty years later, it appeared that Jack Frost had brought his fair to town once more. I took a big pinch of snuff and winced as it tingled intensely in the bridge of my nose. Wally shakily took his pipe from his jacket pocket. With quivering hands he proceeded to fill it with tobacco; I could not tell whether he was cold or shaking from the previous night's indulgences.

'We should go down and explore!' Said Wally, with a grin, 'Who knows what adventures may lay in wait!'

With the road clear, we strode across the road to where the thick barrier wall separated the river Thames from the street.

'How much money are you carrying, Wally?' I said, always finding myself cruelly short. He passed me his pipe and dug in his pockets a while. I took a few sneaky pulls and enjoyed the texture of the rich smoke wrapping around my nostrils.

'Not much.' He said, holding out his hand. 'Not much' would still be plenty for a few cups of hot cider, and some gingerbread. It would not be the fine gingerbread that I was accustomed to, but we had not eaten since the previous evening and I knew Wally would soon be ravenous and whining if he did not eat.

As we walked, I ran my hand over the coarse embankment wall to where a set of large stone stairs led down into the river itself. I felt each grain and ridge of the cold granite tingling under my palm.

The advances in medicine that Walter's father was privy to were truly miraculous; the combination of cocaine and laudanum both sharpened our senses and dulled our pains. It was a blissful, near heavenly combination. Soon no man would have to suffer any ailment again.

I took another big pinch of snuff before stepping hesitantly onto the high snowdrift. We both immediately cried out as we plunged through the soft snow. For a brief second I feared we would plunge through into icy water and drown, but the snow quickly compacted underfoot.

Standing waist deep in the thick snowdrift, we once more forgot our gentlemanly bearing. Walter, being considerably more portly than I, bundled me over into the snow before running away. I surfaced and looked around to see him mincing, arms raised, through the waist-high snow. Moving like an effeminate plough, he cut a path through the snowdrift onto the open ice.

The cocaine drops took full effect and I felt suddenly full of vigour. The laudanum completely cured my aching head and the world was beautiful once more. I leapt after Wally with the cat-like grace of which my dancing master had once been so proud. Scooping up a hatful of snow along the way, I quickly caught up with Wally and showered him in white powder. He tried to return fire, but whereas Walter still opted for a traditional tricorn, my more fashionable high beaver hat could hold a much larger volume of snow. He knew he was beaten and lunged at me, sending us both sprawling on our backs across the ice towards the tents.

'Need a drink gents?' said a sweet female voice. We both stopped our play fighting and looked up from the ground.

There, upside down, looking over me was the most beautiful young woman I had seen for days. Her curled hair framed her simple rosy face against the blue morning sky. She smiled.

'Ginger breads with every drink,' she said.

I shoved Walter off me and struggled falteringly to my feet, slipping on the ice several times as I did so. My grace had abandoned me.

The young maid worked at one of the tent taverns called 'The City of Moscow'. After collecting my hat and cane from the snow, I followed her towards the tent, Walter close behind.

We took a seat at a table outside 'The City of Moscow', and surveyed the bizarre fairground. I thought it would be the ideal setting for a little playful hallucination and Walter agreed so we topped our cider up with a double dose of laudanum wine from Walter's flask. Mixed with the hot sweet cider, the bitterness of the laudanum all but vanished. I politely declined the free ginger biscuit; I did not feel ready for food in my stomach. Wally ate it instead.

The cocaine drops had made Walter bold. They always did. For a normally shy, polite young man, he had a destructive habit of believing in himself when we were taking the drops. He thumped his cider down on the table.

'I'm going to ask the bar maid to dance, whilst I still can!' he announced, and stood up resolutely, striding towards the tent flap. I grabbed his arm as he passed.

'Wait, wait,' I said, and then hesitated. 'Where?' I finished, looking around. There was noisy chaos all around, and I could see no appropriate place to dance.

'Oh, over there somewhere.' He gestured with this free arm to an open snowy area on the ice, away from chaos.

'But Wally… there's no music over there… She may find it… strange.'

'Nonsense,' he said, pulling his arm free of my grasp, 'our beating hearts will be the bass, and I shall hum.' He started humming, then lifted the tent flap and ducked inside.

'Wally, no!' I cried, and stood up from the bench, flailing after him with my cane. 'That is not the romantic gesture that you think it is!'

It was no use. Wally was a man of science, and although we both attended a regular lecture in Classics at the university, he could never quite grasp things of a poetic or artistic nature. During our little forays into the town, his attempts to speak to members of the opposite sex were frequently painful and embarrassing for all concerned. Though, I must admit, he regularly hooked some surprising beauties. I parted the tent flap and popped my head through to watch.

Inside, the tent was dim and close. There were other crude wooden tables and benches, all attended by gnarled cackling root vegetables, muttering at each other with moist lips. They gave off a smell of sour sweet cider and stale sweat. Not one wore a tall fashionable beaver hat like mine.

I looked at my cane and saw that it had lost its usual rigid quality. My hand also looked larger than usual. Knowing the root creatures for what they really were – just simple old men enjoying their drink – I looked around the tent for Wally.

Against one side of the tent, a simple bar had been packed into the slushy frozen river, and behind it were three large barrels of cider. Wally was leaning on the bar, humming to the maid who stood behind it. It was most ridiculous. Her face sheen as though made out of wax, her expression held fast like a bust of a very confused – and slightly alarmed – Aphrodite.

The smell of the awful grizzled old roots was threatening to overwhelm me, and so I pulled my head out of the tent back into the fresh air outside. The vibrant colours of the fair were truly astounding. Every colour of the rainbow stood out sharp and joyful. Everything in the world fitted together like the most perfect artwork.

The cool gentle breeze and the happier light calmed me. I sat back down at our table and waited for Wally.

To my surprise, he came out of the tent a few moments later beaming from ear to ear.

'She said yes!' He did an ungainly dance step and slid across the ice in front of me, spreading his arms victoriously. 'It was most difficult to woo her with all of those stinking mangy dogs lapping so loudly at their tankards, but I overcame them as ever to win her heart. She said that if we stay and drink at 'The City of Moscow' all day, she will meet me when she finishes her shift!'

'Walter,' I said, shaking my head, 'Wally, Wally, Walter. That is not a yes! That is a business proposition. Sit down whilst the wave passes, have a drink.'

He looked a little crestfallen, but eventually had to agree with me.

We discussed the entire world as we drank our hot cider. The French with their revolution as always, the riches to be had in the New World of the Americas, the power of the East India Company, the correct way to load a blunderbuss. Topics we had discussed a hundred times. As always, we argued passionately and with great certainty on things about which we had very little knowledge.

***

Not the barmaid. Surely? I would never seek so base a prize. The barmaid could never have a room like this one.

Unless…did I pay for a fine hotel? I'd done it before to snag a peasant woman on nights when the finer fillies were too stupid. They were always good fun in the bedroom.

No, I wouldn't take a pleb so early in the day.

The girl's arm still around me, I dared not roll over to see. If I awoke her we'd have to do conversation. Frightful!

***

Holding onto each other so as not to slip on the ice, we set off in the direction of the theatre ship where the little man in the barrel still kicked and danced. I was relieved to see my cane almost solid again. It could be quite pleasant to attend a play.

It was not at all pleasant. We found ourselves stood shoulder to shoulder with the peasantry, the horribly unwashed, bunched around the frozen ship. For a time I fought with panic, clinging to Walter's sturdy frame as the crowd heaved and moved around us. The play was truly awful. An interpretation of the classic comedy of manners by Sir George Etherege entitled 'Love in a Tub'. But nobody was really paying attention to the story – there had been very little attempt to follow the original narrative, the troupe had instead opted to leap around to comic effect. The simple commoners loved it.

On the deck of the ship, the small man was still stuck in the barrel. He danced strangely to a frantic tune played on the fiddle as the other actors in their gaudy attire pranced around him. Someone had cut holes in the barrel for the little man's arms to poke through and he used them to beat an ill-timed rhythm on the barrel sides. His small round pea of a head rested on top of the barrel, thrashing from side to side as though it might come loose from his body at any moment. From the bottom of the barrel, his little legs poked out and he kicked them around as though dancing an Irish jig.

The root vegetable faces of the crowd brayed and howled with animal voices. I felt trapped in the madness, unable to free myself. All around me noses seemed too long and too bulbous, dripping from rooty faces like warm candle wax. Ears made of wet clay folded and drooped slowly towards grubby shoulders, whilst eyeballs floated high on mottled lumpy foreheads.

The crowd surged around me and I almost lost my footing on the slippery ice, but we were so tightly packed that I managed to remain upright by pushing over the man next to me. He was a large man with the face of an unpeeled root vegetable, and eyes so black and glaring that I feared for not only my life, but also my soul. Before he could get up from the ice, I turned to Walter, whose frock coat sleeve I still clutched tightly.

'I don't think I'm having a good time!' I yelled at him over the braying of the crowd.

When Walter looked around at me, I could see that his face too was beginning to warp into the same melting, vegetable-like state. The man on the floor was rising unsteadily from the slippery surface. As soon as he could right himself I was done for. I used my exceptionally long leg to prod the large man off balance, sending him crashing back onto the ice, and then urged Walter:

'Run!'

Walter bulled through the crowd with me clinging on tightly. The faces growled and howled at us as we pushed past.

After several paces the crowd began to thin. We need not continue to push people aside; instead we dodged and wove through the gaps, and eventually emerged from that hell into the clear open air.

I breathed deeply.

Letting go of Walter, I stumbled away from the crowd. I threw myself backwards into a snowdrift and by chance found the most tranquil and comfortable position I had ever known.

Suddenly the world felt angelic. I tuned my attention to each element of the moment. In the periphery of my vision, the pure white walls of snow rose up around my head. They cooled my skull, and muffled my ears so that the chaos of the fair was a distant, separate existence. Above the white walls, framed in a silhouette of my head and beaver hat, the blue winter sky looked down on me. A solitary white cloud drifted elegantly past, in no hurry to be anywhere. My own breath clouded in the cold air, and drifted dreamily away to join its larger sibling in the sky. The snuff still tingled pleasantly in my nose bridge.

Breathing deeply and slowly, I savoured the moment as a whole perfect synthesis of its elements. Like listening to a beautiful piece of music, I was acutely aware of time's harmony. Everything made sense.

***

Not so now.

So, she was not from the theatre ship.

She started snoring. Deeply and loudly. Each reverberation seemed to shake the bed and my fragile skull with it.

Be quiet you bovine woman! Damn you!

She had to be quiet. Absolutely!

I shoved her off of me, and onto her side. One quick movement. Then shut my eyes, pretending to be asleep.

I heard her shuffle under the bedcovers and smack her lips loudly.

Where had I found such a creature?

***

Walter's rosy face popped into view, wild-eyed and chewing his lip. My pang of irritation passed when he whispered:

''The ice is on fire over there.'

'What? Are you sure?' I asked.

His face disappeared from the white frame. It reappeared a moment later, nodding vigorously.

'Definitely.'

I sat bolt upright in the snow and looked across the fair.

He was right. On the other side of the fair, defying all logic, a huge fire raged on the frozen river. I stood hurriedly and gathered my hat and cane. The cane was solid!

Leaning on one another for support, Walter and I continued our perilous adventure through the fair. We meandered through the crowds like unsteady skaters. Grinning faces of rich and poor alike rushed past all around us, but we kept a singular purpose on the roaring fire on the ice.

As we approached the fire we saw, like a vision of hell, a whole long-horned ox being turned on a huge spit over the flames. It gave a sweet meaty texture to the air. Its eyes had already melted out, and a fatty liquid dripped from its mouth, gliding down in beads to spatter and sizzle on the hot coals. The man turning the spit did so with a slow but interminable solemn rhythm, puffing and panting as he did so. The meat around the animal's haunches still leaked blood, pumping it out afresh with each turn of the spit, but the shins and hooves had started to blacken. The meat there would need to be sliced off and eaten soon or else be spoiled.

The gathering crowds knew this and looked on hungrily, smacking their moist lips like starved hounds. The sight of their grotesque hanging faces instigated that same pang of fear and nausea that I had felt whilst trapped in the braying madness at the theatre ship. I took a swig of Wally's laudanum wine to calm my nerves, and looked away into the flames.

Slushy snow and water had started to pool around the base of the fire where the frozen river surface was melting. The sharp orange fire danced in those pools. I wondered how long the fire could burn before it melted through the ice and extinguished itself in the murky Thames water.

In this image I suddenly felt the universe speak to me as she sometimes did.

She told me that if I burned hotly enough, perhaps I would melt through the ice and know what was behind it. If I did not, I would only ever burn at the surface and spatter out; consumed by the very slush I had created. Feeling suddenly a little despondent, I thanked the universe for her advice, and turned from the roasting ox to search for the billows that would stoke my own flames.

Wally caught up with me a few steps later.

'What's wrong Henry?' he said.

I could not properly articulate my thoughts. Wally had not seen the watery slush at the base of the fire with the same meaning as I. He was a man of science and would think me insane if I told him that the universe would speak to you if you knew how to hear her.

'I feel a lack, Wally,' I settled for. 'One that no amount of your unerring loyal friendship can fill.'

'You want to meet a woman?' He replied. It was not so simple as that, but he would never understand.

'Not just meet a woman, that is easy enough. I want to get a token printed, like the one your grandparents have. Their whole life as a couple began with that token.'

***

That was what the token was about; maybe in my haze, I had thought this girl was the one to keep me happy for life. What nonsense.

I cringed at the sickeningly romantic gesture. Still…it reeled her in…I got my weekend victory. Maybe the Frost Fair would stay a while and I could try it again.

Slowly, I wriggled up onto my elbows and then sat up in the bed. There was a small dainty hipflask on the floor next to the bed. Carefully and silently I reached down and picked it up.

Sniff.

Wine.

Sip. Ugh!

Laudanum wine!

This girl had her own supply, the little fox. I was intrigued.

Light was breaking through a thin gap in the heavy green curtains, and I could see the girl's face. She was not altogether ugly, but I could get better.

I lifted the covers to look at her bosoms. Hmm…actually they were excellent. Pert and large and full. I cupped one gently in my hand and felt myself stiffen.

Maybe I should wake her? I'd already paid for a token.

Was it worth the awful conversation for one more tumble?

No, my aching head was not ready for it yet.

I sipped a little more wine from her hipflask and winced as quietly as possible at the vile bitterness.

Where did I find this girl? What was her name?

***

'We should join a dance,' Said Wally, 'You were always once of the best dancers in school. Perhaps we'll meet someone that way.' He pointed around the fair at the different boats locked in the ice. 'I'm sure a band will strike up on one of the frozen boats.'

It was true; I was good, but only because my father had sent me to that infernal French dancing master every week. I had no love for dancing.

At length we stumbled upon a cotillon contredanse that was just about to begin. It would be the perfect dance to meet the perfect lady. Only the most refined ladies would know the figures and changes that would be called, and with so many changes of partner I could cast my eye over some of the finest fillies at the fair!

There was a lot of milling about at the front of the stage, so I took up a position at a suitable point for a square, and adopted the opening stance. I bid Walter do the same parallel to me with enough room for ladies to take our arms. Soon enough several others fell into line, and positions were filled. A young dark-haired girl gently took my arm. We smiled at each other and she gave a little curtsey.

The music began and each couple took their first steps in the opening figure. Within five steps the first man had slipped and crashed to the floor. Hilarity ensued. It was clear to me then that this was not going to be a serious contredanse. I looked at my partner and we laughed gaily. Her eyes were unusually large in her skull.

As the dance continued, more people slipped to the floor. It was incredibly difficult to stay upright for some of the more complex figures, but I had rediscovered my cat-like grace and tried to use the ice to my advantage, sliding through each movement to great applause from the onlookers.

Wally fell several times; on one occasion he almost crushed his partner, but always made a joke of it. The dancers laughed loudly, shrill thin whinnying swirling madly through the air almost drowning out the music. With each new partner that took my arm, I flashed my winning smile. Some girls blushed, others looked away coyly. One square-jawed extremely fine girl gave me only a frightful icy indifference, which left me uncomfortable for the whole sequence. Handing her on to the next man was a great relief.

Many of the ladies were very beautiful, but I did not feel that they warranted a printed token; the lady with whom I printed a token had to stoke the dying fire within me.

I looked at my new partner. The girl was my inverse. Where I was lithe and rangy, she was a little flour dumpling. My hair was thin and dark, hers a voluminous mass of fire-red ringlets. It bounced merrily as she stepped, each movement releasing a cloud of rich perfume. Her voluminous chest heaved with the effort of keeping up with my steps… A treasure trove jiggled before my eyes.

***

There she was! That's where I found her. A Cotillon. A good sign.

She might even be a filly of good pedigree. Perhaps it would be no bad thing if she did wake up. It may be the start of something good.

Love? Finally?

I dearly hoped her name was a good one.

***

In her efforts to remain upright, the girl barely took her eyes from the ground. She must have felt my gaze upon her for she suddenly looked up, directly into my eyes. Her face was a picture of perfect symmetry, with pretty dimples in her chubby cheeks. Plump red lips parted in the most joyful beaming smile I had ever seen, revealing a full set of the decent white teeth. My teeth were the most perfect I had known, none in London rivalled them. But her smile was pretty and, impressed; I could not help but grin back at her.

I slipped on the ice. It was her fault; her awkward dance steps.

Unable to unlock my arm in time, I dragged the poor girl down with me. We both crashed to the ground, her on top of me. The impact knocked the wind right out of me, and I lay there gasping for air, the laughter of the crowd stinging my ears. The girl struggled upright.

'I'm so sorry!' she said, hurrying away, hiding her face in her hands. I rolled onto my side just in time to see her disappear through the crowd at the edge of the dance area.

'Wally!' I shouted. He blundered towards me. 'Up, up, up man!'

Walter's strong arms lifted me from the ice and helped me to stagger, panting and wheezing, away from the dance area.

'Did you see where she went?' I asked Walter, when we were through the audience and away from the music.

'She and her friend joined the queue at that printing press over there.' He pointed to one of the huge queues.

'Wally you beauty!' I said, grabbing him by the lapels and kissing his unusually soft cheek. 'Let's have them!'

'Wait,' he replied, looking nervous, 'what should I say? I danced with her friend but she wasn't very friendly.'

'Ask her name, tell her yours. Compliment her… you're an educated man; the words will come naturally in the moment… But *don't* hum a tune for her.'

We took a couple more cocaine drops with laudanum wine, and a big pinch of snuff each. After checking each other's noses for brown stains, we approached the queue that wound through the fairground revelry, meandering between carnival tents towards the printing presses.

My cane wobbled and bowed as I walked along the queue ignoring the bulbous faces of the common people. Those fiery ringlets stood out from the crowd and after pointing Wally in the right direction, we hurried over to the girl and her friend.

The red-haired girl's friend was the extremely handsome girl who had so chilled my soul with her icy indifference. Her elegant jaw had set in a firm scowl and her face seemed to be carved out of rough granite; the texture looked most appealing to touch, just as the granite wall had been at the start of our journey. I steadied my hand and refrained from rubbing her ear. I hoped that Wally's bumbling charm could rouse a smile from her. I struck a pose with my cane and took off my hat.

'Excuse me, fair lady,' I said to my fire-haired girl. She looked around. Seeing me, her beautiful round face dropped with the shame that she felt for landing so heavily upon me. Rightly so. 'Your smile stoked the fire within me that I had given up on fuelling. I hoped that I might know your name?'

***

Eggshell.

Not her name. Her voice. I remembered only the wonderful eggshell texture of that voice. Her words were not important.

In the bed next to me, her breathing changed.

She mumbled and turned in her sleep.

My heart stopped as I thought she was about to wake. Please, no. Not yet!

Maybe her name would be on the token itself? If her name proved to be as important as my name, I would wake her and try to converse

***

The press itself was a large wooden structure with a screwing mechanism to press the ink plate against the paper. The old man who turned the screw was bent-backed, his lips the stiff shape of a long pipe wreathing blue-grey smoke. His hands glistened a wet black from the ink and his fingers seemed to fuse together like cloven sheep hooves. I looked nervously at the girl standing next to me and threw her what I hoped was my most charming smile. She returned my smile with her own perfect one. I wanted to reach out and hold her hand, but in the corner of my eye I could see her looming granite-faced friend scowling at me. Wally's seductive powers sometimes took a while to take effect.

We watched the man's dexterous black hooves splay and refuse as he changed the letters to make our names. When he had done, he straightened his bent back and pulled down the lever that would press the words forever into the paper. An irreversible process. I dared not look around at the girl.

The bent-backed man had just handed us our tokens, when a blood-curdling cry came from behind me.

'Oi! Toffee Nose!' came the sickening sharp voice of the goblin.

As I turned, I felt a bloody rage surge in my ears. There he stood, the foul little beast. He was not alone. Four other twisted demons stood behind him, two much larger than he. They all leered and snarled menacingly at me, gnashing their black teeth, their savage angular features a filthy brown against the snow. My heart raced so fast that I feared it would burst through my chest.

That these foul little urchins would dare to speak to me in such a way drove me to frenzy. I could not let the girl see me stand for their insolence. In a fit of wild rage I raised my father's cane and saw that it was as limp as a leather belt. I cracked it like a whip and ran at the terrors.

'Off with you foul creatures!' I shouted.

To my horror, they did not turn tail and flee; I was perhaps not so menacing as I imagined myself to be. Instead they raised their own arms high and conjured from the realm of hell, a barrage of cannonballs.

***

I jumped in fright as the door handle started to turn. Oh no, no, no. Don't come!

She still slept deeply.

The door opened about a foot. Argh! Who?

...

Wally's fat head peered in. Phew! I put my finger to my lips.

'Sunday hunt?' He whispered.

I grinned at him, nodding, and pointed downstairs.

He retracted his head.

Stealthy, I slid out from underneath the covers.

Tiptoes.

I struggled with my trousers and frock coat, the fabric loud and scratching.

I left her my broken cane, and took her little hipflask of laudanum wine. She'd think she lost it.

In my coat pocket, the paper token crinkled. I looked at it with a wry smile and scrunched it back into the pocket. No name. Something to remember her by.

One last look at that wonderful bosom? No. Too risky. There'd be others.

Away to the Sunday hunt.

IGNATIUS SANCHO'S SHOP

Ignatius Sancho's Shop

2nd June 1780

My little grocery shop sat just a few hundred yards from the Houses of Parliament and through my window I could see the hundred thousand strong mob gathering outside. A river of blue cockades and grimy resentful faces swirled and eddied in the streets. A poor, miserable, ragged rabble. All ages, marauding and tense, ready for any and every mischief. It started as some anti-Catholic nonsense in protest over the recent Papists Act, but for most of the mob it was just an excuse to cause trouble.

The shop was my pride and joy, though I was not proud of what I sold. Tobacco, Sugar, Rum, Tea. The products of the slave trade. For I am an Affrican – with two ff's, if you please – for proud I am to be of a country that knows no Politicians or Lawyers. As a man of Affrican descent and born into slavery I found these items abhorrent. There were other items for sale, but to my shame, slave goods provided most of my very decent income. It would be folly to decline to sell the goods; such a decision would quickly bankrupt me. Yet, with every sale, my heart shrank even as my purse swelled.

My beloved wife, Ann, reassured me that I was using my exceptionally fortuitous situation to the best possible effect. With the influential people who frequented my shop – and I could count some of London's best musicians, artists, thespians, and indeed, politicians, amongst my regular customers – I could strike up friendships with the men who had the power to bring about the abolition of slavery. I had mentioned the horrors of the slave trade in conversations with and several letters to these influential friends.

One such friend, a sculpture artist of some renown, Mr. Joseph Nollekens, paid for his tobacco and bid me good day. From behind my fine wooden counter I watched him wind away through the crowds, pulling his tricorn hat low and trying to be invisible.

It was only just five o'clock but I thought it best to shut early and bolt the doors. I suggested as much to Ann, who sat in all her white-haired wisdom and loveliness, peacefully chopping up the sugar at her neat preparation counter in one corner of the shop. She agreed and began to pack away her things.

Across the street, some shops remained open, daring to risk the mob for the extra custom they might claim from those who closed early. I would take no such risk. As a black man of some wealth and standing – not to mention the only black man in London eligible to vote – I would be an easy target for ordinary working people venting anger at the hardships of their lives.

The gout in my ankles flared painfully as I walked across the cold stone floor to lock the entrance to my kingdom. My door was sturdy and new; it was painted a rich green and had a shiny brass knocker and a black iron number 19. Nineteen Charles Street. My own little haven. An island that was, at long last, a part of the world that I had control over. I slid the heavy metal bolts across to secure the door, and trading was over for another day.

With the soft light of the cool summer evening pouring gently through the display window, I began to take the display items down. Leaving such fine produce in clear view whilst the blue cockade protests were threatening to boil over would only invite looting. I could see some of the mob loitering around near my window. One ragged ruffian met my gaze with fierce hate-filled eyes. Not wanting to provoke a reaction, I looked away quickly and busied myself with gathering the display items.

I heard the glass shatter a mere millisecond before the pain flashed through my skull, and I felt myself falling backwards. Thoughts of Ann and our children upstairs fought to keep me upright, but did not have the strength in my gout-ridden body.

Back and back I fell until the ceiling of my shop was a white plaster sky a hundred miles above me. My two tall lamps reached upwards like great trees, and the display cabinets loomed like wooden cliff faces, each fruit fly a soaring bird. It seemed an age before I hit the cold stone floor. When the moment came, with a soft, inaudible pffft like a crushed sugar cube, the solid stone crumbled to fine grains underneath my great weight. I fell straight through it.

Tumbling down through pitch darkness, I flailed after the circle of light, watching in terror as it shrunk rapidly above me. After my lungs could scream no more, I landed on a thick, grey-white mossy material. The moss caught me carefully and I felt I was cradled in the palm of a giant gentle hand.

I lay there in the moss of a deep dark cavern far below the London streets. On the very furthest edge of hearing I could feel the chaotic rumbling of the protesters mutating into rioters. Lying on my back, I stared upwards, mesmerised by the shilling-sized hole I had made in the shop floor high above me. The shaft of light streaming through it was not enough to penetrate the gloom of the cavern, but cast a single spotlight on the soft white moss where I lay. A few grains of the sugar floor stones tumbled down through the light and landed on my face.

Confused and terrified, I used my elbows to roll onto my side, and then shakily onto my knees. I knelt, blinded, willing my eyes to adjust to the darkness. At length, I saw a faint pinprick of orange glowing on the pitch-black canvas. It moved haphazardly, dancing and weaving like a drunken firefly. I realised that it was steadily getting larger, but in blackness of such pitch I could fix no perspective upon it and there was no way of knowing whether the orange light was growing or moving closer to me. I sat back down on the comfortable moss and watched it as I considered my situation. In the six months that I had owned the shop, the stone floor had always seemed solid and sturdy. I never knew of any cavern below it, and the previous owner would surely have mentioned something. It was most perplexing. There was no way of climbing back up to the hole, and the blackness stretched out infinitely in all directions. There was only the shaft of white daylight far above me, and the faint orange firefly in the distance.

I could lay there in my shaft of light in the darkness, or investigate the mysterious orange glow. Perhaps it would lead to a way back. I was about to stand when I heard the vague, panting breath of a man. At first I thought it was part of the distant rumblings of the rioters far overhead, but it was closer than that. It was here, with me, in the cavern. It was coming from the orange glow. I stood up and stepped forward out of the shaft of daylight.

'Hey?' I called out, my deep voice echoing through the cavern. The orange glow stopped moving abruptly. It waited. Panting.

'Ignatius?' came the thin nasally voice of Joseph Nollekens, my sculptor friend.

'Joseph!' I cried, stepping delicately over the moss towards the orange glow, 'what is this place? How did you get here?'

'Stop Ignatius!' Joseph yelled. I stood still in my tracks. 'Keep quiet and stay in the light. I will come to you. The caverns are full of dangers.'

As he spoke, something long and muscular slid over my foot. I leapt back into my shaft of light and waited for Joseph to reach me.

In his flaming torchlight, Joseph's narrow nose and angular chin stood out from the shadows underneath his low tricorn hat. He wore the collar of his frock coat upturned and pulled right around his ears.

'What-' I started to say when he was within a few yards. He cut me short by pressing his long bony index finger to his lips, and gestured for me follow him. Closely. Silently. Exactly.

As we crossed the moss-covered floor I watched the pool of light at Joseph's feet. The hem of his frock coat fluttered around his sinewy calves, and each of his footsteps left a print in the moss. I did my best to place my own feet in them before the moss sprang back.

For mile after mile we walked like this. A lifetime of weaving left and right through the darkness. At times, I fancied I glimpsed black tendril creatures at the edge of our little pool of torchlight. They glistened wetly in the grey-white moss, snaking back into the darkness even as I glanced at them. In other places, twisted, rotting chains and manacles poked up through the moss. To my horror, some still held hands and feet; their owners long buried under the grey-white blanket.

Walking such distances would usually be impossible for me; my feet and joints would not permit it. Perhaps it was the softness of the moss that made the walk quite painless, or perhaps my fear of the evil darkness pressing against us forced the pain from my mind and kept me within Joseph's circle of light.

Suddenly Joseph stopped. So suddenly that I ran into the back of him, almost knocking him to the ground. He winced and grunted and managed to steady himself, and then held his torch aloft before us. We had reached a wall. A slick, sheen, sheer, sheet of marble.

'Shhhh,' hushed Joseph, turning around to me and raising his hat to look at me with his deep-set eyes. The torchlight reflected in them gave the appearance of a man possessed by a demon.

He turned back to the marble wall and held the torch closely to it, peering at the wall, his narrow nose almost touching the wet marble. After a few seconds he let out a sharp exhalation and planted his long finger on the rock. Squinting, I could just make out a tiny crack, as thin as spider silk. Joseph passed the torch to me and I held it close to the wall. He put his knuckled, skilful thumbs at either side of the crack, and teased it open as though splitting a recently healed wound. Once he had opened the rock wide enough, he put his fingers in the wound, and prised it apart even further. The solid marble was bread dough in his hands, and he quickly opened the crack wide enough for me to see a narrow tunnel beyond. As soon as he could fit, Joseph slipped through the gap and took the torch from me.

I looked back one last time into the darkness, and saw in the furthest distance, the shaft of light through which I had fallen. It was nothing more than a long white hair. The thin, frail hair of a woman. I reached out and plucked it from the cavern ceiling. Tucking the white hair into my trouser pocket, I tried to follow Joseph though the marble wall but my girth was much greater than his and I found myself trapped. To my touch, the stone was not malleable like bread dough, and I felt it tightening around my body.

'Joseph, help me!' I cried, my body half inside the evil dark cavern, and half in the narrow tunnel beyond.

A slick, muscular, tendril creature wrapped around the wrist of my hand in the darkness. I breathed in, I heaved, I tried to force myself through the ever-shrinking gap, but the dark creature around my wrist tightened its grip and tried to pull me back into the cavern. Joseph took hold of my other hand and pulled with all his might. I felt I would tear apart down the middle when, in a snap of cotton, the buttons of my shirt tore off and I fell through the gap, landing heavily on Joseph.

The marble wall was springing back rapidly behind me, but the tendril creature of the cavern still clung to my wrist, pulling me back in with great strength. The part of the long creature still inside the cavern was a slick black eel-like muscle, but where it came into the torchlight of the narrow tunnel it was a simple wrought-iron chain. The marble wall closed around it and the chain fell from my wrist, landing with a heavy metallic clang on the cold stone floor.

I lay panting, my clothes torn, my stomach and back sore and bleeding, lacerated by the sharp marble walls. Joseph had dropped his torch when I fell on him, and it lay spattering on the floor. He quickly gathered it up and stood, waiting for me to follow.

'Joseph, where are we?' I said, almost weeping as I struggled to get to my feet. He offered me his hand and cracked his hawkish smiled at me.

'You'll see soon dear friend,' he said. I took his hand and he pulled me upright, 'onward!'

With that he turned and headed quickly down the narrow tunnel. I felt the weight of the earth pressing down on top of me as I struggled to keep up with him, the painful gout returning to my feet and knees with every step. His torchlight and trailing frock coat disappeared around corners, always just ahead of me. And then, to my surprise, a breeze.

A clammy, tropical-scented breeze. Organic, living, and tremendously old. It was the breath of ancient trees sighing. Joseph turned another corner ahead of me, but I did not need his torchlight now. The breeze had carried a faint light into the tunnel. I followed Joseph around another corner and emerged into a brightly lit, open-mouthed cave.

'My Othello!' cried a regal, booming voice, as I stood there blinking in the daylight. 'Ignatius, my good man I feared we might lose you. Yay, as yet we might.'

When my eyes adjusted, I saw Joseph sat on the floor catching his breath and staring out of the cave mouth, silhouetted by the daylight streaming in. Next to him, stood my theatrical friend Mr. David Garrick. David was an actor of near magical ability and theatre producer of great renown. He had been giving me acting classes in the hope that I could play the leading role in his production of Shakespeare's Othello. I confess that my acting was truly atrocious; I was simply woeful at every aspect of the profession. Even so, David and I had developed a great friendship and mutual respect.

Wearing his usual garishly eccentric waistcoat, large trousers, and ornate cane, he struck a masterful pose in the cave mouth. He bowed deeply at me and strode forwards on long, powerful legs with great elaborate steps, huge outstretched arms inviting me to embrace him.

Missing his step on the uneven cave floor, he stumbled into me. I caught him and was immediately engulfed in the cloud of sickly-sweet spiced rum breath. Never had I known the man to be completely sober. I'll grant that he was always coherent, and could hold his excellent sturdy-framed posture extremely well, but the rum on his breath and his comfortable inebriated smile – a smile he only allowed himself when he thought nobody else was looking – were obvious indications of his vice.

'David! Where are we? Joseph? What's going on?' I asked, bewildered. Struggling under his great weight, I managed to stand him upright. The big man laughed heartily, braying like a donkey, his long face thrown skywards and huge Adam's apple bobbing up and down in his muscular throat. He clapped a meaty affectionate arm around my shoulders.

'My dear, great Ignatius. We are in a place that knows you very well, though you have never seen it,' he said, giving me cryptic, bucktoothed grin as he led me to the cave mouth where Joseph still sat. My mouth dropped open in awe. Before me lay a vast green jungle.

Our cave-mouth overlooked the jungle from a few metres above the canopy. Brightly coloured birds and insects swooped and dived above and amongst the trees, screeching, squawking, buzzing and nattering in a thousand languages. The vibrant cacophony of life rose on a heat haze. Joseph looked up at me from where he sat, and David spread his arms wide.

'Welcome to Africa, my friend,' he said, 'it is as you imagine, I trust?'

I stood speechless for a moment. Tears welled in my eyes. Joseph stood up sharply and dusted himself down.

'We need to go,' he said, 'the others will be waiting.'

'Go? Where?' I looked up at David for an answer. He pointed out across the jungle canopy to where a huge mountain shot up high into the clouds.

'There!' he roared, delivering the word with unnecessary drama. Birds in nearby trees took flight.

Joseph furrowed his brow and tutted at David, who stood statuesque, the image of a great leader; legs apart, jaw set, one hand on his hip, the other pointing his cane at the mountain.

'We've got to get you back to London,' said Joseph, 'the cavern was your shortcut here; the mountain is our shortcut back.'

I wanted to stay in Affrica and find a fellow Affrican to teach me about my land that I had never seen or known, but Joseph said there was still too much to be done in London. He led the way down the rough rubble track from the cave mouth towards the dense forest below.

'I cannot climb such a mountain!' I called down the track to him, 'you know I am afflicted by crippling gout.'

'That is why our dear David joined us!' he shouted back. I turned and looked up at David stood next to me.

'I'm renowned for playing the horse,' he said, with a wink and a buck-toothed grin. He knelt down in front of me, 'Saddle up, my dear Ignatius, Laurence and Foxy have gone ahead!'

It was wonderful to know that my regular customers, and friends, Laurence Sterne and The Honourable Charles James Fox had also come to take me back. It meant my shop was influencing the powerful; it was working as I intended.

Awkward though it was, I had no choice. They would not leave me, and David insisted on carrying me. I was quite a large man with a significant gut, but David carried me on his back with ease. The bloody scrape marks on my stomach left red patches on the back of his waistcoat. He bent forward at the waist and instructed me to sit upright on the base of his spine so that his legs could take my weight and I could see where I was going. With Joseph leading the way, and me following behind on David, we made our way through the dense jungle.

The deeper we went the more humid and close the air became. Joseph removed his frock coat and slung it over his shoulder, and David's neatly curled black hair was matted with sweat. I was almost glad that my shirt had been torn to pieces. I hung it over a tree branch and rode with a bare chest for the rest of the journey. It was ungentlemanly, but no more so than my tattered, bloody shirt. Besides that, we were no longer in a place where gentlemanly bearing had any meaning.

The undergrowth grew thicker, and so David handed his cane to Joseph in order that he might hack a trail through it. The trail that Joseph carved was straight and clear, but even so, David wobbled and strayed from it on several occasions. Whether from the drink or the fatigue I could not be sure, but with a word and a tug on the right or left side of his waistcoat, I soon brought him back to the trail. At each break in the canopy, we checked our position against the mountain and Joseph adjusted our direction accordingly.

I heard things scurrying through the leaf litter as we passed, rustling and sniffling alongside us. The brightly coloured birds looked down on us from the tree branches with great curiosity, their heads tilted at an inquisitive angle. It seemed that the whole jungle was trying to understand what we were about.

We stopped by a trickling stream to drink. The water tasted muddy but to our parched throats it was as holy water. Joseph and I cupped the water in our hands and washed our faces in it. David, an actor forever true to his role, knelt to in the leaf litter and put his lips to the water's sparkling surface, supping like a horse.

A fallen tree trunk by the stream offered a good resting spot and we gladly took a seat. Joseph took out his pipe and tobacco and was soon puffing away merrily, wreaths of blue smoke spiralling up through the canopy. Refreshed, David stood up straight and dabbed his wet lips with an expensive silk handkerchief. He excused himself and walked a little way into the trees to answer the call of nature, and, when he thought nobody could was watching, he took a hip flask from his trouser pocket and drank deeply from it. I pointed David's drinking out to Joseph.

'David, if you're going to drink at least share the wealth,' he said, without looking around. David looked embarrassed and hobbled back over to us, offering his hip-flask around. I had no love of rum and declined his offer, but Joseph gladly took the flask.

'Well, Joseph, I daresay the same applies to you,' said David indignantly. Joseph threw a cold glance at David, and begrudgingly held out his pipe.

We lounged in companionable silence on the fallen tree by the stream. Joseph looked at my bare, scratched torso and patted me manfully on the shoulder.

'One day, good Ignatius, I will carve you in stone,' he said. I wasn't entirely sure how to respond, so I simply thanked him and said I would gladly sit for him whilst he carved. Satisfied, he nodded and plucked his pipe from David's mouth.

After no more than two minutes, a most disturbing noise cut through the harmonious hum of the jungle. It was the soul-searing cry of a man.

We looked at each other and listened intently.

'Help me!' came the cry again. A coarse Irish accent, strangled and full of fear. The voice was familiar.

'It's Laurence isn't it?' I said. Joseph was already stood up and tapping his pipe out.

Laurence Sterne was a literary genius and one of the most respected writers in London, and another of my influential customers with whom I had developed a great friendship. Though Sterne by name, the man was anything but; he had a jovial Irish manner and his writing was famously satirical. He often came into my shop to discuss literature with me, and in my latest letter to him I had urged him to use his pen to lobby for an end to the slave trade.

'Laurence!' boomed David, causing all of the birds and creatures for miles around to take flight in panic. Joseph punched him on the arm.

'Must you announce our presence to every dangerous creature for miles around!' he glared angrily at David.

I climbed back on David's back and we splashed through the stream, plunging through the jungle in the direction of Laurence's cry. No further cries came.

After at least an hour we had still not located Laurence. In our frantic hurry to come to his aid, we grew careless and dashed straight into a thick shadowy swamp. The mud glooped and sucked at David's feet as he tried to push through it, and we were quickly stuck fast. Joseph, just a step ahead of us, was also unable to move. Then, to my horror, we began to sink.

Fear engulfed me as I realised why Laurence's strangled cries had ceased so suddenly. We were going to die here. Here where the daylight barely broke through the canopy. Swallowed up into the stinking, sucking swamp. David began to panic and struggle underneath me, sinking us ever faster. I managed to calm him and looked at Joseph. He was stood still, eyes darting around for anything to grab. There was nothing. From my vantage point on David's back, I could see those slick black tendril creatures sliding through the rotting swamp water. The wakes in the ooze caused by their muscular snaking bodies encircled us as we sank. We cried out for help, but had no response. The mud was up to Joseph's waist, and David's thighs. I looked up and saw, in the branches overhead, a thousand tiny black faces staring down at us. Diminuto![11]

They were small, wiry people, perching on branches with great balance and ease. Their stomachs were bloated and their black skin drawn tightly over their skulls. Each Diminuto had strange lumps in their cheeks.

I threw my arms up to them, imploring them to save us. Joseph, now sunken up to his chest, did likewise, whilst David brayed in terror. For a moment I feared that the Diminuto would simply watch us disappear, but then three long green vines sailed down. On David's back I was highest above the ooze and managed to grab a vine first. I barely had time to wrap it around my waist when there was a flurry of movement above me and hundreds of Diminuto working together hauled me up away from danger. Still dangling on the end of the vine, they swung me from one

---

[11] A fanciful tribe that appear in Sancho's surreal journey. His work for abolition gave him great stature in certain quarters and was of paramount importance in his personal journey.

side to the other like a pendulum until the trajectory of the swing brought me over solid land. Then they dropped me. I landed with a painful thud at the side of the swamp.

Joseph soon landed next to me and together we watched David slowly ascend from the gloop. His huge size was a great struggle for the Diminuto, and more and more of the little fellows joined in hauling on the vine. When all but his feet were out of the swamp, one of the vile tendril creatures leapt from the mud and wrapped around his ankle. Joseph and I watched, helplessly as poor David was pulled back towards the swamp. He howled his terror, kicking at the mud-covered evil thing with his free leg. The Diminuto strained and heaved, all thousand of them working in unison. If the vine should snap David would be lost. He screamed in the pain of being stretched. One of the Diminuto let go of the vine and climbed up to the very top branches of the canopy, there he parted the leaves and daylight surged down into the swamp. The moment it struck the vile tendril, the creature released David's ankle and shrank back into the mud. David shot upwards and the Diminuto swung him over to land next to us with a mighty thud.

The Diminuto surged out of the trees and surrounded us, chattering in a strange high-pitched language that I couldn't understand. I remounted David and, looking down at their big awestruck eyes and the solid round lumps in their cheeks, I realised that to the Diminuto I must seem like a god. I was a large swollen version of them, and I rode upon the back of a giant pale man with another pale man guiding me. One little bare-breasted Diminuto woman tugged at my trousers and gestured for me to follow her, other Diminuto did the same to Joseph and David. I exchanged glances with Joseph, who nodded and allowed himself to be led by the hand. I used my heels to tap David's thighs and we followed the Diminuto through the jungle.

After the elation of escaping from the swamp had passed, I spared a thought for poor Laurence. If the sudden cessation of his cries for help were any indication, the great man had fallen victim to the swamp. Joseph said a prayer for him as we walked and David and I made our amens. The Diminuto were terribly excited, leaping and dancing all around us. One little Diminuto boy even climbed up onto David's great head and sat in front of me on his back, stroking David's hair. I remarked to Joseph about the strange solid round lumps in their cheeks, and he agreed that it was not usual. We had both heard tales of the Diminuto, but never any mention of the lumps in their cheeks. They all looked as though they had two cheekfuls of chewing tobacco, though they did not chew or spit.

At length we came to the Diminuto village and were greeted by yet more excited little people with lumps in their cheeks. The village stretched out amongst the trees in a less densely packed part of the jungle, the little homes were simple twig structures thatched with large leaves, and in the very centre was a much larger, longer hut on stilts. I dismounted from David and the Diminuto took turns at riding him – three and four at a time – in and out of their little thatched huts, they laughed and chased gleefully as he vaulted over their campfires.

Strange gave way to truly bizarre as Joseph and I were led to the central hut and climbed up the short ladder to the door.

Inside, sat cross-legged on the wooden floor, was a Diminuto chief with beautifully coloured feathers adorning his head, his bulging cheeks set in a broad smile. Opposite the chief, sat with his back to us and wearing a loose white mud-covered shirt, was Laurence Sterne.

Laurence turned around and looked up at us. His bright white hair was littered with twigs and leaves, his high forehead shone with sweat, and he too grinned with bulging cheeks.

'Ah, you found him. Well done Joseph. Ignatius, it's grand to see you my lad!' He said, speaking very quickly in his jolly Irish accent. He held out a small paper bag to us, 'Boiled sweet?' he asked.

We both took one and immediately realised the cause of the lumps in the Diminuto's cheeks.

'Laurence, did you give boiled sweets to every Diminuto in the tribe?' said Joseph with a reproachful tone. Laurence was significantly older than Joseph though he did not behave so, and Joseph had the manner and mentality of a headmaster. Laurence started chuckling, revealing his awfully decayed brown teeth.

'Well I had to give 'em somethin',' he said, 'The little fellas saved me life! They seem to like the sugar so I gave 'em two each. This one 'ere's been teaching me the language, so I gave him extra for his trouble.' The chief's cheeks truly were bulging; he must have had at least four boiled sweets stored. 'Where's David?'

With his typical dramatic timing, David's braying laugh shook the whole hut, followed by a chorus of high-pitched laughter from the Diminuto.

'He's giving rides to the Diminuto,' I said.

Such was Laurence's genius that in the short time that he had been with the tribe he had learnt much of their language.

'We need to get Ignatius up the mountain and back to London. Ask the chief if he can help us,' said Joseph.

Laurence and the chief spoke in the strange Diminuto language for a while.

'He says no. We can't go to the mountain. We're sure to die,' said Laurence, always speaking at a hundred miles an hour, 'He says we've to stay here with the tribe. He thinks Ignatius is their creator. Called him the first Diminuto – loose translation of course. They believe they've been gettin' smaller every generation since Ignatius. Eventually they'll all be the size of ants, and their babies born like grains of sand. Then they'll vanish back into the spirit o' earth.' He paused for a breath before finishing with a shrug, 'Somethin' like that.'

Joseph's usual frown had somehow become even more etched into his face. I looked from Joseph, to Laurence, to the chief – whose constant grinning stare was most unnerving – and back to Joseph.

'We won't die on the mountain,' he said, 'Foxy will be there already. He was going straight to the top to prepare for the moon. If we stay here, Ignatius will die.'

'Well, they'll not have us leave. He's gifts for Ignatius. It wouldn't be on, refusin' him.'

Joseph's foot tapped subconsciously on the wooden floor. There was an enormous crash outside, followed by a groaning from David. We all flinched, and the chief looked around in panic.

'I'm going to confiscate that rum before he falls and crushes someone, if he hasn't already,' said Joseph through gritted teeth. 'Start thinking of a way out of here.' He stormed to the door and down the ladder.

Laurence and I stayed with the chief. We heard Joseph berating David outside, calling him a drunkard and telling him to rebuild the Diminuto hut. Fortunately it seemed no Diminuto had been crushed inside it.

I sat against one wooden wall of the hut with the chief to my left and Laurence to my right. One by one, the Diminuto men and women came into the hut and laid gifts at my feet. Some brought ornately carved pieces of wood depicting various jungle creatures, others simply very smooth pebbles. I nodded politely, expressing thanks to each gift bearer and Laurence translated my words.

The size of the lumps in the cheeks of the Diminuto decreased with every visitor. Eventually the lumps were gone completely, and each visitor looked sleepier than the last.

'They're going to want more sweets soon,' I said to Laurence. He looked around at me with his rotten-toothed grin.

'All part of the plan,' he said with a wink, 'there's nothin' saps your energy like your first sugar-low. 'Specially for so small a body as theirs. They'll all need a sleep soon and we'll just walk out of here. They'll reckon they dreamt us.'

'What about Joseph? Why didn't you tell him you planned this?'

'Had to keep him busy.'

After two more sleepy visitors no more came. An eerie silence had fallen over the village. I looked at the little chief to my left and found him sleeping soundly, his head resting on his chest. We left the little chief sleeping in his hut, the gifts spread all around his feet.

Outside, the Diminuto were asleep everywhere, spread throughout the village like a carpet. Carefully and silently we picked our way over their little sleeping bodies. David had finished fixing the hut he had crushed. It was not a good job, but it would have to do. Joseph met us in the trees at the edge of the village. He was stood next to a life-sized wooden statue of me. It was really rather grotesque, not at all an accurate representation.

I was no longer surprised by anything I saw. Such was the surreal nature of my sojourn.

'Did you really think they'd fall for that?' said Laurence, sceptically.

'Well, I don't work with wood. There are no rocks around here,' replied Joseph. 'You knew they'd fall asleep didn't you?'

Laurence smiled and winked at him. We left the wooden statue there amongst the trees and I climbed back onto David. Joseph took note of the mountain's position and led us away through the forest.

When we were well out of earshot of the sleeping Diminuto village, Laurence came to walk alongside me.

'I got your letter about the abolition of the slave trade,' he said, 'I was about to post my letter of response when Joseph called by about your needin' help. I have my letter here.' He pulled a letter from the top pocket of his shirt, it was mud spattered from the swamp but had escaped being soaked beyond legibility; the tide-mark of mud on Laurence's shirt came just below his breast. Unfolding the letter, he cleared his throat and began to read:

'There is a strange coincidence, Sancho, in the little events (as well as in the great ones) of this world: for I had been writing a tender tale of the sorrows of a friendless poor negro-girl, and my eyes had scarce done smarting with it, when your letter of recommendation in behalf of so many of her brethren and sisters, came to me—but why her brethren?—or yours, Sancho! Any more than mine? It is by the finest tints, and most insensible gradations, that nature descends from the fairest face about St. James's, to the sootiest complexion in Africa: at which tint of these, is it, that the ties of blood are to cease? and how many shades must we descend lower still in the scale, 'ere mercy is to vanish with them?—but 'tis no uncommon thing, my good Sancho, for one half of the world to use the other half of it like brutes, & then endeavour to make 'em so.'[12]

My heart soared to hear Laurence's words. He would be a powerful ally in the fight against the slave trade. They all would, David and Joseph too. Even more so since Joseph had mentioned that Foxy awaited us at the top of the mountain. The Honourable Charles James Fox was a prominent member of the British parliament, and had stopped by for tea at my shop on several occasions and was a most amicable fellow. His radical opinions championed the downtrodden, fighting for tolerance and individual liberty. He had the real power to bring about the changes we all lobbied for. I was thrilled that he had come with the others to take me back to London.

At the foot of the mountain I looked up the tower of sharp, craggy rock reaching almost vertically from the jungle floor. The top disappeared out of sight into the clouds and David reared up so high to see that he almost threw me from his back. We walked single-file. I followed behind Joseph, who smoothed the jagged rock into even steps as he walked, and Laurence followed at the rear. As we ascended, the muggy humidity and giant mossy trees at the base of the mountain quickly gave way to dry air and a few scrubby bushes. The sheer angle made it impossible for us to climb straight up the mountainside and so we traversed the slope.

---

[12] Letter from Laurence Sterne to Ignatius Sancho 27 July 1766, first published in *Letters of the late Rev. Mr. Laurence Sterne, To his most intimate Friends* (1776)

Behind me, Laurence constantly sucked and slurped on his boiled sweets, clacking them across his teeth from one cheek to the other after every five steps. Ahead, Joseph's rasping breath grew louder the higher we climbed, his lungs rattling in his chest. These sounds, along with the rhythm of David's movement and the thinness of the air, lulled me into a comfortable trance as we plodded along. The light began to fade and the jungle far below was lit by a beautiful sunset. It seemed such a perfect and harmonious place. Peaceful and primordially simple. I almost didn't want to leave, and fantasised about what my life would be like if I stayed and lived with the Diminuto.

Lightning cracked. I snapped out of my trance. Thunder rolled. We were almost into the clouds when they turned a deathly grey streaked with violent inky black. Huge drops of lukewarm rain pounded down upon us, it felt wonderful on my bare chest, and washed away the blood from my grazed belly and back. Each drop kicked up dust from the dry rock, and soon formed rivulets that raced down the mountainside all around us. I turned around on David's back and looked past Laurence at the way we had come. The winding stone stairs that Joseph carved out had turned into a gushing river, the rainwater pooling at every turn before cascading once more towards the jungle canopy far below. In one of these pools, I fancied I saw an eel-like creature thrashing, but it was too far below to be certain. Even so, it unsettled me. I knew that the searching tendrils might come for us in the darkness, providing there were sufficient foul miasmas to support their rank bodies. The thick cloudy fog that we were entering did not smell altogether holy. Despite his rattling lungs, Joseph increased our pace. The steps he carved became less even and perfect, but this was no time to be lingering in the dark clouds. I kicked my heels into David's thighs to hurry him on.

As the cloud thickened it became very difficult to see each other. There was an undeniable foul acrid tang to the air. We all agreed we could taste it. In order to stay together we formed a train. David took the hem of Joseph's frock coat in his mouth, and behind me Laurence held on to the out-turned pocket fabric of David's huge trousers. Soon I could not see the even the back of David's head. I gripped him tightly with my thighs to be certain he was still there and called out to the others who immediately answered my calls. We kept up this roll call every five steps and trudged on through the wet stinking cloud.

Then came the nightmare. Slick and black it slid across my bare chest. Sopping with sticky mucus like a fat elongated slug.

'They are upon us!' I cried. Grabbing the tendril and flinging it from my body before it could take hold. Joseph increased our pace, and though I could not see the ground I felt David struggling to find his footing with every hurried step.

Looking behind me, I could see one of Laurence's hands still clutching David's pocket, the rest of him lost in the thick fog. A black tendril slid over his hand, trying to wrest the hand from its grip on David. Laurence's other hand shot into view from the fog, spearing the creature with a fine white quill. The creature snaked away into the fog, the quill still embedded in its horrid flesh.

'Not far now chaps!' shouted Joseph, 'I can see Foxy's campfire up ahead! He'll have the kettle on for us!'

The fog began to thin and I felt we might soon be out of it. Then I watched in horror as one of the evil tendril creatures landed with a wet smack on the back of David's neck. David screamed and reared up in terror. He bucked me off and fled up through the fog. I landed hard on the solid ground, pain searing through every nerve in my body. The wind was knocked right out of me and I couldn't speak or move.

Laurence tripped over me and fell to the ground. He scrambled back up quickly and grabbed me under the arms, dragging me up through the fog.

'Ignatius!' I heard Joseph bellow, from the fog just ahead.

'He's here!' Laurence called back. 'Help me with him!'

More hands grabbed me, dragging me upwards on my back over the rough stone stairs. I tried to get my footing but my gouty legs had been rattled by the fall and searing pain shot through me whenever I moved them.

I felt a cold slimy muscle slide around my neck. It snaked in from the side of the track and pulled tight, trying to drag me back down to the thicker fog. Joseph and Laurence had not the strength to fight against it and the tendril was winning out, spinning me around so that my head was towards the base of the mountain. David returned and managed to halt my descent, but the harder they pulled, the tighter the tendril choked me. The taste of blood flooded my mouth and I could hear my heart beating in my ears. I saw a blackened copper kettle held over my head by a pale, chubby little hand. It tipped and a sickly herbal, metallic smell of hot tea filled the air, followed quickly by boiling flesh. I prepared for my end as sizzling smoke rose around my head.

Clang! With the sound of metal hitting rock, the pressure on my throat ceased. Strong arms picked me up, coughing and spluttering. The chain around my neck fell away completely; I heard it tumbling back down the mountain as we emerged from the fog into cool night air.

On top of the mountain David sat me on the ground with my back propped against the tree. It was night. Not the terrifying rotten dark of the cavern or the swamp or the fog. It was a beautiful clear night, with the full moon almost directly over my head. There was a small campfire a few yards away with the copper kettle held over it on a spit.

Through blurry, confused eyes I saw a chubby little hand holding a cup of sharply spiced tea under my nose. I blinked and drank deeply from the brew. It was a strange herbal mix that sharpened my vision and eased all of my pains as soon as it reached my stomach.

Not a foot in front of me, under a bushy mass of grey hair, thick black eyebrows, and wobbling rosy cheeks, little eyes full of sympathy stared back.

'Nearly there good Ignatius,' said The Right Honourable Charles 'Foxy' James Fox, taking the tea from my lips and slurping it loudly.

'Last few steps now,' came the voice of Joseph. I looked around but couldn't see him. His voice seemed to come from above my head.

'Just to climb that now my lad.' Laurence stood by the fire warming his hands. He pointed at the tree above my head. I looked up to see Joseph already half way up the tall tree, his long frock coat swinging behind him as he climbed.

David put a mighty hand on one of the lower branches of the tree and hauled himself up.

'I can't carry you up here my friend, the angle is too steep. You'll be fine. Tally ho!' He climbed through the branches, shaking the whole tree as he swung upwards, 'Mustn't miss our ride!'

Laurence left the fire and followed quickly after him.

Foxy helped me to my feet and embraced me like a brother.

'I have written a speech in favour of a measure to abolish the vile business of the slave trade, and will put it to vote in the Commons. I can't promise it will pass, but we shall try,' he said. 'Now, let's get you back to London! The moon shall take us home!'

He ascended the tree rather elegantly for a dumpy little man full of tea. My spirit soared! Perhaps my humble little shop really had influenced these great men just as I hoped. Perhaps I really would see an end to the slave trade within my lifetime. Eager to get back to London I flexed and stretched, testing my gouty limbs. The pain had vanished entirely under the power of Foxy's herbal tea mixture. I leapt like a young man onto the bottom branch.

Looking up as I climbed, I saw the moon directly over the top of the tree. It was moving fast. Joseph stood, silhouetted on one of the top branches. He reached out his hands and took hold of the rim of the moon. With a great leap he swung upwards through the moon and disappeared. David came next, his great weight and wide shoulders seemed to slow the great globe down. Laurence's old frail frame seemed to shrink before the size of the enormous moon and I feared he would not have the strength in his old arms to haul himself through it, but, never one to let age hold him back he positively vaulted out of the treetop and disappeared.

Foxy and I were a little further behind the others and the moon was beginning to move past the top of the tree. We climbed as faster and faster. Foxy ran along the top branch and managed to hook one finger onto the rim, the hands of the others reached down through the light and pulled him through.

I hurried along the top branch after him, below me the mountaintop stuck out like an island on the sea of swirling storm clouds, cracking and sparking as though angry that I might escape. I tried not to look down and focused on reaching the moon. The others watched me, four black silhouettes framed in the face of the moon. I held out my hand but could not reach by several feet. The thunder rumbled in the clouds below me. I was running out of tree branch. Four arms reached down to through the moon to me but even David's great arm was still a hair's breadth away. A hair. I remembered the strand of hair. The fine silver hair of daylight that I had first fallen through and then plucked from the ceiling of the mossy cavern. I plunged my hand into my trouser pocket and pulled it out. It was still as shiny and silver as it had been in the cavern. I unravelled it quickly and threw one end to the reaching arms. David caught it. I ran out of tree branch and swung out through the open air. Hanging onto the moon by the single hair, the lightning storm raging in the clouds below me, David and the others pulled me upwards. I clung to the thread with all of the strength I could muster, and was hauled into the moon.

Darkness. My senses crept back into my body on tiptoes. First was the pain. Everywhere. I moaned.

A flurry of garbled voices erupted. I could not understand them.

Familiar smells played on my nostrils. Tobacco smoke, spiced rum, minty sweets, and tea. The smells of my little shop.

Cracks of light split the darkness in two as my eyes began to open.

'He's waking up,' said a voice, distant and ethereal.

'Ignatius! We came as soon as we heard dear friend,' said another.

'The mob took some o' the stock, but at least they left you alive. Just about ey!' I knew the Irish accent of Laurence Sterne. My eyes opened further, though they remained a blur.

'We'll find the brutes that did this, I promise you Ignatius.' I blinked my vision into focus. I was laid on my back in my comfortable bed and there they all were. Stood over me looking down with faces full of worry. Joseph, puffing his pipe. David, hip flask to his lips. Laurence, sucking anxiously on his boiled sweets. Foxy, sipping from his bottomless teacup. My Abolitionists.

My jaw hurt to smile; apparently the mob had beaten me near to death. My shirt had been torn off and my torso and back were a mesh of grazes. Bruises covered my throat where someone had tried to strangle me before Foxy struck him and the scoundrel fled the scene. When I could muster the strength to speak, I asked them about Affrica. None had the faintest idea to what I was talking about and adjudged that I was delirious.

The Abolitionists left me to recover in peace and Ann came to tend my wounds. She was more beautiful than I had ever seen her in all our long and happy years together. When the window first smashed and I was falling backwards, I feared I would never see her again. To be alive and look upon that face filled my eyes with tears of joy.

She would not allow the children in to see me in such a state, and had already put them to bed. Together we managed to turn me onto my side so that she could clean the wounds on my back. I lay there still and silent, listening to her humming a happy tune. As she washed my back, I spied a hair resting on the pillow. A thin frail white hair. Her hair. I picked it from the pillow and put it in my trouser pocket.

THE VULTURE TEMPLE

Vulture Temple

Early 1900

I perched on the edge of the Silent Tower in the middle of the jungle, my wings folded in prayer as our White-Back Elders taught me was right. Our four Guardians had been seen carrying a new dead to the tower and so we gathered to give our thanks. The First Vulture, she who laid the land and soared higher than the sky, circling the world for all eternity, sent them at important times each year. My father perched next to me, full of pride at my being there.

The Silent Tower was a sacred place for every vulture. A tall circular stone structure that made a round hole in the jungle canopy, and could be seen for many miles around. A long stone ramp led up to a door near the top of the tower that opened into the central chamber. Inside, the floor sloped gently down towards a wide hole. Each fresh dead was laid there as carcass, a gift from the First Vulture to her children. Vultures of every creed and colour visited the tower at least once in their lifetime.

I had been to the tower once before; my father brought me there when I was young and small. I was probably a little too young, but he couldn't leave me alone in the nest since mother's life had ended. My father and I had been waiting at the nest for her to return, but the she never did. The Elders said she had been too bold at a freshly dead deer, and tried to get to the meat before the tiger had laid it as carcass. On that first visit to the tower, he was very protective of me.

'You wait on the wall, little Kesti,' my father had said to me. 'I'll bring you some food in my crop, and we'll go and have a look at the human carcass when the big vultures have gone.'

It was boring having to wait until every vulture had eaten their fill. I remember being in awe at the power of the White-Back Elders, and how much they were revered. My father told me how they devoted their lives to the First Vulture, and brought her blessing upon us. Since then I had attended many common deer and goat carcasses and now, at five years old, I finally had my adult plumage and was large enough to compete at the human carcass. I was determined to prove myself to the Elders.

The Red-Head vultures were perched on the opposite side of the tower, bunched together in twos and threes. They were similar in size to us, and although they didn't have our long necks most of them did had longer wings. Flaps of red skin around their short necks throbbed with pink veins in the blazing afternoon sun, and they hunched their wings in an aggressive way that to me seemed disrespectful to the Guardians. I did not like their apparent superiority. Though we had agreed a truce – and these were supposed to be strictly observed during the tower ceremonies – many wars had been fought between us and the Red-Heads.

I had always been too young to fight in the wars. My father said that they were about dominance rather than killing. The teachings of the one First Vulture said that no vulture should take the life of another. Even so, tensions were always high around the carcasses, particularly so at the tower where rare, human carcass was on offer.

In the trees nearby, the smaller Yellow-Face vultures waited. They had white feathers right up to the top of their bright yellow-skinned heads, and gathered in small groups on different trees around the tower. Each group seemed to worship at the tower in a slightly different way, and although they did not follow the true First Vulture as we did, we had no conflict with the Yellow-Faces. Besides being significantly smaller, they were not interested in the meat for which we and the Red-Heads fought; they would wait until the end to squabble like crows and ravens over tendon and sinew.

The largest vultures in the land were the Bearded-Ones. My father and I had soared with them once, after my mother had not returned to the nest. He thought perhaps they would know where she had died as they took careful note of each carcass in the land, in order to return for the bones. They were kind to us and did all they could to help. When we could not find her at the carcass where the Elders said she had died, we assumed the tiger had taken her into the jungle.

The Bearded-Ones were soaring high overhead when we first gathered at the tower, but I could no longer see them in the sky. I felt a little relief that they had gone; with their huge size and powerful beaks they could easily dominate all other vultures at the carcass. However, they did not usually trouble us because they disdained meat of all forms. They ate only the bones, breaking most apart with their powerful beaks, and dropping the largest bones onto rocks from a great height to shatter them and get at the sweet marrow held inside. Having noted our gathering, they would return much later once we had left only the skeleton, to worship in their own way.

The four Guardians were seen walking up the long straight ramp to the tower entrance, and Elder Skrim led us through the welcoming worship. Silent reverence is of paramount importance to the Guardians, and our ceremony was conducted with head-tilts and blinks.

The Red-Heads did not respect this silence. Their leader, Mahdolmu, was a large ugly vulture with a savage chip in her beak and huge raw flaps of skin around her throat. She had black evil eyes, unlike the male Red-Heads who had white or yellow eyes. I did not want to meet her at the carcass. She led the Red-Heads in a loud and piercing prayer, squawking and screeching in their shrill guttural accents. Another slight on our beliefs.

Elder Skrim looked at the Red-Heads but did not utter a word for she was most devout and would not offend the Guardians. Skrim was a fearsome sight herself; her neck long and muscular and beak scarred from previous battles. Her wings were the longest of all the White-Backs, and her toughness at the carcass was renown amongst White-Backs and Red-Heads alike. She glared across the tower at Mahdolmu.

I hoped to be like her one day and had devoted myself to learning the plain, forest, and mountain prayers for common carcasses such as bullocks, deer, and goats. Soon I would show the Elders that I knew the temple prayers for humans too. Perhaps they would eventually invite me to their special meetings where they were said to speak with the First Vulture.

The two foremost Guardians, *Beginning* and *End*, reached the top of the ramp and entered the inner chamber: *Beginning* on the eastern side of the tower entrance, with a corner of cloth in his left hand; *End* on the western side, with a corner of cloth in his right hand. Between them I could see the feet of a new dead laid out on the cloth. They were followed by the secondary Guardians; behind *Beginning* came *Mating*, and behind *End* came *Food*. The four of them carried the fresh dead into the tower, and laid it out on the stones with its feet towards the central hole.

Once on the ground, the fresh dead became carcass, but going to the carcass was forbidden when the Guardians were still inside the chamber, and so we waited. I saw the Red-Heads beginning to edge closer. Because of them, we had to edge forward too. I did so as far as I dared without my father noticing. The Guardians took the cloth from the carcass and cut open the swollen torso so that we could get to the meat easier. *End* and *Beginning* wielded the blade together this time, each with one hand on their sharp metal claw. This was not usual. It was supposed to be that one Guardian made the cut, and that would be a single message from the First Vulture for the season ahead. I did not know how to understand this message and looked forward to hearing the Elders speak about it later.

The Guardians turned to leave. I kept one eye on the Guardians and one on the Red-Heads. It was almost time. My heart thundered as the tension mounted.

The last Guardian closed the door behind him, the metal latch grinding against the wood. And then… click. It locked.

Chaos erupted. Elder Skrim shot past my father and me; she always initiated the descent to the carcass. Other Elders followed her. I saw Skrim veer off and fly screeching straight for Mahdolmu, and then the two were lost amongst all the rest in a twisting rage of beaks and feathers.

The carcass was quickly surrounded by vultures; Red-Heads and White-Backs all scrapping for position. Next to me, my father waited; he was quite old and wanted to wait for the pandemonium to die down. I took flight to circle the carcass and see the meleé from all angles, when I saw a perfect opportunity to prove myself. A large Red-Head had its head in the torso. It was bigger than me, but I mustered up my courage and used the momentum of my flight to knock it out of the way. The Red-Head stumbled screeching away from the carcass and I leapt quickly into its place, burying my head and neck into the open torso.

It was bold for one so young to dive straight in, but I thought that Skrim and the other Elders would be pleased with my tenacity. I tore as much meat as I could from inside, holding each mouthful in my crop so that I could offer it to the Elders' families after the carcass was finished. In return the one true First Vulture would bless me and hear my prayers.

I managed four large mouthfuls before a huge Red-Head landed on my back. The Red-Head grabbed my neck in its sharp beak and tugged until I had to get out of the carcass or lose a chunk of my skin. I pulled my head out and blinked away the human blood, screaming my rage at the Red-Head on my back. I turned to face it and found it was not a Red-Head at all. It was Elder Kraak, a stern male and teacher of the word of the First Vulture.

'Elders first you little runt!' he screeched at me, buffeting me away from the carcass with his huge wings and sharp talons. 'The First Vulture curses those who disrespect the Elders.'

'I thought only to-' I began to say sinking my head low in submission, but Elder Kraak lunged at my eyes with his beak.

'Your mother didn't know her place either!' he screamed. Shocked at his words, I hopped backwards onto the rim of the central hole and with one swift kick of his talons, Kraak shoved me over the edge.

The hole was not deep and I did not have the time to fully unfurl my wings before I hit the bottom in a cloud of dust.

It was much cooler in the shaded side of the hole. Stubby white bones littered the dry dusty floor, too small for the giant Bearded-Ones to bother with. The Guardians swept these small bones and bits of cloth into the central hole from the offering surface above.

I stood for a moment feeling guilty that in my eagerness, I had eaten from the carcass before the Elders had finished. My guilt quickly turned to anger at Elder Kraak. I had shown great devotion to him and often attended his teaching. The carcasses were violent places but attacking my eyes with his beak and kicking me over the edge as though I was less than a crow was unacceptable. Wasn't it against the truths of the one true First Vulture? Fighting at the carcass was right and honourable, but not causing lasting damage that would result in the end of another vulture's life.

Ruffling the dust out of my feathers, I resolved to speak to Elder Skrim privately about Elder Kraak's actions. Perhaps she would rebuke him. I stood to fly out of the hole when I caught a movement in the shadows. It was an injured Red-Head. Huddled against the wall of the hole to protect a broken wing, its eyes were closed and its breathing shallow. I hopped closer. It opened one eye. A shining jet-black eye. Mahdolmu.

She weighed me with that piercing glare, but she did not move. Nor did I. We stared at each other, transfixed for a moment, then I realised she could not move.

The First Vulture taught that we should act to assure the survival of our fellow vultures, just as She had intended when She laid the world. With this in mind I hopped closer again.

'Come any closer and I'll tear your throat out.' Mahdolmu screeched at me in her coarse accent, 'Did Skrim send you to finish me off?'

'Did Skrim do this to you?' I asked.

'Who else would even try?' She opened her other eye as she spoke and I gasped at the bloody red hole. Her eye had been torn out.

'But what about the truths?' I could not believe that Skrim would do this, even to a Red-Head like Mahdolmu; she was still a vulture like the rest of us. She laughed at me. Loud and screeching.

'Yes, but she didn't kill me did she?' She closed her eyes again and rested her head on her breast. I didn't know what to say, Skrim had not quite killed Mahdolmu, but she had all but ensured her death. 'What's your name, girl?'

'Kesti.'

'Leave me to die in peace, Kesti.' She said, struggling to pronounce the 'st' sound in my name – the Red-Head accent did not have that sound.

'You need not die here.' I brought the meat up from my crop and lay it all out on the ground in front of her, 'Keep your wing still and when the meat has given you strength, call to your mate. I'm sure he will bring you food until the wing heals and you can fly again.'

Not waiting for her answer, I looked up to take flight and saw the Elders circling above me, watching, Skrim and Kraak amongst them. They had eaten their fill and were overseeing the rest of us. Not making eye contact with them, I flapped up from the hole to join rest of the vultures still going at the carcass.

At the day's end, as the First Vulture passed overhead and the shadow of her great wings gave us night, I settled high on my cliff-face sleepily cleaning my feathers. Other White-Backs close by chattered about the excitement of the Silent Tower and the adrenaline of the carcass. Some had stories of victories over Red-Heads, others nursed the wounds suffered in defeat – though none were life-threatening. My father perched nearby, crop full and sleeping already. At least he had managed to get some meat.

With the Elders sleeping far above near the cliff top, I spoke to the other young vultures about how Elder Kraak had attacked me, and how I had seen the mortal damage that Elder Skrim had caused to the great Red-Head, Mahdolmu.

This caused much debate. Hushed and whispered, for there was an air of nervousness around such talk. Some said I had broken the rules of the tower by eating at the carcass before the Elders and that Kraak was right to teach me a lesson. The Elders represented the one true First Vulture; who was I to think I should be permitted to eat, when everyone else must wait for them to finish? But nobody else had seen the violent intention in Kraak's attack. Surely it was not the way? I was positive that he meant me lasting harm. As for Skrim's attack on Mahdolmu, most agreed that it was probably Mahdolmu who sought to do mortal damage to Skrim first. Others pointed out that the word of the First Vulture applied only to those who followed Her in the true way. The Red-Heads were false anyway and should be punished without mercy. I could not agree that this could possibly be the First Vulture's intention for us.

The whole cliff-face community, which had been happily preparing for sleep not ten minutes ago, was quickly alive with argument. Vultures screeched and screamed their opinions at each other, nobody listening or backing down. It was decided eventually that the only way to settle the argument was to speak with the Elders in the morning. As quiet descended, I hoped that nobody would remember me as the instigator of the argument. The Elders would not appreciate this. I looked at my father; he had slept through it all.

I did not get chance to seek answers from the Elders. They came for me at first light and forced me from my resting place, telling me that I was a blasphemer and a heretic. For my crimes, they said I must leave the White-Backs or face the wrath of the First Vulture.

My cries of protest as they shoved me away awoke my father. He pleaded with the Elders not to punish me, but they would not listen to him. I circled nearby, calling out to him until Kraak and Skrim chased me away, trying to knock me out of the air with their beaks and talons.

From a far distance I could see my father calling out, though his words did not reach me. The Elders enclosed closely around him, preventing him from opening his wings. One of Elder Skrim's children took my place on the cliff face and I was banished into exile.

Distraught and scared, alone and upset, I headed for the Silent Tower in hope that I might find the Guardians. They might not speak to me, but perhaps the First Vulture would use them to send me a sign. I needed something from her. Skrim and Kraak had shaken my faith; their actions proved their words to be lies. For the whole of my existence I had held their words as the truth. I could always find food, and avoid harm, but there was something more to life that I could no longer explain. The sudden emptiness made me feel lost, even in this land I knew well.

With the First Vulture having only just passed overhead and released us from the shadow of her wings, the land had not yet had time to warm. The air was cold and flat, soaring was difficult and I was using too much energy. I was relieved when the tower finally came into sight; a circular break in the jungle canopy.

No fresh dead would be laid as carcass at the tower today and it was much quieter. The Yellow Faces were still hopping noisily around yesterday's carcass, but there was not much left. They plucked and tore at the remaining tendons and sinews, scattering away into the trees as I approached and landed on the tower wall.

'I have not come to fight you for sinew and tendon,' I spoke tentatively, hoping not to cause offence. My rashness of the previous day sat raw on my heart - a red gash on my soul.

The Yellow-Faces perched silently in the trees, their white feathers standing up high on the backs of their heads. In each tree colony, all of the vultures gathered around their largest member. I was unsure as to whether they had understood me, but then they broke out into a hurried discussion. Speaking so quickly in their very odd accents, I could not understand what was said.

They flew down from the trees and landed on the offering floor around the carcass beneath me.

'You have interrupted our incantations, White-Back,' said one of the larger Yellow-Faces.

'Yes, and ours,' said another.

'Ours also,' came a third voice.

'We're about to start but you're holding us up!' Said a fourth. They all looked up at me silently, waiting for me to speak.

'You do not worship together?' I asked, fascinated.

'Of course not,' said the largest Yellow-Face, 'We each worship different goddesses and gods in different ways. It would not make sense to worship together.'

'But who of you is right?' It seemed impossible to me.

'There is no right. That is the only truth.'

'May I stay?' I was gripped by this new idea.

After consulting with each other, they agreed there was no harm in my staying; I was free to do as I pleased, providing I did not interrupt them again.

I watched their strange ceremonies for the rest of the morning as the land warmed. They spread out on the offering surface around the wide central hole, but no single group appeared to desire to be closer to the carcass than any other. There was no clear order to what they did, each small group being led by their largest member through a series of chants and incantations unique to that group. Occasionally a group would hop over to the human carcass and eat some sinew or tendon. The culmination of noise and strong lyrical accents was confusing and I struggled to follow any one ceremony.

One of the younger Yellow-Faces was dancing backwards with its wings spread, looking up towards the sky away from the sun. It seemed to be praising blueness and was lost in prayer when suddenly, with a loud screech, it fell down the central hole.

Some of the Yellow-Faces laughed, others continued their ceremonies. All fell silent when the young Yellow-Face flew out of the hole screeching at the top of its voice:

'Mahdolmu! Mahdolmu! The Red-Head!'

All of the Yellow-Faces quickly abandoned their ceremonies and fled back to their trees around the edge of the tower.

The curved shadow in the hole was cast on a different side by the morning sun, to where it had been yesterday afternoon. Hovering over it, I could see Mahdolmu had shuffled around to be in the shade. I flew down and landed next to her.

'Did your mate not come?' I asked. She looked at me with her one piercing black eye.

'I have no mate.' She said, her voice weak and dry.

'Do not move your wing. I shall return with food and water.'

'No!' She stopped me as I flew upwards, 'Do not help me. Just leave me to die with dignity.'

'You do not want to die, or you would have not moved to the shade. There is no dignity in dying in the discards pit.' I said. She had no answer for me, but tucked her head into her chest in resignation.

I flew up and stood on top of the human carcass on the offering surface. The Yellow-Faces, perched in the trees around the tower, stared down at me. I spread my wings wide to address them all at once.

'Mahdolmu is injured and I want to help her to heal.'

They all looked at me, unblinking and expectant.

I took flight and let the warm air now rising from the land carry me higher. I did not look back because it did not matter if any Yellow-Faces had followed. Alone or not I would bring some food back to Mahdolmu. I soared in the direction of the plains where I was likely to find more carcasses.

The first carcass I came across was a large goat. It had only been dead for a few hours judging from the redness of the meat. I knew it had been killed by a tiger or leopard by the way that it had been eaten from the rump first. Other vultures were gathering, and so I knew that the killer must have left the area. White-Backs, Red-Heads, and Yellow-Faces. Some I recognised, most I didn't; there were thousands of vultures in the land. I noted that the huge Bearded-Ones passed overhead, keeping track of all of the carcasses to return when the bones were ready.

I tore as much meat as I could, eating some and storing more in my crop. I had to fight with other White-Backs and Red-Heads, but none were so ferocious as Elder Kraak or Elder Skrim. With only a few minor scratches and some missing feathers I returned to the tower. On the way back I stopped at a pool to drink, storing water in my crop with the meat; Mahdolmu would need the water.

Back at the tower's central hole, the shade had moved around and Mahdolmu was sat in the scorching sun. I spread my wings and shaded her as she ate the meat and drank the water from my crop. She did not want to feed like a newly hatched chick, but there was no way of getting the water to her without spilling it on the dry dusty ground. After feeding, I continued to cover her in shadow as she slowly moved to the other side of the central hole where the shade would last for longer. She kept her broken wing as still as possible, though was clearly in pain with every step.

'Thank you,' she winced.

Sat in the shade, with her stomach full of meat and water, I left Mahdolmu to sleep and heal. The Yellow-Faces had finished with the sinews and tendons of the human carcass on the offering surface above, and were nowhere in sight. I perched on the edge of the tower's central hole where I could see Mahdolmu in the shade below, and dozed in the afternoon sun, thinking of my father.

I awoke to the sound of Yellow-Faces returning. They chattered loudly to each other as they landed all around me.

'Sinew and tendon holds the world together,' said one of the larger group leaders as it sidled over to stand next to me, looking down at Mahdolmu in the pit, 'without their binding force, nothing works.'

He flapped down and laid the sinew and tendon from his crop in front of Mahdolmu. Others did the same and Mahdolmu stirred from her slumber, thanking each vulture for their offering – though she did not eat the food until much later in the evening.

I stayed in the tower for my first night away from the White-Back cliff. It was safe, being enclosed from the surrounding jungle, but I felt desperately lonely. I missed my father dearly, and wondered how he was coping without me. The Elders would no doubt be cautious that he might seek revenge for my exile, and so I prayed for his safety, though I was not sure to whom.

For the next week I continued to bring food back to the tower for Mahdolmu. The human carcass on the offering surface remained with us, but was little more than a skeleton. The Bearded-Ones would arrive soon for the bones. Some of the Yellow-Faces remained with me and though Mahdolmu did not enjoy their sinew and tendon, she did seem to be getting stronger. It saddened me to see her have to turn her head this way and that in order to see from her one remaining eye.

Twice I tried to return to the White-Back cliff to see my father, but the Elders had declared me an ostra[13] and I was chased away aggressively whenever I came close. At each carcass that I found, I looked for him. I even asked other

---

[13] Fanciful word for 'unclean'.

White-Backs about him, but any who might know him would not speak to an ostra, and any who would speak to me did not know him.

One day when I returned from a scavenge, Skrim, Kraak, and the other Elders were waiting at the tower for me, hidden in the central hole so that I couldn't see them as I approached. Mahdolmu was crouched submissively in the arc of shade against the wall. She did not seem to have been harmed yet.

They took flight and surrounded me, pecking at me and jostling me in the air. I screeched at them and fought back, but they were too many and too strong. They forced me to land in the central pit and stand against the wall next to Mahdolmu. Other White-Backs emerged from the trees and perched on the rim of the central hole, with more still on the tower wall. Hundreds of piercing eyes encircled me, staring down at me from behind sharp beaks. Each held a heavy rock in his or her talons. Terror gripped me when I realised what they had come for. The Elders stood on the floor of the pit, surrounding Mahdolmu and I. Skrim stepped towards us.

'In the eyes of the one true First Vulture, I-' She began, but was cut off by a shrill screech from overhead. I looked up but could see nothing for the brightness of the sun. 'She condemns you to death by breaking for-'

A huge bovine skull, complete with heavy curled horns, fell out of the sky and landed on Kraak, crushing his head into the dusty floor of the pit. His wings twitched and then he lay still. The Bearded-Ones had arrived.

The other White-Backs erupted in panic, fleeing from the tower in all directions. In the sky above, the silhouettes of the Bearded-Ones were enormous against the sun. More large pieces of bovine skeleton landed in the pit, sending up huge clouds of dust and crushing the Elders who did not flee quickly enough. Mahdolmu and I pressed tightly against the wall to avoid suffering the same fate. Skrim herself was knocked out of the sky as she tried to take off. She landed heavily, breaking one of her legs. From the angle of her wing, I guessed that to be broken too. She cried out in pain.

I looked up, and there, soaring with the great Bearded-Ones, was my father. He looked small and frail and old alongside his giant companions, but my heart swelled with pride to see him screeching instructions at them as they rained down their huge bones.

By the time they had finished, all of the White-Backs who could do so had fled. The eerie quiet of the Silent Tower returned, broken only by the whimpers of the injured Elder Skrim who lay on the floor before Mahdolmu and me. Kraak was crushed under the horned skull, another Elder had her neck broken by a large horse pelvis, and yet another lay unconscious but breathing, her beak shattered by a large femur.

My father and the Bearded-Ones circled down to the tower. The leader of the Bearded-Ones was called Lammergeier. She was a huge female, twice the size of Skrim or Mahdolmu. Whereas our necks were long and bald, her neck and legs were shaggy and covered with gold and brown feathers. Her eyes were grey with bright red rims, and a black beard curled underneath her powerful beak.

She and my father landed on the floor of the central pit, whilst the other Bearded-Ones ate the bones of the human skeleton on the offering table above. They hopped around Kraak, and Skrim and my father hurried over to me, greeting me with excited calls and twitches of his head. I called back and returned his twitches happily.

'Your mother would have been proud of you, Kesti,' said Lammergeier. Her voice was soft and peaceful. It made me feel calm.

'Did you know her?' I asked. Lammergeier bowed her head sadly, and my father answered for her

'Before her life ended, your mother was a great friend of Lammergeier. They had been exchanging ideas about the world and our place in it.' My father looked around at the injured Elder Skrim, 'Perhaps that is why her life ended. We will likely never know.'

Sadness rested heavily on the wings of my father and Lammergeier at the thought of my mother. I was a mere hatchling when her life ended and, having never known her, had made my peace with the loss.

'Thank you for coming to our aid, Lammergeier,' I said, 'What will you do now?'

'We are about to begin our ceremony of bones at the skeleton,' she replied, 'you are welcome to join us.'

'I fear I have neither the size nor the stomach to eat the bones, but I will gladly watch.'

For the rest of the afternoon, my father and I perched on the edge of the tower watching the Bearded-Ones conduct their bone ceremony. Some of the Yellow-Faces who helped me take care of Mahdolmu came back from their scavenging and joined us. The Bearded-Ones cracked the thinner bones and carried the larger bones high to break them open by dropping them with great accuracy on the stone, offering surface. I could not fully understand what was going on, but Lammergeier explained afterwards that the ceremony was not about worship for the Bearded-Ones did not believe in any god or First Vulture that could be worshipped. It was about attentment[14], focusing the mind to every moment of preparing the bone, and fully experiencing every detail of its creation and consumption. This was very interesting, but I still struggled to understand why they were doing it.

With the help of my father, Lammergeier, and the Yellow-Faces, we nursed Mahdolmu and Skrim back to a semblance of health. They would not be the dominant vultures that they were, but after a month they could fly and scavenge again.

I set up a new home with my father at the Silent Tower. Mahdolmu, Skrim, Lammergeier and some of the Yellow-Face leaders also set up homes around the tower. It became a place that vultures could visit to learn about the beliefs of others, and we had hundreds of visitors from far and wide, mostly juveniles or those in their first year of adult plumage.

Even the crows and ravens started joining us.

---

[14] Fanciful word for 'mindfulness'.

STOLEN FROM INDIA

Stolen from India

c. 1750

Excitement buzzed around the staff as we stood in front of the Manor House. For the first time in ten years the Master was home from India. It was a wet but bright April morning and the fine lawns in front of the house had been freshly cut giving an earthy smell to the air. Small birds whistled merrily in the trees as the rumble of carriages drew ever closer. After a minute that felt like an hour, the heavy iron gates at the end of the long driveway were slowly opened. A large black carriage drawn by four huge horses rumbled in followed by a second carriage loaded with large trunks.

I had never met the man, despite working in the manor as a gardener's boy for over five years. The older staff had a lot to say of his aggressive temperament, and I found myself more and more nervous as the carriage drew nearer. I suppose it was at least partly his temperament that had seen him rise through the military ranks to become Major General of the English East India Company. Everyone said I should be grateful to that military temperament for keeping me fed and in a job.

The carriage ground to a halt on the gravel in front of us. William, the stern house steward, put the small stepladder in position and opened the door.

We held our breath as a thin wooden crutch poked out of the dark interior. Followed by a single polished black boot. And with a grunt of pain, the master hauled himself out into the light. We cheered as he stood for a moment on the stepladder looking at the house and his staff, a bored expression on his thick-bearded face. His left leg was missing from just below the knee, and his right arm from the elbow. There were brown-stained bandages wrapped around the stumps of each limb, and his smart military uniform was ill-fitting around his shoulders. He was not the strong, powerful man depicted in the portraits throughout the house. His face was drawn and pallid; his eyes sunken and rheumy.

He forced an awkward smile at us and lowered himself out of the carriage. William reached forward to offer a hand, but was met with a fierce glare and backed away quickly.

To our surprise, behind the Master a beautiful Indian woman climbed out of his carriage. Wrapped in colourful blue and gold robes, she moved with dreamlike grace and elegance. Her lips were full and moist, her lightly tanned skin, soft and inviting.

At that moment large ladybird landed on the front of my gardening overalls, I took it gently in my hand and released it onto the ground. When I looked up again, the Indian woman's deep brown eyes met mine and lingered for the briefest second.

'This is my Daayan,'[15] the Master barked, his gravelly voice more used to addressing soldiers than servants. I did not know what a Daayan was, but it seemed she was some sort of healer, 'She is healing my wounds. Do whatever she

---

[15] An Indian word for a type of witch originally associated with the worship of the mother goddess.

asks. If I hear any different, you will be thrashed and dismissed!'

With that he continued slowly towards the front door of the house, William at his elbow speaking hurriedly and the Daayan following a few metres behind. As they walked, William looked around and signalled for us to get back to work.

As the youngest lad on the staff, at sixteen years, I was required to help unload most of the heavy trunks and crates from the second carriage. The first one I came to was a crate large enough to contain a full grown man and too heavy for me to lift alone. It was made of solid wood and had small round holes in the side. I took hold of a handle on one side of the crate and one of the older servants took hold of the other end.

A thick black hairy finger poked through one of the small round holes. I yelped and dropped my end. Something in the crate yelped too. Piercing and high-pitched.

The Master had reached the front door and turned around to glare at me.

'You!' He shouted. Pointing at me with his one remaining hand. I am sure he was about to have me thrashed and dismissed, when the Daayan suddenly spoke.

I could not understand her language, but her musical voice seemed to carry through the damp morning air and wrap around my head. The master responded, speaking in her language. They had a brief conversation and then the Master turned back to me, 'She wants you for her assistant. You will report to her after lunch.'

She fixed me again with her deep brown eyes, and smiled warmly before entering the house. That smile melted my fear of the thing inside the box, and filled my soul with love. I was so excited to be working for a woman so peerlessly beautiful and kind as the Daayan. She had saved me from the Master's wrath and taken me under her protection. I would be forever at her service; my heart was hers from then on.

The rest of my morning was spent moving the Master's luggage into the house. In many of the crates I felt things moving inside, or heard breathing and scratching. The older lads who helped me with the largest boxes gossiped to the other staff and rumours quickly spread that the Master was to open a menagerie in the Manor grounds. It would be most exciting to see all of the strange and wondrous creatures from the other side of the world. I was eager to open the crates and witness the oddities that lay within.

The Daayan was given a whole wing of the house. She had a bedchamber, a drawing room with wide doors opening onto the garden, and a long gallery room that ran along the entire first floor. Strangely, the Master also assigned her a kitchen to use as she pleased. I thought perhaps she would want to teach the staff to make the food of India so that she might feel more at home.

The crates were moved into the Daayan's long gallery and William sent a man to purchase some large cages to contain the animals whilst the menagerie was built. William said that building the menagerie in the grounds could take some months, and until it was complete the Master desired that his creatures be on display in the long gallery. The gallery stretched the whole length of the first floor of the eastern wing and the cages would run down either side, with space for a walkway through the middle.

After lunch, William gave me an old servant's uniform to wear instead of my gardener's clothes and I went to the Daayan's drawing room. Stood nervously in the vestibule outside the drawing room door, I straightened my simple uniform and felt a little embarrassed that it was stretching at the seams and shirt buttons – I had grown significantly over the past year and William had given me a very small outfit. My knock seemed to echo around the quiet sparse vestibule.

After a few seconds the Daayan's voice permitted me to enter. She did not speak the words, but her warm musical voice came to me as a tingling feeling at the base of my skull, where the neck bones join.

Inside, the Daayan sat in on of two high-backed chairs by the wide double doors that opened onto the garden. One of the doors was open and a cool spring breeze blew gently into the room. I knew the room well. It was one of my favourites in the house as it was aired regularly and always smelled like the fresh garden outside. I had placed some extra plants in there to give me an excuse to linger when doing my watering rounds in the house.

The Daayan had changed her clothes. She wore a pale cloth of fine silken mesh, draped around her elegant shoulders like the Romans wore in some of the classic paintings around the house. As the gentle breeze blew in, the silk swayed around her beautiful body, riding up above her ankle and exposing her long graceful calves. Seen this closely, I guessed her to be in her mid-thirties at the most – though her brown eyes were deep with the wisdom of someone much older.

She pointed for me to sit in the chair opposite her and I did so, hesitantly and awkwardly, for it seemed strange to sit informally opposite this mysterious beautiful woman who had arrived so unexpectedly with the Master of the house. I had never been permitted to sit as equal to one whom I served.

There was a small tea set on a table between the two chairs and the Daayan reached for the pot to pour a cup.

My heart raced as she leant forward pouring the tea; the gentle breeze swayed the light fabric of her robe, revealing and then hiding a large portion of her left bosom. To my shame, she looked up at me as she poured and caught my wandering eyes. I felt my face redden and was about to apologise when to my surprise she flashed me a suggestive smile and continued to pour a second cup. Though I dared not risk another glance at her bosom, I could feel its bare presence pulling at my eyes.

She finished pouring and handed a cup to me. For the briefest moment as I took the tea from her, reflected in the surface of the tea I thought I saw the faint reflection of a haggard old woman. With a blink it was clear that some tealeaves had fallen through the strainer and must have distorted the Daayan's reflection.

'What do you wish for, Daniel?' She said. I was taken aback by her use of my name. She must have got it from William, the house steward.

'Ah-um,' I stammered, 'I don't need for anything Ma'am. I am well taken care of.'

'I can see that you need new clothes. You are almost bursting out of those,' she said, running her eyes over my body. I felt naked under her stare. 'But that is not what I asked,' she continued, 'What do you wish for? What do you want from life?'

I thought for a moment. Looking out of the window I could see the head gardener tending the exotic flowers in the beds around the perfect lawn, and swallows dancing in the blue sky. Inside the room I looked at the grand high ceilings and fine chandeliers, the portraits of the Master, mighty and powerful in his commanders' uniform, the antique weapons mounted on the walls, the expensive teacup from which I drank. Finally I looked at the Daayan.

This goddess of a woman brought all the way across the oceans from the other side of the world, to be here in the Master's house, by his side, healing his wounds.

'I want to be the Master.' I said. She shook her head and drank her tea.

'The Master is a cruel, violent, foul-tempered, beast of a man. He has lost two limbs because of his war-mongering. You should not want to be the Master.' I was shocked to hear her speak so brazenly about the Master, and looked around sharply to see if any other servants were in earshot. Thankfully there was nobody else around. 'But, some day,' She continued with a smile, 'perhaps you will be like him.'

For the next hour she told me about my duties as her assistant, and warned me that her healing would not be as I might have seen in England. Some of the animals were to be used in healing the Master, and I was to take care that they were properly fed. Though I could not fully understand the reasons behind all of my duties, I vowed to obey the Daayan's every command. I would be at her constant call.

She saw me to the door and asked me to meet her in her kitchen early the next morning. Before I could leave, she leaned in towards me and kissed my cheek. The sweet floral scent of her hair filled my nostrils, and the moist warmth of her lips on my skin made the hairs of my neck tingle. The door shut behind me and I crossed the vestibule with a spring in my step. Everything about my life felt so much better than it had done before I met her. Even my uniform seemed to fit a little better.

The next morning I went to her kitchen and knocked on the door. No answer came and so I waited outside. I had been waiting some five minutes when there came a distant screeching cry from the long gallery on the floor above me. I listened intently and there it came again, short sharp screeches. Thinking the Daayan may be in some sort of trouble with one of the animals, I set off at a run for the gallery, but then the screeching stopped abruptly and I could hear slow footsteps walking overhead. I returned to my post by the kitchen door and soon heard the same slow footsteps approaching along the corridor, this time accompanied by the scraping of metal against the marble floor.

The Daayan appeared from around the corner, ashen-faced and walking slowly with a long metal chain trailing behind her. She smiled at me with sad eyes when she saw me waiting loyally by the kitchen door. Her chain led around the corner and I could hear other shuffling footsteps approaching. There was a clacking of wood against the marble too, and the wheezing of a man.

'Do not be alarmed,' whispered the Daayan. Despite the early hour she still looked as beautiful and vibrant as she always did.

From around the corner, a small hairy human-like creature came. It dragged big powerful fists along the floor, using them as extra feet, and waddled half upright on stumpy bowed legs. Its face was dark and leathery, with a flattened nose and wide bulging mouth, its head hung by its chest like a scolded child. I stared in amazement as this hairy, stocky little creature approached us with its subdued waddle. It looked up at me, and though its eyes were too close together, there was a definite human quality in them. The Daayan's chain was fixed around the creature's neck.

I was crouching down to look more closely at the sad little thing, when the Master followed around the corner. He swung himself slowly on his crutch and remaining leg.

'Don't touch it. You stupid boy,' he said to me, 'If my Daayan wasn't here, the gibbon would tear your throat out with one hand.'

'Sorry sir!' I said, standing bolt upright. The Daayan opened the kitchen door and led us in.

It was the oldest kitchen in the house, made of cold grey stone and mostly underground but for the small ventilation grates that ran along the top of one wall near the ceiling. Bright morning light streamed through these, casting a strip of gold and black stripes across the room. This kitchen was only intended as an extra space to cater for large feasts. It hadn't been used for many years whilst the Master had been away, but it had been cleaned just last week in preparation for his return. Knives and cleavers hung sharpened on hooks along the wall, woodpiles for the roasting fires were stocked, and the chimneys swept. A huge oak carving table dominated the centre of the room, long enough and sturdy enough to lay a whole cow on for butchering. It was ready to be used again.

Whilst the Master lowered himself onto a chair by the table, the Daayan said some strange words to the gibbon and he climbed up onto the table. She had me light the fires, and set a cauldron of water to boil, and then sent me to fetch some fruits from the main kitchen for the gibbon.

When I returned with a bowl of chopped pears, the gibbon was still sat obediently on the table. The Daayan had removed the bandage from around Master's arm stump and was cleaning it with warm water from the cauldron.

The stump was not neat. It rested on the table, loose strips of flesh spread across the wood like squid tentacles around the severed bloody end. I thought that the wound would have healed at least partially during the voyage from India, but it looked fresh and raw as though it had been severed within the past hour. Blood was soaking into the wooden table. I felt my stomach turn and my face pale at the sight.

'Don't just stand there gawping like an imbecile boy!' said the Master. I blinked my eyes and offered the bowl of pears to the Daayan. My hands shook uncontrollably as I held out the bowl to her. She put down the cloth that she had been using to clean the Master's bloody stump and walked towards me. Her beauty tore my eyes from the grotesque stump, and I felt instantly a little better merely by looking upon her face. She laid her hand lovingly on my chest and my nerves calmed completely; I felt strong and determined once more.

From the sleeve of her colourful robe, she took a vial of white powder and sprinkled it on the fruit, then took it from me and placed it in front of the gibbon.

The creature gorged hungrily on the fruit and then promptly fell into a deep sleep. It lay out on the table, breathing very shallowly. With the Daayan's help, I wrapped the long metal chain across the beast's chest and under the table, securing it tightly. The Master stood up with his crutch, and leaned forward to feel the creature's muscular right forearm and huge powerful hands.

The Daayan stood at the opposite side of the table and spoke calmly to the Master in her language. His brow furrowed in anger.

'Daniel,' said the Daayan, her sweet voice tingling in the base of my skull, 'You should wait outside of the door and turn away anyone seeking the Master.'

'Nonsense!' roared the Master. 'The boy stays, this shall harden those weak nerves!'

The Daayan spoke to the Master firmly in the Indian language. He replied several times, becoming angrier each moment, and pointing forcefully at the creature's powerful right arm. Suddenly, he slammed his fist down on the table.

'You are my Daayan!' He yelled at her, 'You are mine to command!' It made me furious to see her spoken to like this. I wanted to attack the Master, but the Daayan turned her eyes to meet mine and softened my rage. He stared at her across the table, wild eyed and panting.

'Even so, I cannot harm the creature,' she said, calmly.

The Master turned angrily and pulled a huge cleaver from the wall behind him. He held it aloft in his left hand, the morning light from the ventilation grates flashed off of the sharpened blade. I gasped as he brought it down heavily on the gibbon's right arm, severing it at the elbow. The creature awoke screaming and flailing its bloody stump, writhing under the chains. The last thing I remember was the severed arm twitching on the table and the Master's booming laughter ringing in my ears as I hit the floor.

I dreamt of making love to the Daayan. Her soft warm thighs wrapped tightly around my waist and her moist lips kissing my bare chest.

I began to wake up on a bed. It was soft and warm and smelt like the Daayan. I enjoyed the blissful comfort of the place for a moment longer as my mind came back from sleep.

With a start I realised I was on the Daayan's bed. I sat upright and looked around, rubbing my eyes. The heavy royal red bed curtains had been drawn around me, but I could see through the gaps where they joined. In the room outside of the bed, she sat with her back to me in a deep copper bath. I watched enchanted as she washed her shoulders and arms with a cloth and then slowly stood up. I could see the shape of her bare hips and bottom. I swallowed hard as she stepped out of the bath and strode on long legs to a changing screen.

'You fainted and hit your head.' She said suddenly. I did not know that she was aware of my presence and kept perfectly still and silent, hoping she would think I had been awoken by her voice. 'He wanted you dismissed for lack of stomach, but I reminded him of your young age and persuaded him to be lenient. You need to take him his evening meal in his room. He won't allow anyone else to see him yet.'

'Yes Ma'am.' I said, massively embarrassed I shuffled off of the bed and climbed through the curtains. I hurried towards the door, still feeling a little groggy and with a pounding headache, but eager to be out of the awkward situation.

'Wait.' She stopped me as I reached the door. I turned around to see her stood suddenly right beside me, dressed once more in her colourful blue robes. She looked younger and more beautiful than she had done when I first met her. 'Did you have nightmares? You moaned most alarmingly in your sleep.'

'N-no Ma'am,' I said, feeling the heat in my cheeks.

'Oh, then dreams? They were moans of pleasure?' She raised her eyebrows at me and smiled knowingly.

'I-I, I don't recall Ma'am.' She laughed at my awkwardness and kissed my cheek.

'You mustn't keep the Master waiting,' she whispered, her hot breath tickling my ear.

In the main kitchen, a roasted leg of lamb had been prepared and I quickly carried it up to the Master's room on the first floor of the west wing. At the top of the stairs outside his room, I caught sight of myself in one of the long mirrors. I looked so much older and stronger than I had done two days ago. My shoulders seemed heavier set, and the usually soft downy hair on my face was now coarse and black. I would need to shave before long.

Pleased that I was becoming a man, and more confident for it, I rapped on the Master's bedchamber door.

'Enter,' boomed the Master's voice from within. I backed through the door, the roasted leg of lamb steaming on the tray in my hands. It smelled delicious.

The room was in darkness but for a fire crackling under the mantelpiece. Facing that fire, sat in his deep armchair, the Master stared entranced into the flames.

'Your supper, Sir.' I strode over to him and placed the tray on a small table next to his armchair, and then turned to leave.

Suddenly his arm shot out and grabbed my wrist. His missing right arm. I looked down at it. Covered in wiry black hair, it gripped me with such force that I feared my bones would crush. The strength of the gibbon's arm made me feel like a boy again. The Master fixed me with a mad grin, a strange savageness in his fire-lit eyes.

'Bring me a razor and some hot water, boy,' he said through bared teeth, 'It's time I taught you how to shave.' He released my arm and I hurried away, confused and horrified. I ran back to the main kitchen, unable to rid myself of the sight of the gibbon's arm attached to the Master.

It must be the work of some great evil to make such an abomination possible. I thought about going to the Daayan and confronting her about the dark arts, but I could not believe it so. One so beautiful and pure as the Daayan would not engage in such evil. With every step, I felt her purity tingling pleasantly in the base of my skull. That tingling presence calmed me and helped me to see that the

Master had surely bonded her to his will by some vile and despicable magic. I resolved not to scurry to her like an upset child. The tingling pulsed in my skull and told me that she would respect me as a man if I behaved as such.

I returned to the Master with a bowl of hot water, a bar of soap, a towel, and a sharp blade. He had eaten his roasted meat very quickly and was chewing on the leg bone, his lips shining with grease in the firelight. He used his powerful gibbon's arm to snap the bone in half.

'If you cut me, I'll do the same to you,' he said. He slurped noisily, sucking the marrow out of the middle of the bone, and then discarded it on the tray. 'I want all of the hairs gone from the arm. Understood?'

'Yes, sir.' I said, my voice weak and juvenile. I took the bone-littered tray away, replacing it with the bowl of water.

He held the gibbon's arm out over the bowl and I doused it with warm water, then worked the soap into a lather on the hair. My fingers trembled as I held the sharp blade and I could feel the Master's eyes willing me to make a mistake. My whole hand began to shake, but then the Daayan pulsed in the base of my skull. She flooded me with calm and I managed to steady my hand as I pressed the blade against the wiry damp hairs.

The hairs came away smoothly and fell into the water, exposing tough leathery brown skin beneath. I shaved the arm from the elbow where the strips of the Master's original flesh joined it, sewn on like a roughly darned sock heel, all the way to the thick wrinkled knuckles. When I had finished the bowl was full of matted hair. I dabbed the exposed flesh dry. The Master held the bare arm up to the firelight, and compared it with his human arm. The gibbon's arm was darker in colour and much more muscular, but the two were not overly dissimilar.

'Now go and clean the Daayan's kitchen,' he said, and then patted the stump of his left leg, 'We've got a busy day tomorrow.'

I gathered the bowl of hairy water and the chewed lamb bones, and left the Master alone testing the strength of his new arm. As I closed the door, I saw him smash the little wooden table with his new powerful fist. His laughter chased me down the corridor.

It was quite late when I returned to the Daayan's kitchen where I had seen such horrors earlier in the day. The long carving table was stained with blood. The Master's and the gibbon's, the two bloods mixed and fixed into the wood grain in one large blot. I felt confused and horrified by what I had seen. It should not be possible. There was something deeply sinister happening and I wanted to know the truth about the Daayan, but as soon as I thought about her all of my questions vanished.

Exhausted, it took me several hours to scrub it clean, the Daayan pulsing and tingling in the base of my skull to keep me strong. Occasionally I would hear a growl or a shriek from the animals still in their boxes in the long gallery. I felt sorry for the creatures but trusted that the Daayan was taking care of them. The poor gibbon would be amongst them. When I finally reached my bed in the servant's quarters, everybody else was asleep and I was quick to join them.

The cages arrived the next day. The other servants and I positioned them along the sides of the long gallery, some were quite tall and covered the portraits on the walls, and others were short but long. William stood at one end of the gallery directing us as to which cages should go where, and the Daayan sat on the animal crates in the middle of the room. The banging and clattering of the cages had made them very vocal and excited, but the Daayan hummed in a strange rhythmic chant and they quietened down. The Master had not yet emerged from his room.

The other servants were jealous that I, despite my youth and relative inexperience, had been chosen as the Daayan's assistant. They laughed at my new beard claiming that I was trying to look like the Master, and they teased me about being the servant of an Indian woman. I would see them glance at her with lust and longing, but she was an ever-present pulsing tingle in the base of my skull. Their glances at her and their mocking did not trouble me in the slightest.

With the cages in position, the Daayan dismissed the rest of the staff. She and I were alone in the long gallery. My muscles were burning and swollen from lifting the heavy metal cages, and my shirt stuck to my broad chest with sweat from the hot spring morning. I felt more powerful than ever. I had not found the time to shave, and my facial hair had grown during the night to be thick and manly. It would soon be mighty like the Master's beard. The Daayan walked to the gallery door and I followed her curvy, petite frame and beautiful swaying hips. I yearned to pick her up and wrap her legs around me as I had in my dreams. She locked the door and turned to me, deep brown eyes peering into my soul, reading my thoughts.

'Shall we let the animals out of the boxes?' she said with her suggestive smile. I dared not respond to what, in my lustful mind, I felt was her intentional double meaning. Before meeting her, I would never have thought like that about so simple a question but she had changed me. I simply nodded and selected one of the boxes.

I unlocked the box and carefully slid the side panel upwards. Inside, the brown leathery face of the gibbon looked up at me with sad suffering eyes. Its missing stump of an arm was wrapped in bandages. I felt pain in my heart for the poor creature and felt my eyes welling. The Daayan put her hand on my shoulder and I blinked away the tears.

'I've made sure that he is not in pain,' she said, and held out her hand to the gibbon. The creature took it, and the Daayan led him along the gallery to one of the larger cages.

We transferred scores of strange animals from their boxes to their cages for the next few hours. Miniature horse creatures with long snout-like noses, tiny monkeys with huge eyes, a large pig with huge flapping ears and a long snake-like nose, a type of large goat or deer, numerous colourful birds, a large spotted cat, a striped pig, and a kind of rat with a hard scaly shell. Some tried to bolt and flee when the box was opened, but with a few sharp Indian words from the Daayan, they walked obediently at her heel.

The final box was the largest of them all; it was as tall as a man and twice as long. Inside I could hear a heavy creature stalking up and down. The box could be opened from one end and I could hear a deep throaty growl as I undid the latch. The Daayan urged me to move aside quickly in case the creature should leap straight out. She began to speak to the beast within using an even stranger language that did not sound like the Indian I had heard her speak before.

I cautiously creaked open the door and saw two large golden eyes staring back at me. The size of the beast within made me gasp; a huge striped cat. Twice the size of a man, it crouched, ears flattened back and teeth bared like a mouth full of knives. The beast was ready to pounce.

As soon as I opened the door wide enough it sprang through the air straight at me. I dodged out of the way and it landed elegantly in the middle of the room. Still speaking to the beast, the Daayan pointed at it and raised her voice in command. It turned around, tail flicking and faced the Daayan. I thought it would attack her, and so I moved to block its path, staring the beast down with all the ferocity I could muster.

But the beast did not pounce. Instead, it sat obediently and let the Daayan stroke its head. I feared that it would snap her hand off in one bite, but it was completely peaceful. She led the great animal to the largest cage at the far end of the gallery. It prowled with great power in its legs and there was a regal expression written across its majestic face.

I felt a terrible sadness as I slid the heavy iron lock across the cage door behind the tiger. As soon as the lock was secure, the Daayan stopped her muttering and the beast let out a terrifying roar that seemed to shake the whole house. It slashed at the metal bars with its huge claws and when they would not shatter it lay down, defeated.

'This is a tiger,' said the Daayan, her voice strangely choked. I looked around and to my surprise, saw that she was crying.

'He can't take its limbs, he can't!' I said to her as we stood before the tiger cage. She shook her head and wiped away her tears. 'Why do you obey him?'

She could not answer for a few seconds. Eventually she told me how the Master and his soldiers came to her isolated village in the Indian jungle. The soldiers held her sister Daayan at gunpoint and the Master threatened to kill them all and burn down their jungle if they would not use their healing powers to make him immortal. She vowed to serve him to save her sisters and their jungle, travelling with him during his battles to keep him strong and heal his wounds. After the latest battle he lost his arm and leg to cannon fire, and the Daayan had not been able to heal what was no longer there. He ordered her to replace the limbs with those of the most powerful animals in India, and brought her back to England to where he could recuperate and get accustomed to the new limbs.

When she finished her story I was shaking with rage; furious that the Master had treated one so pure as the Daayan like that.

'He should not have the leg,' I said, looking at the mighty tiger in its cage.

'I cannot refuse.' She looked up at me with those beautiful sad eyes, moist with tears. I should have slit the Master's throat with the shaving blade last night. The Daayan put her arm around my waist and rested her head on my chest. I felt my fury calm under her touch. 'I swore a vow.'

In the afternoon we led the tiger solemnly down to the ghastly kitchen. It padded along softly next to the Daayan, a chain leash around its neck as a precaution. The Master was there already, and had obviously been using the facilities.

There was the bloody savagely hacked carcass of a huge wild boar on the table. A cauldron of water boiled over the fire, and I could see bits of the boar bobbing at the surface. The salty metallic smelling steam from the boiled meat clouded the air and flowed upwards through the ventilation grates. The Master sat at the table amongst the carnage, gnawing on a roasted boar's snout. The tiger growled hungrily and I thought it would attack, but a touch on its head from the Daayan subdued the beast once more.

'I took this boar apart, and it seems that the boar's power is mostly in its neck and front shoulder muscles,' he said, without looking up from his roasted snout. 'Humans are such weak animals by comparison. It gave me a few ideas.' He nonchalantly threw the snout to the tiger, and looked up at the Daayan, the mad sparkle in his eyes, 'We've got a busy day ahead.'

'Yes, sir,' she said, and sprinkled the boar carcass with her white powder. The tiger leapt up onto the table and began to gorge on the powder-covered meat. The Master looked at me as if noticing me for the first time.

'Oh dear, boy,' he said darkly, shaking his head at me, 'She's got to you hasn't she?'

'Sorry, sir, I don't understand,' I replied.

'Look at yourself, you simpleton. You've aged twenty years already!' Confused, I looked at the Daayan for an answer but she would not meet my eyes. The tiger stopped eating and fell asleep heavily on the table next to the boar carcass. The Master laughed at me, 'You've been lying with her haven't you?'

'No, sir, I swear I haven't!' I said.

'Oh really? Had any sinful dreams lately?' He looked at me accusingly. I reddened and could not respond. 'I thought so,' he continued, 'You are dismissed lad, for your own good. I want you gone from this house immediately!'

'No, sir! Please!' I protested. I could not bear to be separated from the Daayan, 'I did nothing wrong!'

'Out!' He roared. I looked at my hands, now hard and masculine where they had once been soft and juvenile. I could have easily strangled the Master with them, but he had his powerful gibbon's arm and forty years of combat experience. I looked to the Daayan for help, but she could do nothing. She fixed at me with her beautiful sad brown eyes and gave an almost unnoticeable shake of her head. I felt her tingling in the base of my skull, warning me. The Master was trying to turn me against her.

I flashed the Master an angry glance and stormed out of the room. His smirking face and vile laughter lingered in my mind as I strode down the corridor.

I did not leave the house. The Daayan still pulsed in the base of my skull, begging me not to leave her. She did not need to beg, I would never leave her. Instead I went straight to the Daayan's drawing room to wait for her to return.

There, I paced around the room looking at the weapons on the wall. I took down a light cavalry sabre and swung it as I walked. Despite having never wielded a sword before, the thing felt right in my hand. It was a powerful feeling to hold a weapon. I could feel all of the portraits of the Master, staring at me from every wall.

One particular painting in the Daayan's drawing room rankled me more than the rest. It showed the Master in his full uniform, looking mighty and dominant. Behind him a battle was taking place in a jungle; trees were on fire and tigers and other animals, as well as Indian men and women, all fled before his army. It was perhaps how he had captured the Daayan. I slashed the painting with my sword, severing the Master's head from his shoulders.

As I turned from the slashed painting, I caught sight of a mirror and jumped. I could not believe what I saw. There, staring out of the mirror at me was a full-grown man, mighty and regal like the man in the paintings. He had wrinkles around his eyes, and a thick black beard. Very much how the Master had looked before he turned grey. I stroked my face to feel my own powerful beard, and cried out in horror as the man in the mirror did the same. It really was me. The Master was right; I had aged twenty years.

I walked towards the mirror, touching my face in disbelief. Terror began to take hold of me as I thought of the years that I had lost. I cried out in rage and hacked at every mocking portrait on the walls, slashing them to pieces one at a time. Amidst my destruction I heard a great sickening roar from the tiger in the ghastly kitchen below me and knew what was happening down there. I was about to charge downstairs to stab the Master through his evil heart, when I suddenly dropped to my knees and wept. It was as though a strange force had pulled all the hate out of me.

The Daayan was pulsing her calm from the base of my skull, telling me I should wait for her to return. My rage melted away and I was filled with sadness. The tiger in the kitchen below ceased its wild roaring.

I dragged myself to the high-backed chairs facing the wide double doors that opened out onto the garden. Flinging the doors open, I slumped down heavily into the same chair that I had sat in as a love-struck boy not three days ago. With the sword across my knees, I stared out into the beautiful garden, missing the peaceful work with nature that my gardener's boy duties had entailed. My raging and slashing had made me hot and so I took off my servant's jacket and sat in my shirt, allowing the cool spring breeze to calm my shattered nerves.

Throughout the afternoon I heard more animal wails from the kitchen below me. All different voices filled with the same wild terror. I focused instead on the pleasant tingle of the Daayan. Thinking about her beauty and purity made me forget the fear of my inexplicable ageing, and the horrors of the ghastly kitchen. I bathed my aching mind in thoughts of her to block out the screams of the animals below me.

As the light began to fade, the head gardener walked by outside and waved at me. It roused me from my thoughts and I raised my arm, returning his greeting with a friendly wave. The man smiled broadly and went on his way. Without my servant's jacket, he must have thought me the Master.

The room had cooled during the afternoon and so I started a fire in the fireplace. The animal screams below had ceased and the Daayan would surely be returning soon; I wanted it to be warm and welcoming for her. I lit the oil lamps, and closed the doors to the garden.

It was late night before she returned. The room was warm and comfortable, lit golden by the dancing flames of the oil lamps and the fire. I was dozing in one of the chairs when I felt her tingle draw nearer. The door handle clicked and I stood up as she entered.

She was crying and shaking, blood stained her robes, and spattered her beautiful face. I took her in my arms and she buried her head in my chest, sobbing openly. I tried to ask her why I had aged so much, and what the Master had meant by saying that 'she has me', but each time I tried to phrase the question my lips could not form the words. It was as though between my thoughts and my mouth there was a force blocking me from asking those questions. The Daayan pressed her supple body against me and pulsed in my skull. Suddenly, she was all that mattered.

'He's coming,' she whispered, and quickly locked the door.

Fear sprung from my backbone as I heard the slow thudding of footsteps outside of the door. I pushed the Daayan behind me and held out my sword. It felt heavier in my hand than it had done before. As the footsteps grew closer, I could hear the Master's wheezing breath. He stopped outside of the door and I watched the handle slowly turning. The Daayan placed her hand on my shoulder and I felt my mind clear, strength returning to my sword arm. The door rattled against the lock.

'We're not finished Daayan!' came the hoarse deep growl of the Master.

The door flew open, splintered from its hinges by brute force. I dodged out of the way as it fell past me.

There in the doorway stood the Master, now a nightmarish mishmash of creatures. He had tried to put his military uniform on over the top of his new limbs but with little success. The lower leg of the tiger had replaced his missing one, and the tiger's claw had torn through his black leather boots. The other foot was a hoof, sticking out of the bottom of his white trouser legs. The trousers were ripped at the thigh revealing short brown hairs where a muscular deer leg had burst through. He still had his gibbon's hand, but the claw of a large spotted cat had replaced his remaining human hand. Stout black boar hairs pocked through the gaps in the fabric of his red military jacket where he had taken the powerful shoulders and neck of the boar. His great full beard ran wet with saliva, dribbling from his gaping mouth where the spiked tusks of an elephant stuck out like two swords.

He threw back his head and laughed loudly at me. The laugh became a roar and he leapt forward at me, striking out with his tusks.

I managed to throw myself to the side and deflect the tusk with my sword, backing away towards the fireplace. Thankfully he was still getting used to his new legs and the claw of his tiger foot got caught in the rug as he lunged. He stumbled to his knees and growled in pain. Before he could rise I swung the sword as hard as I could at his head, but he quickly turned his tusk around to meet my blow. The sword slid down the tusk and sliced through the Master's cheek sending a spray of blood high into the air. The Master howled in pain and staggered to his feet. He grabbed a huge two-handed highland claymore from the wall with his mighty gibbon's arm, and swung out wildly with the long blade. He knocked other weapons from the walls; halberds and battle-axes spun through the air smashing ornaments and furniture.

I ducked and danced backwards, avoiding the blows. There would be no point in parrying that huge blade; it would simply shatter my own light sabre. With two wild swings he shattered the oil lamps, plunging us into gloomy dimness.

By the light of the small fire under the mantelpiece, I could see his snarling face advancing on me. He seemed twice the size and ten times the strength of the crippled man who had first arrived in the carriage. Madness sparkled in his eyes, and wet saliva glistened in his beard. Lisping from his sliced cheek, he shouted something in the Indian tongue, some sort of command aimed at the Daayan. I grabbed a half flaming log from the fireplace and held it out at him with one hand, my sword in the other.

Behind him, the Daayan began to shout back in her Indian language. I could not understand what she said but he roared in fury, splitting his cheek even further, and turned to face her. I saw my chance. With all of my might I raised both arms and brought my sword down on the Masters' neck and the flaming log on his head. The sword merely stuck fast in the thick boar muscle that had replaced his human neck. The flaming log, however, shattered into a million fiery embers and the oil in his fur from the smashed lamps caught fire.

The Master howled and roared as his oil-soaked fur leapt in flames. He dropped his giant claymore and tried to beat out the fire. When this did not work he dropped on all fours and charged in panic through the big double-doors into the garden. The cool night air fanned the flames higher and I watched the flaming beast bound on all fours, howling over the manor grounds and disappearing into the night.

When I turned from the open doors back into the dimly lit room, sat in one of the high-backed armchairs was a very ancient woman. Her wrinkled skin hung loose from her bones, and her long white hair reached down to her waist. She looked up at me with the same striking deep brown eyes that I had first fallen for, and pointed at the other chair overturned on the floor opposite her.

'I owe you answers, Daniel,' said the Daayan, with a sad smile. For all her great age, her eyes and smile were still as perfect and beautiful as they ever had been.

'Who are you?' I said, picking up the chair and sitting down.

'You may think of me as a Mother of Nature. Before your master came to my village, young men would often visit to love me and my sisters, gladly sacrificing the energy of their youth so that we could live on and care for the world's plants and animals.'

'So it was you, not the Master, who took my years?' I asked, shocked and betrayed. I could no longer feel her calming tingle at the base of my skull.

'You wished to be the master. Now you can be.' She said, gesturing with her frail old hand at my face, 'You have all of his possessions, but thankfully will never have his violence. What more would you want as master?'

Looking out of the window, by the light of the moon I could see the exotic flowers in their beds around the perfect lawn and bats dancing in the clear night sky. Inside the room I looked at the grand high ceilings and shattered chandeliers, the slashed portraits of the master hanging limply from their frames, the antique weapons strewn across the floor, the smashed remnants of the expensive tea set crunched under my boot. Finally I looked at the Daayan. This goddess of a woman brought all the way across the oceans from the other side of the world, thousands of miles from her home, alone and sad. Even without her mask of youthful perfection and without her tingling pulse in the base of my skull, I still saw all of the beauty of the world in her sad brown eyes.

'I want you,' I said, 'I want to stay with you in your village. I want to be always at your side. Teach me how to care for the jungles and the rivers. Make me a Father of Nature.'

Her smile lit up the room and the sadness disappeared from her eyes. My heart swelled. I took her aged hand and kissed it.

The next day, in my new role as the master, I informed the staff that I would be returning to India and taking the young gardener's boy with me. Nobody would miss him.

The gamekeeper brought me the smouldering corpse of a huge disfigured creature, the light sabre still buried in its shoulder. I told him that one of the large carnivores had escaped last night and that I had been forced to slay it. The remains were buried under the foundations of the new menagerie.

I had the cages removed from the long gallery and instead ordered that the animals be kept in temporary outdoor enclosures until the menagerie was built. Many of the larger animals had lost their limbs to the previous master's hunger for physical power. They could never be released back into the wild, but I ordered that they have as much space to roam as my grounds would allow. I sent for an expert from India to care for them, and when it was complete the menagerie was opened to the public. People came from miles around to learn about the animals of India.

The Daayan and I returned to her village deep in the jungle. Together we took care of all the world's plants and animals. Young men and women would often visit to love us, gladly sacrificing the energy of their youth so that we could live on.

Glossary of Terms

The Alexander

The convict transportation vessel carrying the most male convicts in the First Fleet.

Barque

A large sailing vessel with three or more masts.

Beaver Hat

The name first given to what we now know as the Top Hat. It was originally made from beaver pelt.

Coolie

During the 19th and early 20th century, Coolie was a label applied to a person from Asia, particularly if they were from Southern China, the Indian subcontinent, the Philippines or Indonesia. Today, this may be used as a racial slur, particularly in South Africa, but is used in this collection for historical veracity.

http://en.wikipedia.org/wiki/Coolie

Charles James Fox

(24 January 1749 – 13 September 1806), styled The Honourable from 1762, was a prominent British Whig statesman whose parliamentary career spanned thirty-eight years of the late 18th and early 19th centuries.

A close friend of Ignatius Sancho.

http://en.wikipedia.org/wiki/Charles_James_Fox

Daayan

The Daayan cult refers to a secret society which emerged during the 15th century in Harangul, a village in the Latur district of Maharashtra. The cult was associated with worship of the mother goddess.

In Harangul it is believed that a sect of women known as Daayans lives in an area of the village. Assuming the form of a young, attractive female, they hunt for young men on roads and seduce lone travellers into accompanying her. Imprisoning the man, she feeds on his blood or sweat. One legend says that a Daayan will hold a young man captive until he is old, using him sexually until he dies and joins the spirit world.

The Daayan is said to be culturally derived from shamans and healers, the original healer, counsellor and stateswoman of her community in a matriarchal society. Belief in Daayans has existed in most regions of India, particularly Jharkhand and Bihar. It is prevalent in rural and semi-rural areas, with "witch-hunts" causing women to be killed or ostracised.

http://en.wikipedia.org/wiki/Daayan

David Garrick

(19 February 1717 – 20 January 1779) was an English actor, playwright, theatre manager and producer who influenced nearly all aspects of theatrical practice throughout the 18th century and was a pupil and friend of Dr Samuel Johnson.

A close friend of Ignatius Sancho.

http://en.wikipedia.org/wiki/David_Garrick

First Fleet

The name given to the 11 ships which left Great Britain on 13 May 1787 to found a penal colony that became the first European settlement in Australia. The fleet consisted of two Royal Navy vessels, three store ships and six convict transports, carrying more than 1,000 convicts, marines and seamen, and a vast quantity of stores.

http://en.wikipedia.org/wiki/First_Fleet

Joseph Nollekens

(11 August 1737 – 23 April 1823) was a sculptor from London generally considered to be the finest British sculptor of the late 18th century.

A close friend of Ignatius Sancho.

http://en.wikipedia.org/wiki/Joseph_Nollekens

Laurence Sterne

(24 November 1713 – 18 March 1768) was an Anglo-Irish novelist and an Anglican clergyman. He is best known for his novels The Life and Opinions of Tristram Shandy, Gentleman and A Sentimental Journey Through France and Italy; but he also published many sermons, wrote memoirs, and was involved in local politics.

A close friend of Ignatius Sancho.

http://en.wikipedia.org/wiki/Laurence_Sterne

Laudanum

A tincture of opium, prescribed by doctors during the 18th and 19th centuries as a curing any and every ailment. Commonly mixed with wine by the upper classes.

Packet Boat

Small boat designed for domestic mail, passenger and freight transportation. They were extensively used for much of the 18th century and 19th century.

http://en.wikipedia.org/wiki/Packet_boat

Paiute

A group of indigenous people from the Great Basin in North America between the Rocky Mountains and the Sierra Nevada.

Penzance Promenade

Street along the sea front in the Cornish town of Penzance. The first part of the promenade was built in 1844.

Quicksilver

The name given by miners to the liquid metal Mercury. Mercury could be used to extract gold and silver, but is deadly poisonous.

Sharp Rifle

A large bore single shot rifles that began with a design by

Christian Sharps in 1848 that are renowned for long range accuracy.

http://en.wikipedia.org/wiki/Sharps_rifle

Silent Tower

A Dakhma, also known as "Cheel Ghar" in Hindi and "Tower of Silence" in English. A circular, raised structure used by Zoroastrians for exposure of the dead, particularly to scavenging birds.

http://en.wikipedia.org/wiki/Dakhma

Stiletto

A knife or dagger with a long slender blade and needle-like point, primarily intended as a stabbing weapon. The stiletto blade's narrow cross-section and acuminated tip reduces friction upon entry, allowing the blade to penetrate deeply. It was a popular weapon of criminals, gang members, and assorted assassins.

http://en.wikipedia.org/wiki/Stiletto

Bibliography

Web Addresses

Each story from Dead Men's Teeth and Other Stories from Voices Past was inspired by an untold life from the British Library archive collections. For more information, see the links below:

Dead Men's Teeth:
http://britishlibrary.typepad.co.uk/untoldlives/2013/07/smiling-with-dead-mens-teeth.html

Quarantine:
http://britishlibrary.typepad.co.uk/untoldlives/2013/03/cholera-on-the-emigrant-ship-sheila.html

Arrowhead: (distantly, from one letter in the Bentham collection)
http://britishlibrary.typepad.co.uk/untoldlives/2014/03/meet-the-benthams-an-extraordinary-georgian-family.html

Mary March:
http://britishlibrary.typepad.co.uk/untoldlives/2014/03/mary-march-of-newfoundland.html

How I Did Long fer a Tattie Pasty!:
http://britishlibrary.typepad.co.uk/untoldlives/2013/10/aw-how-i-ded-long-for-a-tattie-pasty.html

Death or Australia: http://britishlibrary.typepad.co.uk/untoldlives/2012/10/a-phantom-burglar-and-the-hulk.html

Printed on the Thames: http://britishlibrary.typepad.co.uk/untoldlives/2014/02/printing-on-ice.html

Ignatius Sancho's Shop: http://britishlibrary.typepad.co.uk/untoldlives/2013/11/black-georgians-an-affrican-in-georgian-london.html

Vulture Temple: http://britishlibrary.typepad.co.uk/untoldlives/2013/12/the-tower-of-silence-a-zoroastrian-detective-story.html

Stolen from India: http://britishlibrary.typepad.co.uk/untoldlives/2013/10/without-a-leg-to-stand-on-victorian-prosthetics.html

http://britishlibrary.typepad.co.uk/untoldlives/2013/08/ghastly-kitchens.html